CW00484830

PRAISE FC
THE
SLYE TEAM BLACK OPS SERIES

"I could not put this book down. Once again Dianna has thrilled my suspense taste buds with an extra dash of spicy romance." ~~After Hours Rendezvous

"Engrossing, thrilling and wonderfully steamy...a pitch-perfect suspense that will keep readers breathless from the first nerve-racking scene to the last shocking revelation."~~The Romance Reviews

"It seems with each book this series gets better." ~~The Reading Cafe

"A FREAKING AWESOME continuation of the Slye Team series by Dianna Freaking Love!!! She did not disappoint." ~~Goodreads

"This is one of those books where your body tenses, you stop breathing and you just can't read fast enough."~~ Amazon

DIANNA

NEW YORK TIMES BESTSELLING AUTHOR

LOVE

Kiss THE ENEMY

THE **SLYE TEAM BLACK OPS** SERIES

KISS THE ENEMY: Slye Team Black Ops Romantic suspense
Copyright © 2014 by Dianna Love Snell
All rights reserved.

Please Note

This is a work of fiction. Names, characters, places, and incidents either are the product of the author's imagination or are used fictitiously, and any resemblance to actual persons, living or dead, business establishments, events or locales is entirely coincidental.

The reverse engineering, uploading, and/or distributing of this eBook via the internet or via any other means without the permission of the copyright owner is illegal and punishable by law. Please purchase only authorized electronic editions, and do not participate in or encourage electronic piracy of copyrighted materials. Your support of the author's rights is appreciated.

AI RESTRICTION: The author expressly prohibits any entity from using this publication for purposes of training artificial intelligence (AI) technologies to generate text, including without limitation technologies that are capable of generating works in the same style or genre as this publication. The author reserves all rights to license uses of this work for generative AI training and development of machine learning language models.

Cover Design and Interior format by The Killion Group, Inc
http://thekilliongroupinc.com

DEDICATION

For my husband, Karl, who has always been my champion and is the reason I can chase my dreams. I can do anything with him by my side.

CHAPTER 1

Margaux Duke exited first from the unmarked van parked on an empty side street in east Atlanta two blocks from tonight's target. She lowered her night vision monocular into place as the rest of the six-person team spilled out behind her.

Black figures melded into the dark shadows and chilly night, all armed and deadly.

All moving on her intel of a meeting for payoff on a suspected terrorist attack to be carried out in Atlanta.

Wednesday.

Today, as in less than twelve hours.

The meeting was going down in sixteen minutes. Margaux had shared every detail her snitch provided, with the exception of her hunch on who was making that payment.

At one time, her intuition would have mattered.

Not these days.

Sabrina Slye's voice came through the comm sets everyone wore. "You're absolutely *sure* about this intel, Duke?"

If this was about getting retribution for Margaux's dead cousin, Nanci, she'd go on much less dependable intel. But this was about stopping a terrorist and she would not walk the team into danger for just a gut feeling. Sabrina had never questioned Margaux's resources.

It rubbed that she did now, but Margaux pushed the mic switch clipped to her black molle vest and answered, "Yes." She spoke in a soft whisper. The throat mic picked up the vibrations, and the sound came clearly through the earbuds of the team. "This came from my number one contact. He's never been wrong in three years."

No one else said a word. Tension pulsed through the silence.

That was telling in itself when any other time Nick and Dingo would have been ragging on her that she was picking up the beer tab if this was a bust.

She hadn't been invited to share a beer in months.

She added, "This is the same informant who gave us accurate intel on the submarine sabotage we averted in Kitsap last December." An attack planned for Naval Base Kitsap on the Kitsap Peninsula in Washington, no less.

"Ten four." Sabrina's brisk voice moved on with, "Time check. O-one-hundred." She counted seconds until everyone on the team gave an affirmative.

Sabrina ran covert teams for secret national security operations under the cover of Slye, an elite corporate security agency. A tough, but fair, leader who had zero tolerance for her agents going rogue for personal vendettas. She'd leveled Margaux with a steely gaze when she'd reminded the entire team of that unbendable rule just ten days ago.

Message received.

Stop focusing on the Banker, a broker for international terrorism.

Ryder Van Dyke's deep voice cut in on the comm unit. "One vehicle just arrived at Strident Global Imports." There was a pause while they all waited to hear more, then Ryder said, "No one's getting out of the car yet."

Ryder was team member number seven. He had a sniper position on top of the building across the street from an import company where the meet was expected to happen.

The snitch had discovered a link between Tio Giovanni, the ruthless leader of a New Jersey crime syndicate, and this import company, which accounted for the location of this meeting.

What was the mob doing for a terrorist?

Margaux could feel Sabrina's gaze drilling through her confidence. She could not screw up the deal she had with Sabrina, the only person left who knew Margaux's true identity. More than anything, Sabrina had helped her reclaim her life and had known how much Nanci meant to Margaux.

The team knew Margaux based only on what Sabrina had built for her identity. As for FBI Special Agent Nanci Tyler, the team had only known that Margaux had a rapport with a contact in the agency, but one that had to be kept secret. They understood her loss when Nanci was murdered, but not that it had been like losing a limb.

Margaux had been spending her off-time—and her money—hunting for the Banker. But when Sabrina finally made it clear that Margaux had to let go of her quest for vengeance, Margaux paid heed, because Sabrina was right.

The Banker had cost her enough.

That's why Margaux had told her snitch she was no longer paying for intel on the bastard.

Tonight was about protecting innocent people and doing her part.

If this operation went sideways, which was always possible with one pulled together this quickly, she would take a bullet for Sabrina or anyone else on this team. Of the six elite operatives in this unit, Margaux was the only one truly expendable. With Nanci gone, no one would mourn her death.

She shoved that load of guilt back down in the cavity her heart used to fill and checked her Sig Sauer M11-A1 holstered beneath the black windbreaker. Her jacket might look like the FBI type, but hers had no agency initials and this wasn't a sanctioned government mission.

Hell, this hadn't even been a mission eighty-two minutes ago.

Ryder came back on the radio. "Three males exiting the sedan. One is staying by the vehicle. The other two are at the door of Strident and ... they're entering the code for the alarm system. No other vehicle yet."

That meant the first group was connected to Strident.

Sweat trickled down Margaux's back with total indifference to the cold front sweeping Georgia in early May. Adrenaline pumped hard enough through her veins that she was numb to anything as insignificant as the temperature continuing to drop since midnight.

No mistakes.

Sabrina's tone sharpened. "Heads up. Dingo goes with me. White Hawk backs us up at the entrance. Nick's with Duke at the rear with Tanner as backup."

A bad feeling niggled at Margaux, that sixth sense an

operative paid attention to if she wanted to walk away to fight another day. Maybe it was a case of doubting herself after Sabrina had questioned Margaux's intel. She shook it off, getting her head in the game where it belonged when the team needed her.

Ryder had an update. "Second vehicle parking in the lot. No one exiting yet."

"Everyone ready?" Sabrina asked.

Affirmatives followed all around, but Sabrina would hold off sending them until both men were in the building in case one decided to blow up the other.

Nick Carrera stepped across Margaux's line of sight, standing a couple inches taller than her five-ten height. The only part of him showing through the black ski mask was a flicker of white around the eye not covered by his monocular, and his unsmiling mouth.

Margaux would question Sabrina's choice for her partner du jour if not for Margaux's having butted heads with everyone else for months.

Not that she didn't like Nick. He was a solid partner, and he didn't butt heads. But Nick played by Nick's rules and was a bit of a wildcard on a mission. It was hard to say exactly what he'd do in any given situation, but he did make things happen that often defied all probability.

Of course, he just as often did so in a way that created a lot of chaos along with the positive results.

Dingo Paddock stepped over to show Sabrina something on his smart phone. The Aussie's ski mask covered spiked blond hair that looked out of place against skin the color of weak tea.

White Hawk, a Cherokee female operative and new recruit, stood off to the side. Dark brown hair cut short on one side and chin length on the other framed an oval face with high cheekbones passed down from generations of Native Americans. She was quiet, but in a way that said she was constantly engaged in threat assessment.

Word was that White Hawk had a knack for languages.

And for tailing a suspect.

Nick said she practically turned into a ghost when she shadowed someone.

Ryder finally said, "Three suspects exiting the second car, leaving one man out front, two heading into the building."

Sabrina announced, "Move out."

Dingo, White Hawk and Sabrina left as one pack. Margaux, Nick, and Tanner Bodine took off in a different direction to approach the building from the rear. Out in public, Tanner was a big rambling cowboy with an easy smile, but at night he could move like the wind when stealth was key.

Margaux entered a dark stretch of alley that had been used as a john for the homeless if that stink was any indication. She widened her stride until she reached the tall chain-link fence surrounding the back lot of the global marketing company. Tanner stepped up and snipped an opening large enough for his wide body, which left plenty of room for her and Nick to slip through.

Sabrina's hushed voice came through the comm. "Guards at entrance contained. Ryder has confirmation on identity of the New Jersey suspect as Tio Giovanni. Black hair, slender build, five-nine. Both guards positively identified as known enforcers for two separate crime syndicates."

Margaux blinked at that news. Dingo could run facial recognition software *if* he was at a computer and *if* he had decent images. Had Sabrina sent someone ahead to set up a live feed at the front of the import company? Even so, Dingo didn't have that access at the moment, and Josh Carrington, the other techno whiz on the Slye team, hadn't been available tonight. Amanda, the research dynamo Sabrina had snaked from MI6 last year, was on vacation.

That would mean the images were very likely being sent to Ryder's personal electronic superpower, an electronic analyst genius at the FBI who also happened to be his wife.

Sabrina would be pulling out all the stops to confirm as much as possible before sending in agents.

Tanner hung back as Margaux and Nick approached the building.

Nick spoke softly, asking, "Alarm status?"

Dingo's voice came right back. "All clear, mate."

If the alarm had been reset once everyone was inside as a security measure, Dingo had just disarmed it.

Nick moved silently up the metal steps to the rear door of the warehouse and went to work on the lock while Margaux covered his back.

When his hand touched her shoulder, she turned to enter a dark space that would be impossible to navigate without night vision gear. She took the lead, weaving her way with soft steps around forklifts and pallets stacked with merchandise covered in plastic wrap.

She stopped at the corner of tall metal shelving lined up in rows. A mirror set of towering gray structures loaded with inventory ran along the other side of the building, creating a wide walkway down the center.

There was enough space for two forklifts with eight-foot-wide loads to easily pass each other.

Or for two men to meet in the center of the building sixty feet away and discuss destroying parts of this city. A single mercury vapor light glowed bluish-white overhead, leaving the rest of the warehouse in pitch dark.

Nick eased forward and peeked over her shoulder. A guard stood two strides behind each respective boss.

Margaux assessed the room. Lots of metal angles for bullets to ricochet against.

But there were only two exits.

Dread clawed along her neck. *Why?*

This felt rushed, which couldn't be helped since there was no way to plan for when intel would arrive. Besides, this was what Slye excelled at—moving on a hot tip without red tape, then fading into the shadows so alphabet agencies took the credit.

And taking on missions that stopped powerful criminals.

Margaux's snitch had given her pieces of intel that alluded to the Banker making the payoff tonight. But not enough information to say for sure.

Eight months ago, Sabrina would have been open to the possibility of going after that bastard on a good hunch, but not after a source—translation, Sabrina's friend in the CIA—said agencies had been tracking the Banker's ties to international terrorist events for years. According to her source, there was no intel to support the Banker having entered the US at any point in the past or present.

There were no known photographs of the Banker, and Sabrina's CIA friend had shared that the Banker was believed to presently be holed up in Germany.

That settled that, which was why Margaux didn't bring up the bastard's name and draw Sabrina's ire again.

Margaux's new goal was regaining the respect she'd once enjoyed before she'd let an obsession make her team think she'd gone rogue. She hadn't, and no way would she allow her personal issues to end with letting her team down.

Sabrina ordered, "Stand down. The second suspect can't be confirmed as a known terrorist."

Nick muttered, "Fuck."

He took the word right out of Margaux's mouth. She eyed the two men who were now shaking hands as if their business was concluded. The pause that followed stretched until Sabrina said, "Margaux I need any other intel you've got on this guy. *Anything* else from your snitch I can use."

Son of a bitch. Decision time. Margaux swallowed and made a leap of faith, whispering into her mic, "My snitch said this *might* involve the Banker, but he did *not* have confirmation. I dismissed that as insignificant since we were told the Banker is not in this country."

But the snitch had argued that this terrorist was rumored to have put out a hit on an FBI agent eight months ago for interfering with his operation. That fit the description of the hit on Nanci.

"What are you saying?" Sabrina asked.

Margaux regretted all the months she'd focused on the Banker, because right now everyone had to be thinking he was at the core of her investment for this op. She said, "There *is* a chance the unidentified suspect could be the Banker, which would explain not being able to confirm identification as a terrorist. I didn't tell you because it was only speculation and that was never the point of this op. This is about stopping an attack on Atlanta."

Silence answered her.

She glanced at Nick.

He rolled his eyes, an action she was sure the rest of the team mirrored at this same moment.

Nick didn't activate his mic when he whispered right at her ear. "How long have you been suicidal?"

Margaux left her mic off as well to answer him in a hushed voice. "How is this suicidal with an entire team?"

"I didn't mean this." He nodded to the left toward the targets. "I meant stomping on Sabrina's last good nerve."

"I'm not saying it's him." She paused, wishing she were anywhere else right now. "But what if it is?" Regardless of what happened eight months ago, if this was the Banker, they had the chance to take down someone who brokered the deaths of thousands, and they all knew it.

"Hey, I'm in."

And just like that, Nick was at the top of her favorite partners list.

Ryder's voice came on the comm. "We've got company. A sporte ute pulling into the drive. I count at least four inside. Time to move or get out."

Margaux held her breath, not sure what she hoped Sabrina would decide, but if they pulled back, they'd lose the terrorist and Giovanni, and maybe sign the death warrants for thousands of innocent people.

Sabrina finally said, "Op is a go." She paused then ordered, "Move in."

Margaux nodded at Nick then she slipped around the corner with Nick on her left side. She aimed at the guard on her right. Nick would take the one on the left.

Giovanni turned to speak to his guard.

Dingo and Sabrina would be approaching from the front,

one covering the terrorist and the other watching Giovanni. It was imperative to bring those two out alive.

Everything sharpened in Margaux's surroundings. Time took on a life of its own, slowing until everything came into laser focus.

Sabrina's booming order ripped through the room. "Hands in the air. Now!"

Did they do that? Of course not.

That would have been too damn easy.

Both guards spun, shooting toward Dingo and Sabrina's positions as they did.

The terrorist sank into a squat, and Giovanni dropped to the floor, rolling away, but he had nowhere to go beyond the shelves.

Margaux took out her guard with one shot to the head.

Nick hit his target but missed the kill shot only because Giovanni knocked the guard into the shelves where he continued unloading his magazine.

Bullets pinged against metal and the smell of gunpowder filled the air.

With the rapid-fire reverberating, the unknown terrorist must have decided the only threat was coming from the entrance, which had to be why he made a dash for the rear of the building.

He was in his forties, twenty pounds overweight, and must not have been able to bring a weapon into the meet because he had yet to pull one.

Even better? He was heading straight for where Margaux waited. This was too good to be true. Finally, something was going right.

She told Nick, "I got this."

The shooting stopped. Pounding footsteps were the only sound interrupting the sudden silence.

Eight feet from where Margaux hid in the shadows, the suspect looked up as she stepped out. His eyes bulged with shock then rage. She moved forward before he could react and put her weight into the motion, taking advantage of his forward momentum. She hooked an arm around his neck to clothesline him to the ground.

He hit hard. Crack-your-skull hard.

"Get up you piece of shit," she ordered and kicked him in the side.

He groaned and grabbed his head. "You fucking …"

"The word you're looking for is bitch."

"You're a woman? You *fucking whore*. You're gonna burn for this."

She smiled at him and squatted down. "We'll see who burns."

Sabrina came striding up with an HK 416 in her hands. "All clear. Guards inside neutralized. Giovanni is contained. Backup has the four new arrivals restrained and hooded outside. "

Margaux searched his face for something that screamed merciless killer, but nothing magically pinged to identify him. Was this the Banker?

"Do you have any fucking clue what you just screwed up?" the suspect on the ground mumbled in a pain-filled voice.

Margaux prompted him. "By all means. Tell us what you were here to negotiate."

He turned to her, his face twisted with more hatred than she thought a human was capable of expressing visually. "You just fucked a two-year deep undercover DEA operation that was one day from success. I'll see every one of you buried for this."

Sabrina demanded his superior's name. When he gave it, she looked straight at Margaux and cursed.

The agent's eyes rolled back in his head just as Ryder's voice came over the comm in clipped, urgent tones. "Four Atlanta police units pulling up out front. Two unmarked units in back. Alphabet agencies. We're burned."

Blood rushed from Margaux's head so fast she saw stars.

She was alive because no one knew she existed.

If she got arrested, she was as good as dead.

CHAPTER 2

Sabrina still wore the same black outfit when she walked into Margaux's apartment at six in the morning, five hours after the busted op, but her ski mask was off, and her black hair fell loose around her shoulders. For a deadly operative, she had a Catherine-Zeta-Jones look about her that made men who didn't know her act like idiots.

The ones who did know her had enough sense to respect a lethal weapon even when it wore a dress.

Margaux shut the door and turned to lean against it with her hands in the pockets of her favorite jeans. Her hair was still damp from the shower she'd finally taken after trying to find Snake Eyes.

He couldn't hide forever.

At Ryder's word that the op was blown, Sabrina had turned to Margaux and given the signal that meant "get the hell out." Margaux had used her skills at stealth and evasion to do just that, but as far as she knew, the rest of the team had stayed on site. Maybe even gotten arrested.

Sabrina stopped in the middle of Margaux's living room that she thought of as Shabby Chic but accepted that it was just shabby. When Sabrina finally turned to her, she asked, "Did you find him?"

Margaux knew she meant Snake Eyes. "No."

"Snitches go bad all the time."

"It's illogical. I was paying him well."

"To hunt the Banker," Sabrina said, finishing the unspoken part of that sentence.

Margaux shook her head. "I've paid him for all kinds of intel that we've used for good busts all over this country." Finally, she shrugged.

Sabrina spoke in her uber-pissed quiet voice. "I gave you warning after warning."

Here it comes. "I know."

"I let you leave the scene when the DEA agent passed out."

Margaux nodded, giving Sabrina the floor, because repeating "I know" or saying "I'm sorry" while she spoke would only make things worse.

If that were possible.

"I spent the last three hours pulling out every trick I could think of to keep my people out of jail and to convince the DEA that we had solid intel that those two were meeting to discuss a terrorist plot. Thankfully, White Hawk made it to Ryder's van before the APD showed, because the minute that agent wakes up in the hospital tomorrow, he's going to start screaming for the head of the woman who cracked his skull."

More head nodding. How could Margaux possibly make this up to Sabrina and the team?

Sabrina crossed her arms. "I understand about Nanci's death, but we all lose people. Especially in this business."

"Wait a damn minute," Margaux snarled. "I would never, and *I mean never*, put the team in jeopardy for my own benefit or for anything less than solid intel. I told you everything I knew about that meeting. I was *not* chasing the Banker."

"But you thought he'd be there."

"Snake Eyes had a hunch and told me so, but I shut that down because it had no bearing on going after a terrorist with plans to kill people in Atlanta."

"There was a time that I'd have taken that at face value, but what happened eight months ago changed you."

Margaux started to argue, but Sabrina wasn't finished. "I know what it is to lose someone that feels like losing a part of your body. I *tried* to get you to take some time to grieve, because you can't help what it does to you. But you don't have anyone besides this team. I made the mistake of allowing you to stay at work the entire time, and I told myself it was okay for you to spend time searching for a terrorist instead of climbing into a bottle or drugs. But you went too far this time for vengeance."

No matter what Margaux said, no one was going to believe that tonight hadn't been about retribution for Nanci's death. And, to be honest, that was her own fault for not talking to

Sabrina and letting her know that she'd let it go.

Margaux had actually *never* been after vengeance so much as trying to quiet the voice in her head that accused her of doing nothing as Nanci died alone. She had to explain to Sabrina. "Nanci transferred here to help on *our* case. I don't regret asking her, because we saved Ryder from a murder rap, but I pushed her to do things that went against her oath as an FBI agent. She did all that because—" *Because she loved me like a sister.* She took a breath. She never let her emotions show. Ever. In a firmer voice, she said, "Nanci did everything I asked, even when it reached the gray area of her job and all because *I* asked her to. She got a bullet between the eyes for it and I'm having a hard time getting past the helpless feeling of doing nothing."

"I haven't forgotten her sacrifice and neither has the team."

Margaux heard the compassion, but also a hard line in Sabrina's voice. "I know you've been patient and given me space, Sabrina. I'm telling you the truth that I let it all go earlier this past week. I swear to you I did not mislead you tonight."

Sabrina shook her head with disbelief. "But you didn't tell me that you *suspected* the Banker would be at this meeting, did you? Then we break up a drug operation and there isn't one terrorist involved."

Margaux had no idea how this could have happened. She'd gone over it in her mind a hundred times already. She'd also tried calling and texting Snake Eyes, but he hadn't returned her WTF text messages.

Sabrina let out a sigh loaded with disappointment. "The problem is that you've lost the ability to think beyond any tip on the Banker, no matter how slim."

Margaux seethed over the accusation, but this was the time to stop arguing and start putting out fires. "I hear you. And in hindsight, I can see how you think that." Only if she wore Coke-bottle glasses, but this was her mess. She'd accept responsibility. "How bad is it with the DEA?"

"FUBAR, but I made a call I save as a Get-Out-Of-Deep-Shit-Free card and agreed to comp the DEA two missions ...

regardless of the details."

Ah, hell, that sucked. Sabrina was judicious when it came to accepting or declining government jobs. Now she'd not only have to run an operation for free but take ops that she might otherwise pass on.

If Sabrina could do that, Margaux could grovel.

"Sorry, Sabrina. I mean it. I'll do whatever you want whenever you need it for *free* until that's paid off." Margaux wasn't wealthy by any standard, but she had no life beyond being an operative for Sabrina and saved every penny. She could afford to go without pay for a while.

"You don't understand, Duke. I can't fix this, not this time."

Margaux had come to recognize that slight variation of anger in Sabrina's voice as concern. "I'll disappear."

"Really. Then what? You'll eventually have to tell someone the truth because your fingerprints aren't in the system, and you have no identity other than the one with Slye. The days of easy cash for legitimate work are gone. Once someone figures out you're hiding your identity, they'll either sell you out to law enforcement or to—"

Margaux held up her hand. "I know the risks, but I brought this on myself."

Sabrina's gaze held something she was hesitating to say. "I made a deal with you that I'd protect your secret, but only as long as you stayed on the straight and narrow with me."

The first hint of true terror stirred in Margaux's chest. "I have. I've been on the right side of the law the entire time with you."

"You don't understand. You've hidden in plain sight as one of my people. The DEA agent you took to the ground tonight will be demanding your head. If suddenly, you're no longer on my team, someone will put two and two together. I could lie to them for three or four months, tell them you're off on a mission, but eventually it would catch up with me and that would destroy the trust I've earned. That would be the end of my teams."

"What are you saying, Sabrina?"

"That the safest place for you might be in the WITSEC program."

Margaux couldn't speak for a moment past her shock. "You've got to be kidding me. I go there and I'll be in lock down or I'll end up dead."

"Not if we create a new identity and I pull some strings to get you in the system as a witness on a top-secret case."

Margaux argued, "If the Feds don't know I'm the one who called in the bombing in Arkansas six years ago, they won't know to watch for Lonnie's father." The man had led a group of anarchists who were fueled by rage against the government. Lonnie had said he wanted to build a better world, and after the one Margaux had grown up in that sounded wonderful … until she found out the truth about their "freedom" group. When she'd balked, Lonnie had shown her just how little her love and her life meant. One bomb had gone off, and the only reason more people hadn't died was because Lonnie and his father's men had left her for dead.

She'd called in time to prevent detonation of the other bombs.

Sabrina had been the one to find her.

Margaux pointed out what she saw as obvious. "If I go into WITSEC and end up working a normal job out in the open, Lonnie's father will eventually find me and make me pay for his son's death. And if I tell the Feds the truth about being Lonnie's girlfriend, they'll lock me up with crap about it being for my safety and I'll never be free."

Her dad had been a single parent and a mean bastard. He'd constantly pointed out how her two brothers were *something* because they played football, and she was *nothing* because she barely pulled average grades in school. One brother killed a person while driving drunk and the other one got a girl pregnant then disappeared. Yeah, they were something. Then Lonnie came along and convinced Margaux she was special, that together they could change the world.

He'd only changed her world and in ways she shuddered to remember.

Sabrina said, "I've thought about the Feds and Lonnie's father. Give me time to work something out."

No way would Margaux put her life in the hands of law enforcement, not even WITSEC. Lonnie's father had been a policeman once, and he still had friends on the force. He'd use those resources to find her. But saying so to Sabrina now would only double the guards outside. "So, I'm under house arrest until you work that out?"

Sabrina's tight features eased, meaning she assumed Margaux was on board with waiting for a plan even if it ended up being WITSEC. "Yes. If you leave this apartment, I'll have to report you."

That was straight-shooter Sabrina. She didn't try to deny that those people downstairs in surveillance cars that had been here when Margaux arrived home were around for any other reason than to ensure that Margaux stayed put.

"That all?" Margaux might not show emotion, but it was ripping her insides. Sabrina had been her one friend, the one person besides Nanci who knew how much this pitiful life meant to her.

And just how much it would cost Margaux to give it up.

Sabrina's jaw was rigid, all business. "I'll be in touch. I expect you to be here when I do."

Margaux nodded. "Don't leave town. Got it."

"I'm not joking, Duke. Make one step outside this building and I'll consider you rogue. Don't leave this apartment for anything short of a fire and go out the front windows even then." That was an order.

"Whatever," Margaux muttered. She opened the door but when Sabrina stepped through, Margaux said, "Wait."

Sabrina stopped. "Yes?"

"Tell the team thanks for everything and—" Margaux hated to ask for anything, but she was asking now. "*Please* ... tell them that I told you exactly what I knew to be true. I would never hold back information pertinent to a mission or play games with the team."

"I'll tell them." But from Sabrina's tone, she didn't expect many to accept that.

When Sabrina left, Margaux stepped over to peer out the opening between the blinds and her window.

Sabrina drove off in her Hummer. The dark sedan still parked outside appeared to hold one male and one female, but Margaux didn't recognize either one.

How many others had Sabrina ordered to watch her?

Margaux's burner cell phone finally buzzed. Only one person should be calling. She answered, "What the fuck was tonight about and where the hell have you been?"

"Calm down," Snake Eyes growled in a low voice that warned he was on edge, too. "I just found out the cops busted the place. What the hell happened?"

Snake Eyes thought she was a hired assassin who did an occasional snatch job, because she let him think that. It was her persona, to be part of the criminal world. For that reason, she had to say, "What *happened*? You screwed me. You said it was a payoff for a terrorist attack going down in Atlanta to-*day*! Not a fucking drug deal."

"I got screwed, too, but this is as much your fault as mine."

She wanted her gun. "How do you see that?"

"If you'll calm down and kick the attitude to the curb, I'll explain, Duke," he said, using her street moniker The Duke, but neither Margaux nor Duke were the names on her real birth certificate, or on her death certificate.

"*This!*" She pointed a finger at herself even though he couldn't see it. "Is not attitude. This is pissed beyond sanity. Tell me something worth hearing or I'm hanging up so I can hunt you down." False threat, but only until she was mobile again.

"You hang up and we both die. We have to move fast, or we'll lose your Banker."

How could her heart jump with hope after what had happened tonight? She really was a nut case if she got sucked into this again. "Forget it, Snake Eyes. I already told you that I'm done with that bastard. He's cost me more than I'll ever recover."

"Bull. Shit. You aren't bailing on me now. Not after the shitstorm you've dragged me into."

"What do you mean?"

"We were *both* set up. I heard from an associate that the Banker caught wind of me hunting for him."

"How'd you let that happen?" She didn't work with just any informant. Snake Eyes had been tough to bring to the table the first year she'd found out about him. He had to have far-reaching resources for some of the things he'd handed her, which was why she'd been surprised that the Banker had been so impossible to find at first.

"I assure you, Duke, that I intend to find out where the breakdown in my network is, but I have to be breathing to make that happen. Back to our problem, and it is *ours* to fix. The contact who passed the information for tonight's meeting was double tapped at close range while the meeting was going on. Cost me a significant amount of money to discover I was fed bad intel on purpose."

"Why?"

"To find out who's been hunting the Banker. That would be me and you."

Margaux turned and slid down the wall to sit on the floor. She propped her elbow on her bent knee and gripped her forehead. Talk about a sucky night. "If that's the case, how is it that you're still alive?"

"I wouldn't have survived this long if I didn't have friends in this business. We watch each other's backs. So, the hunter is now the hunted. You have to take out the Banker before he gets to you, Duke."

"He won't find me." She started mentally going over everything she'd stashed just in case she ever had to make a run for it alone. She had another ID and plenty of cash, but walking out of this apartment would destroy the trust Sabrina had placed in her.

"Oh, he'll find you," Snake Eyes said without hesitation. "I can disappear, but eventually someone will give me up for the right price. From what I understand, the Banker has more than enough. If he finds me, he finds you. I have two choices. I either help you get him, or I go to him right now and give him everything on you."

"What's stopping you from going to him?" she asked, curious to know what he'd say.

"Because I'm not stupid enough to think he won't send someone to kill me once he has what he needs from me." Snake Eyes added, "You strike me as a loner, but know this. As I understand it, the Banker will not just hunt us down, he'll go after everyone we've ever known."

The ramifications hit her in the solar plexus. She could sit here like a goat tied to a stick for slaughter, or she could run. But either way, the Banker would go after Sabrina and the rest of the team.

She had to call Sabrina.

And say what? That she'd gotten new intel and if Sabrina didn't turn Margaux loose that Sabrina and the team would be at risk.

Oh, yeah, that would fly. *Not.*

Sabrina would think Margaux was making a last-ditch run at freedom. If Margaux brought everyone in on this, there would be no way to shield them from the Banker. Every person on Sabrina's team was exceptional and capable of handling a threat, but once the Banker discovered any connection between Margaux and the Slye team, he had the resources to wipe all of them from the face of the earth.

At this point, there was no reason for the Banker to target Sabrina and the team unless Margaux brought them in on this. That wasn't happening.

No one else was dying because of her mistakes.

"Duke?"

"I'm here. How the hell am I supposed to get to the Banker if I can't find him?" Successful Assassin 101: must have target.

"I've been very busy tonight and put the full power of my resources on this. I have a hard lead on him."

Her heart double-thumped at the words she'd been waiting to hear from Snake Eyes for eight months. "How could you have it now?"

"I received a call from my contact's phone *after* I found out he was dead. The person calling was my contact's people. They're pissed and threatened to come after me until I told them the whole score about being set up."

"You mention me?"

"I don't share information without an incentive, and they had no reason to ask about you." He kept his voice down. "Evidently, my contact was the brother of a powerful man in New York who immigrated from Turkey. He wants whoever was responsible for offing his brother, and he has impressive resources."

Coming from Snake Eyes, that was high praise.

He continued. "This brother in New York needed time to make some inquiries, which was why I didn't call you until now. I just hung up with him. He didn't have a lot of information, but what he did have is quite valuable. The Banker *is* here in the US, but I don't know why. Yet. However, he's meeting with an operator—a mercenary with the skills for whatever the Banker has in mind. We have one shot at finding him before he finds us. The location where the Banker will meet with the merc is being passed off at a nightclub in San Francisco."

"When?"

"Tonight."

She'd have to hand this intel over to Sabrina. "Where?"

His chuckle was dark and deadly. "You know as much as you need to know right now. I'm not risking anyone screwing this up before you have a chance to take your shot. Call me when you reach San Francisco."

If she stepped outside this building, she'd become a fugitive. Sabrina would take a bullet for any one of her team, but when she warned she'd report Margaux to law enforcement she meant it.

"If you can't do this, say so now, Duke, so I can make other arrangements."

He'd find another assassin, who might or might not succeed,

and with no motivation beyond money.

Margaux closed her eyes and considered the end result of defying Sabrina, but it didn't matter. She'd brought death to Nanci's door, but she could stop it from reaching Sabrina and the team. "I can do it."

CHAPTER 3

The elevator doors parted, exposing the Trophy Room, one of San Francisco's best-kept secrets.

Logan Baklanov stepped forward and scanned the space. A pair of sultry female twins in ocean-blue gowns were playing a piano and alto saxophone. Both of their faces were uncovered. No Venetian-style mask like the other women in the room wore. Subdued lighting meant to flatter the clientele gave the upscale décor a warm glow.

An inviting setting to some.

All the makings of a death trap to Logan.

Limited exit strategies. No way for any of his team to get close enough to backup him and his partner. He couldn't bring in a weapon, but that didn't concern him much.

There were plenty of ways to kill a person.

Staying in character as the bodyguard, Logan stepped aside and nodded at Jamie "Nitro" Johnson that he could exit the elevator.

Decked out in a custom black suit and tan silk shirt tailored to his muscular body, Nitro played the role of cocksure Dragan Stoli, or Mr. D as he would be addressed here, right down to his swagger.

As of right now, Nitro *was* Dragan.

Dragan paused as though observing the dazzling assortment of around fifty women mixed in with twelve men wearing power attitudes.

Logan stifled a snort.

If these men were truly powerful, they wouldn't risk *anyone* knowing they shopped in a high-end meat market. These were power-wannabes who rolled in the high seven-figures playground, but a step below the top dogs in their world.

They wanted a safe place to play and prime selection.

Dragan took his time, turning his head with an admiring smile on his lips. In truth, he was taking stock of the layout through a pair of five-hundred-dollar sunglasses that were tinted just enough to hide his eyes but allow clear vision.

Logan was doing the same from behind a pair of iconic-looking Oakley sunglasses most people associated with modern security.

Once Dragan had drawn a gaggle of attention from the pool of beauties, he strode confidently toward three women holding martini glasses. Cookie cutter babes, all dressed in designer chic right down to exquisite jeweled and feathered masks that covered the top halves of their faces.

The Trophy Room was a private—and secret—venue owned by three international businessmen. Their hand-selected stable of women were brought in from all over the world, including some from this country.

The mask indicated availability.

Once a deal was struck, the mask came off, which prevented confusion and allowed the predatory male to show off his "catch."

Dragan spoke with a smooth Russian accent. "Good evening, ladies."

While Logan's partner did his job of making an entrance and charming the women, Logan moved to a quiet spot at the end of the thirty-foot black granite bar. He picked a position close enough to keep an eye on Dragan's back and observe the room at the same time.

The Banker had said to arrive early, and his woman would contact Dragan before 0030 hours. But the bastard wouldn't commit to a code message that would have made it simple to confirm who the correct woman was. The Banker was known for playing games until you were accepted inside his circle of mercenaries. He felt that any operative worth his salt should be able to spot a contact inside a room full of prostitutes.

He had a point.

It still pissed off Logan.

A muscle twitched between his shoulder blades. Would the Banker really show himself when the time came? Logan hadn't found anyone within the Banker's circle of resources, but the

Banker had been credited with enough successful attacks to prove he hired capable muscle.

Logan knew of two mercs who'd *tried* to sign on and failed the Banker's initial tests.

Failure coming in the form of torture, then death.

Logan's failure would put his men at risk and leave his brother Yuri to die in a Russian prison where he was being held. *Held* was an innocuous term for what Yuri might be suffering every second of every day.

Worry fisted in his gut, but Logan had to force it away and stay on task. If anything went wrong tonight, he could forget getting a second chance at a meeting, based on the Banker's known MO. No, this was his one opportunity to capture the head of a snake that slithered through the world, leaving a swath of destruction everywhere it went.

That snake had to be handed over alive in trade for Yuri.

A woman in a sweeping, deep-blue gown strolled up to Logan. Brunette hair fell to her waist and the design on her mask matched a swirl of rhinestones down the front of her dress, drawing his eye to the cleavage on display. He had the advantage of taking her in without notice from behind his dark glasses. And she had a lot of fine real estate, but he would have expected the Banker to at least send a statuesque blonde, based on the rumors Logan's team had leaked about Dragan's female of choice.

Not a five-foot-four, dark-haired hooker.

Full lips painted cherry red smiled at him. "Would you like something to drink or is alcohol off limits when you're working?"

He wasn't picking up anything from this woman that registered needle movement on his *operative* meter. Would the Banker send a novice? Logan didn't think so. This woman was only looking for a shortcut to the man with the money.

Dragan.

Logan kept his head turned toward Dragan but watched her out of the corner of his eye when he answered. "No, thank you."

Her smile slipped. She glanced over her shoulder to where Dragan held court. "I'll have a tough time fighting my way through that crowd." She turned back to Logan. "Tell you what. If I'm not unmasked later, want to hook up?"

Maybe he'd been wrong about her.

He gave her a second consideration. Was this one of the Banker's famous "tests"? Logan's heartbeat ticked up a notch. One wrong move and the Banker might pick up his toys and go home.

Logan lived and died by his gut, and right now it was telling him she was not his contact. The one thing he couldn't afford was to be indecisive. Maintaining an unemotional face, he said, "Thank you, but no."

She stood there a moment then smiled and shook her head as if she'd refused him, which the women could do, and walked off. She strolled up to a man who hadn't warmed up to any woman since Logan had entered.

The brunette didn't seem the least bit deterred.

Business as usual.

Logan stretched his arms out and crossed them over his chest, doing a covert time check as he did. Eighteen minutes to 0030.

He'd have come at the very last moment, but that would have been a risk if the Banker sent his contact early.

If one of the women around Dragan had pinged for Dragan by now, he would have given Logan "the sign" of adjusting his glasses on his face and holding his chin with his left thumb and finger.

Hadn't happened yet.

Logan never rushed an operation, but this one had been taking too long from the first minute he'd devised it. His team had endured eleven hellish months of establishing a reputation in the underworld as a team of elite mercenaries behind two deadly attacks in Bangkok and France. They'd also eliminated the group who had actually executed those attacks.

Still no word from the Banker when Logan had put out word he had the best team for the right money.

Then his reputation got unexpected help in the form of his team being blamed for an attack his people hadn't committed.

Timing was everything.

The next thing he knew, the Banker was shopping for an elite mercenary group. With the groundwork Logan had laid, it was clear to anyone serious in the terror business that there was no better team on the current market than Logan's.

The Banker clearly needed him after that failed attempt on the Pope and Vatican eight months ago.

And Logan needed the Banker.

One man inside INTERPOL knew the truth about Logan's team and the deadly underworld reputation he'd *created*, because Logan had carried out covert operations for that agency in the past. But he couldn't tell his INTERPOL liaison what he was really doing this time. Not when Logan was going after someone INTERPOL wanted badly and Logan had other plans for this package.

He'd lost too many people in his life to risk any of his men who were brothers in belief. He wouldn't have brought them on this mission if they hadn't cornered him and demanded to be included.

If this was only about himself, he'd have refused, but this was about Yuri facing a brutal death, and soon.

Eleven grueling months came down to tonight. Logan cut his eyes down at his watch. Seventeen minutes to go.

The brunette came strolling back up.

Persistent little thing. Could this *really* be the contact and he'd missed a cue?

His uninterested bodyguard expression never changed. "Can I help you?"

She smiled. "No, but I can help you."

Dragan hadn't given him a signal and no other woman had approached Logan, so he gave this one his full attention. He was ready to get the hell out of here as fast as he and Nitro could do so without drawing attention. Logan shifted his head to face her and allowed the hint of a smile in his expression. "In that case, I'm listening."

CHAPTER 4

Margaux had arrived six minutes early for tonight's meeting and taken a strategic position near the roof edge of this thirty-seven-story building. Snake Eyes finally stepped into the chilly darkness shrouding the access door ten strides away.

Should she pay him or kill him?

Tough choice.

Her ass was in a sling because of this prick, despite his protesting otherwise.

White LED lights spaced along the parapet offered enough light beneath the hip-high wall to traverse the outer boundary of the roof, but the snitch didn't move a step. Predators preferred shadows. Salt-laden air rolling off San Francisco Bay blew his duster, making it snap against his legs.

He called out, "Why are you over there?"

"I like the view." *And I might want to find out if pigs really can fly before I'm done tonight.* Margaux held her position, leaving her exposed to the midnight breeze that cut her to the bone. The damned shiny dress she wore for tonight had better be worth the effort. It barely covered the essentials.

And she meant barely. Her cashmere cape offered little additional insulation against the brittle temperatures.

He stood still as the Grim Reaper waiting for his victim to make a move. Short black hair ringed the crown of his head and a beak nose overpowered his narrow face that had picked up a few lines in forty plus years.

Vultures were more attractive.

He sounded almost amused. "I'm impressed that you know I don't like heights."

If I only gave a shit about impressing you. "We've played by your rules. I'm here. Time to give me the rest of the information so I can be on my way."

"I hear a note of hostility that I find curious since I'm here to help you."

*No, you're not here to help me, but to help yourself to the
bag-o-money at my feet that will allow you to disappear even
faster if I fail to stop the Banker.* "Neither of us is here to make
nice. Move this along if you want the money, and the Banker
dealt with so you can live long enough to spend it."

"I hope you're as capable as your reputation," he muttered.

"I am." She hoped so, too. Her gut didn't like any part of the
game she had to play tonight. It had better be worth walking
away from Sabrina, who would unleash a team of elite
operatives to hunt her down as soon as she found out Margaux
was gone.

He studied her intensely and declared, "You'll pass for
Violet."

"I'd better, for what I paid a makeup artist who could turn
you into Brad Pitt." Margaux could pull off masquerading as
an expensive call girl, but that didn't guarantee she wouldn't
be made if anything went wrong. "Tell me about the exits and
security."

"Again?"

"I'm paying to hear it as many times as I want." Margaux
had too much at stake not to put Snake Eyes to the test of
repeating the details while she watched for an inflection, any
sign of lying.

"There is no logic in my lying to you at this point, but you
are paying for this."

The secret club was in the basement level of a privately
owned hotel. Affluent men, celebrities, anyone who wanted to
enjoy a nightclub atmosphere could go there without worry of
public exposure. The women on display were the best that
money could buy, guaranteed clean and skilled in every sexual
game imaginable. Three corporate power players were behind
the club. They vetted members and the female entertainment,
changing access codes daily to assure security.

Snake Eyes finished covering the exit points, then he
repeated that the jagged roof design had no chopper access.
Security personnel held the elevator keycard access. "Everyone
passes through a metal detector so don't walk in there with a

weapon, Duke."

She opened the cape, exposing the dress that stopped just below her thong, and snorted. "Like I could hide a gun in *this* getup?"

"I wouldn't put anything past you."

Smart man. She'd tried to tuck just one knife somewhere, but no chance.

She'd found aerial photos showing the only flat area up high was a penthouse patio with a pool. It was huge, but not big enough for a helo pad. "Where're the key card and mask?"

He reached back inside his bulky coat as he stepped forward slowly and withdrew a red, satin bag the size of two hands. "Violet's ID key card works only tonight, and this mask is worn once then replaced."

Margaux held her hand out.

Snake Eyes eyed her with contempt. "If you force me to come over there, I won't forget."

She held her spot, willing to take her chances by pissing him off.

He stuck the card in the satin bag and tossed the bag to her.

She snagged it from the wind and looked inside. Gold mask with decorative carving. Black, red, and gold feathers poofed out the top. She pulled the drawstring on the satin bag that weighed nothing and dropped it next to the parapet.

Margaux asked, "What about Violet?"

"She's tied up neat as a Thanksgiving turkey. The men I sent were covered head to toe."

Margaux let an edge of steel cut through her quiet voice. "Did they hurt her?"

"No. She's fine. The police will be alerted at daylight about strange noises coming from her apartment. Her employer will have no reason to think she was in on this, as we agreed."

Nodding, Margaux went on. "Now, about this merc meeting the Banker."

"Dragan Stoli. A Russian who's built a name for himself rather quickly over the past year. He runs a team of elite operators, no tie to any one political group. Explosives and tactical experts."

"What's he doing here if he's out of Russia?"

"As I understand it, the Banker doesn't recruit until right before an operation. As this is supposed to be his first venture in the US, he's clearly wanting to meet with those who can insert without detection. He has something planned on the West Coast and soon. My new contact in New York indicated the Banker would be interviewing more than one group. It's a shame I'll miss the opportunity to work with him."

This butt wipe didn't give a piss about the danger the Banker presented to thousands of innocent people in this country. And it would be thousands because this terrorist only got involved with large-scale destruction. If she tossed Snake Eyes over the edge, she'd be doing the gene pool a favor.

She asked, "What kind of mercs is he looking for?" *There were thugs then there were deadly operators with no morals.*

"The kind that keeps the Navy training SEALs."

This got more complicated by the minute. There would be no time to follow a tracker to the Banker. The minute she had the tracking chip in place on Dragan, she'd have to risk calling Sabrina. With a major operation in play, there was too much at stake now to take any chance of losing the Banker or Dragan.

Who do I have to kill to get a real break?

She hated seat-of-the-pants ops, but it wouldn't be the first time. At least, the Trophy Room rules worked in her favor with the masks. "Did you come up with any description of the Banker?"

"*If* I had that, it would cost you far more than is in that bag."

"I shouldn't be paying for anything considering this is *our* problem to solve and I've paid you plenty for him already."

He waved that off as insignificant. "I gave you a deal. Appreciate that and don't quibble."

"What do you know on the Russian?"

Snake Eyes ran a finger over his bony chin that had a patch of beard the size of a silver dollar. "I don't have a lot on Dragan, but he was behind that commando assault that went down at a hotel in Pakistan four months back, and he delivered a stolen load of missiles to Abri A'duazam nine months ago."

This Dragan character needed to burn, too. If Margaux had a team with her, she could bring him in. "What else?"

"Dragan is almost as hard to find information on as the Banker. *But* I did get something personal on him. He doesn't go anywhere without his bodyguard. Big sucker. Dragan will be known as Mr. D at the club tonight *and* Dragan's got a thing for women."

"*That's* intel on someone with a dick?" she asked in a wry tone.

"You have a point, but what I'm saying is that he has an insatiable appetite, so you should get an opportunity to get close to him even if you have to stand in line."

In her experience, men who talked about how much sex they got usually didn't, but she could use the insight on Dragan's ego to her advantage.

Snake Eyes warned, "Don't try to talk to Dragan without going through his bodyguard first. That's a standard Trophy Room rule for anyone who brings a bodyguard."

"Why do these men need protection in a room full of hookers?"

"It's a power image thing, I suppose. And when I say Dragan goes nowhere without his muscle, I mean *nowhere*. I would assume it's to cover him while his guard is down when he's otherwise engaged with a woman."

Ah, hell. That would make inserting the tracking device tricky.

Place the tracking device on the bodyguard? She'd figure that out when she got there. "Photo of Dragan?"

"Unfortunately, no, but I do have a description. He's five-ten, has short black hair and a scar running from his right ear to his collarbone. He prefers tall, blond women, which is why Violet was the perfect choice."

Margaux's auburn hair was tucked beneath a blond wig styled to emulate Violet's long, straight locks that hit just below her shoulders. "How is the meeting being arranged?"

"The Banker's person is supposed to contact Dragan

between 12:30 and one tonight, or technically tomorrow morning. And there's a line the women use in the Trophy Room to let the men know they're interested."

"I thought the whole point was for the men to do the chasing."

"It is, but some men prefer aggressive women who won't give it up easily. Dragan supposedly enjoys role-playing with leather and chains. Approach the bodyguard and say these exact words. 'Tell Mr. D that I'm interested in speaking with him alone. I'll allow him one minute or I'll move on.' That informs Dragan you're interested and should get you close enough to do whatever you have planned. That is, unless you piss off the bodyguard."

"Think I can manage that," she assured him.

"One last thing. Two of the three owners are out of the country. Sergio Santiago hired Violet and he's the only one that will be around tonight." Snake Eyes scratched his chin again, taking her in with an analytical eye. "You look very much like Violet, but I wouldn't plan to stay in view much longer than ten minutes, and definitely avoid any contact with Sergio."

Icy fingers gripped her stomach in warning. Sergio might have taken Violet for a test ride first, which meant that he'd know a hell of a lot more about the new girl than her face. "Fuck. Picked the best one for me to imitate, did you?"

Snake Eyes made an exaggerated sigh. "She was the only one who fit the tall and blond description, plus was somewhat close to your shape. The owners normally observe via cameras. Just don't let Sergio get you alone."

Or you're royally screwed, she finished silently.

"If you miss your 12:30 window, this is all down the drain, Duke."

"I can tell time." All Margaux had to do was find the man the Banker wanted to meet and tag a tracking device on the operative before he went to the meeting. Piece of cake with a team, but she didn't even have backup. "Is that it?"

"Yes."

"Then come get your money."

His face was shadowed, but she could feel anger surging off of him at having his phobia tested. He took one slow step at a time, breathing harder the closer he came to the wall.

A couple more seconds and he'd be in perfect position. He stopped two feet from the bag and bent over, jaw clenched and arm shaking as he reached out.

Margaux kicked his feet out from beneath him.

He fell toward the gritty surface face first, jerking a gun from his coat.

She was ready and disarmed him before he hit the ground. Then she tossed his weapon aside and dropped a knee down, hitting the middle of his back with her full body weight.

That knocked the kick out of him.

Wind howled, blowing her hair around and muffling the curses he was yelling.

She grabbed a pair of plastic cuffs hidden next to the bag and secured first his hands behind his back then his feet. She stood up and used a foot to shove him over on his back, then placed her spiked shoe on his chest.

He twitched and jerked, cursing between gasps for air. "What the ... *fuck*!"

"You wouldn't sell *me* out to someone with a fatter wallet, now would you?"

He shook his head. "You're making a mistake, Duke."

"If you've given me even one piece of faulty intel tonight, or if I find out I've been played in any way, I *will* come for you. And when *I* get through with you there won't be a part worth donating to science ... unless someone wants to make a change purse out of your nut sack."

"You should never make unnecessary enemies, Duke."

She glanced at the delicate women's watch she'd normally never wear. 12:17. Thirteen minutes until showtime, but the hotel was a five-minute walk. She pulled the sheer sleeve that hid her muscular arm back down over the watch. Not that the women in this nightclub weren't in shape, but she kickboxed regularly and it showed.

Reaching inside her cape, she pulled out a switchblade and flipped the blade open.

He didn't flinch, just watched her with the gaze of a man considering murder.

She picked up the satin bag and reached over to the ledge where she'd left her silver purse. It held a cell phone, a miniature camera that doubled as a tube of lipstick, and a tiny EPIRB unit the size of a grain of rice that would send out a signal the minute she activated it, much like tracking units on a deployed life raft. It had a sticky surface and she intended to plant it somewhere it would stay.

Dropping the knife on the ground next to Snake Eyes, she walked away.

Eleven minutes to go. Her timing was perfect.

Sabrina had accused Margaux of being reckless, but the minute she learned that Margaux had walked into this viper pit without backup, Sabrina would change that assessment to mental.

That wouldn't matter unless Margaux walked out alive.

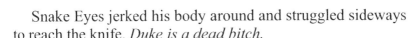

Snake Eyes jerked his body around and struggled sideways to reach the knife. *Duke is a dead bitch.*

By the time his fingers touched the cool metal, his long-legged client had strutted across the rooftop and disappeared through the exit door. He nicked his fingers and cursed while he turned the knife into position to cut through the plastic cuffs.

The minute his hands and feet were free, he reached over for his bag of money, dragging it with him as he crab-shuffled across the rooftop. He rolled around into a sitting position next to the exit door, panting. His heart pounded like a freight train coming down the tracks and he could smell the stink of his own terror.

No one humiliated him and got away with it.

Pulling out his cell phone with one hand, he hit the speed dial button. He used his other hand to check the cash—all there.

After two rings, a click at the other end of the line was the only indication the phone had been answered.

Snake Eyes had to swallow his fear before he could croak out the words, "All done."

"Where is she?"

"Headed to the club. My debt to you is cleared?"

"As long as you did everything I said."

Snake Eyes wiped the sweat off his brow in spite of the freezing-ass weather. "I did. She bought every word."

CHAPTER 5

If this was a trick, Logan wasn't taking the bait. The petite brunette had just finished telling him how many ways she could rock his world once they left the Trophy Room.

He kept the irritation out of his voice and maintained his Russian accent. "I doubt your bosses would approve of you giving it away for free and I have never been a fan of leftovers."

Her smile faded, but she was too tough to be insulted. "I didn't realize you couldn't afford this menu." She walked way. Finally.

One minute before 0030 hours. Was the contact here already?

The elevator doors swooshed open and for the first time tonight a woman caught Logan's eye.

A long-legged fantasy emerged, entering the room slowly like a secret thought. She didn't sashay around in her shimmering gold dress, dragging tongues out in her wake as several others had. No, this one strolled through, letting it be known that she was here, she was available, and she was not going to be easy.

Talk about hot.

That kind of confidence turned Logan on faster than big boobs and pouty lips.

Blond hair flowed around a sleek neck and graceful shoulders. Sheer sleeves covered her arms, but she appeared more buff than soft. Her legs flexed with cut muscle. Not the kind earned from a steady diet of aerobics. He might be the rare man in here who appreciated a woman with serious muscles earned from hours of hard workouts. Those legs would fit perfectly around his waist.

She paused to speak to a man standing with another woman. Madam Amazon's perfect lips offered the possibility of a smile, but no more, as she moved on.

Legs wrapped around him and those lips on his. He wanted

a taste. He wanted ...

What the hell? He was getting hard as stone, and he blamed it on going without for almost a year. Logan balled his hands against his arms and thought of ugly hookers, his brother in prison, anything but how much he liked the way the long-legged beauty moved.

She made it around the room and her gaze shifted toward Dragan for a moment, then returned to surveying the rest of the room. But that one flicker of notice was enough to jack Logan's spidey sense into high gear.

Tall, blond, and moved like she'd had serious physical training.

Could this be the Banker's contact?

Calculating her physical appearance, the time factor, and the way she watched the room as she navigated her way around, Logan would bet his left nut that she was the one.

Another man detained her. She leaned in, listened, considered, and gave him some answer that managed to leave him smiling even though she walked away.

Her gaze had been hidden inside the slits of her gold domino mask until she turned toward the aquarium and the fish cleared. Those intense purple eyes peered through an opening between rocks and fish to meet his. He didn't so much as twitch beneath her perusal, but keeping one body part in particular under control was a test.

Think ugly old hookers.

He had a rule against hookers, no matter how hot. He'd never been that desperate.

On the other hand, this was a mission, and he needed the Banker.

Dragan and his attack bodyguard were here.

Margaux hid her flash of relief that Snake Eyes hadn't screwed her so far. As she walked the room, keeping the aquarium between her and the bar, she gave polite smiles, trying to ignore the men as they ogled her the way cowboys admired prime beef. She took her time weaving through the group of hardtails, who hallucinated her into their current sexual fantasies, and the array of stunning women who paid her no mind.

If Dragan was here, that *should* mean whoever the Banker was sending to make contact had not arrived yet. That's how it would work in a perfect world.

Lately, in her world it could mean the Banker's person had already made contact and Dragan would just walk out once he tired of the female attention.

Margaux might have already gambled everything on tonight, but something told her she wasn't through placing bets.

Women with invisible price tags surrounded Dragan.

Every masked woman in this place had one.

Including Margaux. But only for tonight.

Choosing to play a role was far different than actually being used that way. She'd never let someone hurt her physically again.

Never let herself get in the position where someone she loved could trade her for—

Stop it. Unproductive thinking was dangerous on a mission.

She kept moving, taking her time getting around the room, building interest. At least she *hoped* Dragan was noticing since he was turned this way with his back to the bar.

Dragan Stoli had no reason for a place like this.

Most of the men were of the same cut as the gray-haired fiftyish guy she'd just passed who had a paunch, manicured nails, and sported a diamond-encrusted watch.

Gray-hair gave her a lifted-eyebrow invitation.

She tilted her head and returned his leer with a taunting smile but turned away. A discreet no.

Better than the *eww* screaming in her mind.

How long could she avoid getting cornered by one of the men without someone on staff noticing?

This would have been a hell of a lot easier with backup.

Even a weapon would be nice, but her razor-thin dress wouldn't hide a freckle and security had scanned her, head to toe. And taken her coat.

But they'd cleared her purse and shoes.

Keeping watch on Dragan with sly glances, Margaux made the turn around the far end of the room and proceeded toward the bar behind him.

She'd caught sight of her watch—12:32—when she lifted her hand to wave over the male bartender, who wore an expression that was a combination of interest and distance. His six-figure income depended on maintaining selective memory and not engaging with any of the female guests.

She ordered a martini.

If Dragan hadn't been contacted yet, she had time to get the tracking device in place.

But he was still smothered in women.

Margaux lifted the martini she had no intention of drinking and let her gaze travel to the back of the bar where layers of mirror had been cut in an abstract pattern.

She had a clear image of Dragan.

A couple inches under six feet, he had brown hair cut hot-guy short, but the muscles in his neck hinted at a solid body beneath the black Louis Vuitton suit jacket. The identifying scar slashed from his left ear to his collarbone just as Snake Eyes had said. Dragan had an attractive, but otherwise uninteresting face, much like all the others shopping for an expensive party girl for the night.

On the other hand, Dragan's bodyguard was anything but uninteresting.

He stood off to her right, with Secret-Service-looking eyewear and a coal-black designer suit that had to be custom-tailored to fit shoulders as wide as his.

That was one big man.

Just her flavor if she had any interest in a taste.

Surprisingly, he still managed to blend into the shadows, motionless as a tiger waiting for his dinner to stroll by. Power rolled off him in silent waves. She couldn't discern much about his face with that thick, but neat, black beard and his eyes hidden.

Handsome was too simple a word to describe him, too civilized. Like admiring a wolf for its lush coat or a shark for its grace in the water, a woman would find this man attractive in a deadly way.

A woman who enjoyed playing with fire or dancing with lightning.

A woman who was a fool.

Good thing he was *not* the one she needed to engage in pre-mating rituals. Nothing about that man invited sexual banter, which she found even more appealing. No, he was not one to play with and that presented a problem.

Right now, she had to get to Dragan and the bodyguard was her only route.

The bartender drew her attention when he paused near her but turned away. His fingers went to the wired receiver in his ear. He spoke softly into the mic attached to his collar. "Give me a minute to check the masks for tonight so I can identify Violet. Tell Mr. Santiago I'll send her up as soon as I locate her."

Shit.

Margaux raised her martini and moved away from the bar toward the dark alcove where the bodyguard stood. When she reached him, she waited for the bodyguard to acknowledge her, but he didn't drop his chin or angle his head. Nothing to indicate what was going on behind those dark glasses.

She felt the seconds screaming in her ear with each pulse of her heart. This was it. She forced calm and confidence into her voice. "Tell Mr. D that Violet is interested in speaking to him alone. He has one minute, or I'll move on."

Dragan's bodyguard just stood there.

Who did he think he was? The Queen's guard at Buckingham Palace? Now what?

She leaned in and whispered, "If you think I'm offering twice, you're wrong. I'm here for one reason and talking to you isn't it. You're wasting seconds that I don't think Mr. D will be pleased about if he misses this one-time opportunity."

Her gaze traveled to a mirrored wall that picked up the bartender's profile as he leaned down to study a laptop computer screen. He lifted his head to look around. His gaze stalled when he turned her way.

She was the one running out of seconds and ideas.

CHAPTER 6

The best Nick could figure, Margaux must have mentally snapped to openly defy Sabrina. He'd have thought she had more natural survival instinct.

Nick let his gaze drift over to Tanner, his partner in this fiasco, who had his arm propped on the door of the rental they'd picked up at San Francisco airport.

"We just missed her, and she was tough to recognize," Tanner said to the cell phone he had on speaker.

Nick smiled. He'd been the one to point Margaux out to Tanner, who hadn't recognized her in a wig and a fourteen-carat dress that stopped just short of showing off her goods. Once Tanner sucked his tongue back into his head, he'd called Sabrina to report in.

Sabrina muttered a curse. "Was Margaux alone?"

"For now."

"What the hell does that mean?"

He looked at his phone like the thing might jump up and bite his head off any minute, which was possible with Sabrina on the other end. He gave Nick a look that suggested it was his turn to take some shit.

Nick sighed. "Margaux was decked out in a gold designer dress that just covered her ass and fuck-me heels to match, long blond wig, and a shawl that stopped at her waist. She walked into the Trigon Millennia Hotel like a woman ready to do business."

"Margaux would rather have her spleen taken out without anesthesia than wear a dress, much less heels. She's going after somebody." Sabrina had been up for two days straight, and the strain was starting to come through in her voice. "Nothing on the street here about any significant action going down in San Fran tonight. Haven't heard back from our people on the West Coast. You got any idea what might have set her off, Nick?"

"Not really, but I'm not surprised. She just wants to nail the bastard."

"Don't even try to justify her actions to me. Dingo, Josh, Tanner, and I want to nail the CIA spook who sold us out in the UK two years ago, too, but I won't tolerate those three going rogue any more than you, Ryder, or anyone else."

"What are you going to do about Margaux when we catch her?" If Nick could find out what Margaux faced, maybe he could talk her off the ledge if the opportunity arose. He didn't recommend what Margaux was doing, but he knew how demons drove a person and probably understood her better than the rest of the team did.

His own demons rode his shoulders every day.

"Tell you what, Nick. Get your hands on her and I'll answer that."

Nick got the "don't push me right now message" in Sabrina's reply. *I tried, Margaux.*

Sabrina added, "Do not let her walk past you two again."

Tanner's face warped with a scowl. "If the tail you put on her at the airport *here* hadn't lost her, we'd have her in hand by now."

A pause on the other end must have been Sabrina counting to hold her temper. Her voice gained a sharper edge. "If they were half as good as White Hawk or any of you that wouldn't have happened, but I was stuck with using a contractor. Margaux must have found out something right after I left the apartment, because given more time to plan, I doubt even White Hawk could have tailed her as far as she did."

Nick couldn't argue with that.

Margaux probably thought she'd made it out of Atlanta without anyone finding out, but Sabrina had instructed the surveillance teams to sit tight if they realized Margaux was leaving her apartment. White Hawk had been positioned nearby with eyes on every inch of the apartment exterior. When Margaux was spotted exiting via the roof, her route was relayed to White Hawk who picked her up on the ground.

Then Margaux stopped by a high-security storage facility for ten minutes on her way to the airport. Nick knew that's where she'd kept her go-bag with a new identity and cash. When the tail in San Francisco lost her, Sabrina tapped resources few people had at their fingertips and got a lead a half hour ago. About five minutes too late, or Nick could have intercepted Margaux before she entered that hotel.

Sabrina said, "Hold on. Josh is telling me something." Their muffled voices came through then she was back on the line. "We have intel from the coast. That hotel is owned by three men who run a secret club in the basement."

"Can't be very secret if some snitch knew about it," Tanner interjected.

Josh's voice came through next. "Wasn't a snitch, but people I've rubbed elbows with when I've had a job in that area. Once I found out who owned the hotel, I made a couple of calls to men I wouldn't turn my back on, but if anyone knew about high-roller action, they would. This private nightclub is invitation only."

Nick lifted an eyebrow at that. He'd picked up a little here and there about some of the team members. As a kid, Josh had run the streets of New York with Sabrina and Dingo, but a wealthy couple had adopted him. Insanely wealthy.

On occasion, Sabrina sent Josh to use his GQ looks and social status to ferret information from those with blue blood or celebrity ranking.

Nick asked Josh, "Did *you* get an invitation for tonight?"

"No. The place is called the Trophy Room. Very tight security. They schedule the women every day and change security cards just as often. Clients are booked in advance no closer than forty-eight hours out. Getting inside that club tonight isn't going to happen."

Tanner tapped his fingers on the steering wheel. "So we wait for her to come out?"

Nick shook his head. "Someone has to at least try to get in."

Josh argued, "You aren't going to make it into the Trophy Room. There's only two ways in and out. Heavily guarded. We make a wrong move and it could get her killed. Until someone comes up with more than we have right now, waiting is the safest thing to do for Margaux."

For now. Nick had never known Margaux's background. She was a solid agent, but tight-lipped when it came to talking about anything but the present and the future. He had a feeling that whatever she hid was going to be her downfall when they grabbed her.

Tanner sat up, stretching his neck. "At least we *found* Margaux. That was more than any of us would have thought possible with her skills. So, it's not that bad."

Yet, Nick added silently.

Sabrina was back on the phone. "The DEA agent is awake and screaming for her head. Margaux's in a heavily guarded location with no backup where the women are party toys for men with no financial boundaries, and she's chasing a man known for brokering the deadliest terrorist attacks in years. Think the Banker is going to just sit back and let her walk up to him? How much more *fucked up* does this have to get before it's bad, Tanner?"

The cowboy blew out a breath, taking his time to answer and pouring on his Texas charm when he did. "Come on, Sabrina. I'm just sayin' to give the woman some credit. This could be all about gaining intel. She might have walked into that hotel dressed like a high dollar call girl, but the Duke isn't going to let any man get the upper hand on her."

Josh interrupted. "Sabrina's got a call coming in that might be what we've been waiting on."

"Which is?" Nick asked.

"Intel on whether the Banker is in this country."

"Local intel?"

"No." Josh didn't elaborate, but Nick could guess. Sabrina had friends in every government agency, and she refused to take anything that even hinted of being connected to the CIA, but ... she had a friend who had helped with intel the last time the Banker was involved.

While Sabrina took her call, Josh went over all the resources Nick and Tanner had at their disposal then cut it short, saying, "Dingo and Ryder will be there soon. Hold on, Sabrina's coming back on the phone."

"I don't want to believe it, but the Banker is here. Actually, he's there. He's supposed to be meeting a merc in San Francisco."

Tanner tensed. "Here? Like at this hotel?"

"No confirmation that they'll meet there, only that a merc has been looking for the Banker and he's supposed to get meet instructions in the Trophy Room. At the price of admission, it's hard to imagine he'd be going there for any other reason unless he likes to pay high five figures to spend the night with a woman he's never met."

Tanner whistled. "Da-yam. Who pays that kind of jack? Of course, there's no doubt the women are all gorgeous. Hell, if they held a Miss Hot contest, the Duke would take first place tonight."

"Are you through having your fantasy break?" Sabrina snapped. "Still think she's only going for information?"

Nick answered her. "No. Margaux would never have walked away for anything less than getting her hands on the Banker." The way Sabrina had explained it, Margaux knew the minute she stepped outside her apartment she would be marked as rogue. He gave another shot at boosting Margaux's side of this. "But I'm betting Margaux plans to contact you as soon as she has a definitive location on the Banker."

"Let's hope so." Sabrina didn't say anything for a moment. "I want her yanked as soon as everyone is in place."

"I should go inside the hotel and do recon," Nick interjected, causing everyone to quiet. He found it amusing that they never knew when to expect him to say something or had any idea what he might say.

"Wait for *your* backup no matter what happens," Sabrina said, canceling his suggestion. "I don't want to lose any of you tonight. If I didn't have this damn threat at The Governor's Mansion, Josh and I would be there, too."

Tanner took over the conversation. "We can handle this, Sabrina, but delaying is dangerous. Margaux's been inside there for a half hour already. If she was after information only, she'd have had an exit strategy and should have come out by now."

"I know, but nothing happens until Dingo and Ryder arrive. That's final."

"If she hands you the Banker, are you going to cut her some slack?" Nick wouldn't go so far as to say he understood the crazy woman entirely, but they were hacked out of the same shitty cloth. They'd shared a few beers over rounds of shooting pool. He never pried into her life, and she showed him the same respect. As fucked up as he was, he had a feeling she might just be worse.

For that reason alone, he felt the strange need to take her side in this and offer help she wouldn't accept if she were standing here.

He liked that about her, which was totally screwed and why they got along.

A stifling silence hung inside the car until Sabrina said, "Let me make myself clear, Nick. I don't give two shits about the Banker right now. One of my people has gone rogue and has her ass hung out in the wind. I want her brought in. Alive. What I do with her at that point is not your business. I put you in charge because you've partnered with her so you *should* be able to get close to her. Do you have a problem bringing her in?"

"Nope."

"Then find a way inside there as soon as everyone's ready and don't let anyone die."

You don't ask for much. Nick just answered, "Got it."

Tanner thumbed the phone off and tossed it on the dash. He cracked his neck that had to feel as stiff as Nick's even though they'd rented a Yukon. Ops with Tanner required a big vehicle. Tanner had three inches of height and another twenty pounds of muscle over Nick who came in at six feet tall and could box heavyweight.

Had boxed heavyweight, but that was back when he'd fought according to the rules and cared about rules. Nick played out every possibility in his mind as he wiggled the earpiece of his comm set in place. "One of us has to stay here and call when Dingo arrives."

Tanner rocked his head to one side and gave Nick a look that questioned his ability to discern reality from fantasy. "So now *you're* going to defy Sabrina? You either got some titanium balls or you're just as suicidal as the Duke."

Nick would tell Tanner which one it was if he knew himself. "I'm following orders. Sabrina said we couldn't go into the hotel yet. Way I see it, if we stay out here we have only two possibilities for grabbing Margaux. She either walks out of the hotel under her own power and we grab her then, which I seriously doubt will happen, or we get lucky monitoring the cars leaving the private garage, and *if* we spot her, we go after her then."

Probability for either option had suck-ass odds.

The most likely scenario would end with her cold body locked in a trunk and driven out for disposal.

"Let me get this clear. Are you saying you want one of us to get inside the garage?" Tanner surmised.

"Exactly. That way, the minute Dingo gets here, we can move in faster."

"I'll go. You're supposed to be running this op so you stay here and play boss."

Nick would rather be the one going into the garage, but Tanner was right. Someone had to be out here to talk to Sabrina and take the rap if this op went south. He checked his watch.

Dingo should be here in another eight minutes, but this wouldn't end well.

Either way, Margaux was fucked.

If she came out with no intel, she'd made the critical error of crossing Sabrina.

If Margaux bagged the Banker, Sabrina would pull her from the team for going after a vendetta.

Taking Margaux in was going to suck, but better him than the others even if he did end up looking like he'd betrayed her. Margaux had once told Nick that she could never have anything more than what she had with Slye. She would do whatever it took to stay on the team.

That's why he'd known she wouldn't stay put if she had a chance to prove herself and hand over the Banker. He knew how she thought, which was why he was the one who'd seen her when she escaped the apartment.

He'd considered letting her go, but he doubted she'd survive going up against the Banker alone.

In hindsight, he might end up wishing he'd let her try.

CHAPTER 7

Logan turned his head just enough to let this Violet know he was listening. She'd said, "I'm here for one reason."

He was going with his gut on this one and his gut was screaming that she was an operative by the way she moved and her choice of words. She hadn't given him the sentence he'd been informed the masked women would use for requesting a meeting with Dragan.

If she was one of the working girls, she'd have said, "Please inquire if Mr. D would consider sharing a drink with me. My treat."

Also, *if* Violet was one of the hookers, she wouldn't waste time on Dragan when he was covered up with women and two available prospects were threatening her up with their eyes.

Yeah, she might be *qualified* to be a hooker, with a body that would set sheets on fire and a sexy mouth that quirked up on one side when she talked and ... wait a minute. He got a niggle of something at the back of his mind but couldn't put his finger on it. That mouth reminded him of someone.

Did he know this woman?

Was she an operative he'd encountered somewhere before? He didn't know those eyes, but she was wearing purple contacts.

Determined to flush her out, he pulled out his Russian accent and laid it on thick. He could replace it with an Italian, French, British or American slant at any time the need arose. "Mr. D is clearly busy."

"In that case, his loss. Make sure you tell him there will be no second invitation."

Ah, hell. This had to be the contact. "Follow me."

"Where?" Violet's eyes narrowed inside the mask.

"Somewhere private."

Those lips barely moved into a Mona Lisa smile, taunting him. "I'm not paid to do the hired help."

Did she think she was going to meet with Dragan alone? Not happening. "That is good, because I am not interested in the hired help *either*."

Her mouth ticked with a tiny flinch.

Shit, now he felt like a bastard. And he was a liar to boot. His fingers itched to remove her mask and see the rest of that face. He'd never been much for blonds or brunettes. He preferred the fiery personalities that came with all shades of red.

In a different situation, he'd make an exception for this one. She raised his curiosity and his dick at the same time. No woman had done that in a while. Definitely not a prostitute. "Follow me to the elevator."

"No."

Had she just refused him? "I thought you wanted to meet Mr. D."

"I'll go somewhere private with *him*."

"It does not work that way," Logan told her with no sugar coating but kept his voice down. "I am here for a reason. First, you follow me to his suite. Once I know it is secure, I will bring him up."

"Are you going to stay at that point, too?"

"Probably."

She didn't have to look up much to meet him eye to eye. "No one told me Mr. D preferred ménage à trois."

He wanted to chuckle at her obvious fishing trip but put plenty of steel in his voice when he said, "What Mr. D does in private is no one's business. Now, do you still wish to meet with him or not?"

Her gaze glanced past his shoulder, staring at what he recalled was a mirrored wall at his back.

What had drawn her attention?

Logan searched past her shoulder and caught the bartender looking their way while he spoke into the mic at his collar, nodding, then he turned and started toward the far end of the bar where he'd be able to walk around to exit. The last thing Logan needed was a nosy bartender telling this Violet to stay away from the bodyguard and make herself available to the real clients.

Before he could come up with a way to convince her to leave with him, she said, "What are you waiting for? Lead away."

Never look a gift horse, or a compliant contact, in the mouth.

He walked toward the elevator, sliding a look at Dragan—Nitro—as he did. Nitro lifted his hand to his right ear, the sign that he'd noticed, and plan A was in effect.

Nitro would continue talking to his bevy of women—as Dragan—for the next thirty minutes in case this didn't turn out to be the contact. If Logan hadn't returned at that point, Nitro was to move to plan B, which was basically get the hell out of the building any way he could since plan A was FUBAR.

At the elevator, Logan told security he was going up to examine Mr. D's suite.

Security had been informed of Logan's position in advance, so the man stepped into the elevator car and used his key card to activate access to the top two hotel floors. As he did that, he spoke to another person through his mic, explaining that Mr. D's personal security was on his way up to Mr. D's suite with one of the ladies.

The ride up was quick, the whole point of an express elevator to the top floors.

Violet held herself in check the whole way.

Security led Logan the short distance to Mr. D's penthouse suite and unlocked the door, telling Logan he would be at the elevator if Logan needed him. In other words, no return without keycard access, but Logan didn't plan to be here very long.

He held the door for Violet, who walked in ahead of him and stopped in front of the wall of glass. On the other side, a clear night back-dropped an impressive balcony lit with a hundred candles, a pool with blue lighting beneath the surface and decorative trees scattered around the perimeter.

She turned as he strode up to her.

He still needed confirmation.

He had twenty-three minutes until Nitro would have to find his own way out if Logan didn't return. This was the point where Logan hoped he hadn't left Nitro's back exposed, but if the Banker was ready to meet, then Logan should be the only one at risk once he explained that *he* was Dragan Stoli, not Nitro.

Violet clearly hadn't anticipated being separated from Dragan, but she probably figured once they had an agreement, she'd have Dragan isolated up here on the second floor with no escape route.

"Aren't you going to secure the suite?" Violet asked, letting him know he was imposing on her time.

Logan didn't like turning his back on this one, but he moved away carefully. He checked every room and closet, including the bath, before returning to the living room where she'd seated herself.

He confirmed, "All clear. Time to talk."

"I'm not paid to talk." She waved her hand at him, sending him away. "Hurry back down and bring up Mr. D. He's paid dearly for this opportunity and deserves a *full* service."

When Logan failed to move, she made a huffing sound. "If Mr. D doesn't come up here soon, Sergio will come for me. So either take me back down or bring him up. I need this job too much to let a paranoid bodyguard screw it up."

Tell me I didn't fuck up and bring one of the whores up here. There was no time left to spend on playing any more games. He crossed the room to her and bent down, noticing that she didn't flinch.

Not the least bit intimidated by him.

Why did he find her cool poise so fucking hot when it was frankly getting in his way right now?

That was it. He knew what he could do to make her show her hand.

He'd take five minutes to find out one way or the other if she was the Banker's contact. He dropped his voice into one he used in the bedroom. "Here is how this will work. My employer prefers his women ready."

She snickered. "Doesn't get much more ready than the Trophy Room."

"Stand up."

Her eyes narrowed. He wanted that mask off, but the rules were that the victor unmasked the woman. She wasn't standing. He spoke in a soft voice, but the power behind his words made it an order. "Stand. Up. Or this meeting is over."

Her gorgeous mouth lost all playfulness. She popped up easily, even in that gold fuck-me dress and on stiletto heels. He still had a couple of inches on her, but hot damn, what a woman.

"Is this ready enough?" she said with just enough threat in her voice to let him know not to confuse her with a submissive woman.

He leaned closer until he could smell her skin and whispered, "You are not even close to what he considers ready." Logan ran the back of his finger lightly along her jaw and slowly, very slowly, down her neck. "You will be once I peel you out of that dress and bend you over the back of this sofa. When I lean in close, you will feel me, feel how hard I am for you and know that you cannot have me."

Her nostrils flared. Anger and passion riding a razor edge.

He let his finger glide along the smooth skin of her shoulder and kept explaining. "I will cup your breasts and carefully pinch those nipples that already pebble in anticipation. My fingers will slide between your legs and tease you until you are wet and begging. If you ask nicely, I might even push them inside just to feel how tight you are."

A muscle ticked in her jaw. Her breathing gave her away, coming in shorter pants.

He was so hard his dick ached. He wanted her.

That hadn't been the plan.

This was backfiring on him. He'd thought if she was a hooker, she'd have come on to him by now just to get things moving so he'd bring up Mr. D. She hadn't done that, but neither had she copped to being the contact and ordered him to back off if he wanted to meet the Banker.

Fuck this. If she touched him right now, he wasn't sure he wouldn't give her everything he'd just promised.

One thing that always worked with the enemy was to threaten them. While he still had her caged between him and the sofa, he said, "If you have a message for Mr. D, then spit it out or prepare to be disappointed."

Everything about Violet shifted subtly into the calm, defensive mode of someone ready to kill if necessary. She had steely nerves found in those who had faced dangerous situations enough times to wait for the right moment to react.

He'd been right. She was no fucking prostitute. Time to cut the pretense on both parts and get down to business.

Echoing her words, he shifted into an American speech pattern and said, "I'm here for one reason and talking to *you* isn't it. Tell your boss that *I'm* Mr. D. If he wants to meet, then let's meet. If not, I'm leaving. What's it going to be because you're running out of seconds?"

Her eyes widened with understanding the mask couldn't hide. He could swear her lips moved with the word *shit*.

Real concern crawled up his neck. Something was off. Way off.

When she spoke, her voice held enough chill to frost the windows. "I don't know what you're talking about. Move. I have to go back downstairs. My boss isn't going to be happy that I walked out with you instead of a client. And if you're telling the truth about being the real Mr. D, my boss is going to be pissed because he doesn't like to be played."

She sounded so unbelievably natural.

Thoughts were having a train wreck in his brain. He'd never been this far off fingering an operative. She had to be one. "Who the fuck are you?"

"Move."

Logan glanced at his wristwatch. In nine minutes, Nitro aka Dragan had to get out of this place alive. What if the real contact was down there right now with Nitro, taking advantage of no bodyguard to get Nitro out of the room?

"Let's go." Logan grabbed her arm.

She snatched her arm away, but not before he felt her strength. "Don't touch me again unless you think you can still bodyguard with one arm."

"Take off that mask."

"Dream on."

"You have ten seconds before I take it off of you."

"Your insurance had better be paid up," she scoffed back at him.

Harming a woman galled Logan, but he'd fought alongside skilled females who could take down a terrorist cell. Still, he could unmask her without doing much more than bruise her. He reached for her mask.

Her hand shot out to stop him.

Glass exploded into the room from the balcony at the same moment the door to the hallway burst open.

Four figures cloaked entirely in black, including their heads, entered. Two from each point, weapons drawn, but not shooting.

Violet yelled, "You take those. I've got these."

Was she crazy? Logan grabbed her and swung her around behind him, backing her up to a wall. Violet shoved him aside and yanked up a lamp and swung at the two men coming in on Logan's right from the balcony.

Why didn't they shoot her?

Why weren't any of them shooting?

Logan didn't have time to find out because he had his own two to battle and lunged at the pair who had entered from the doorway. Thuds and grunts were the only sounds. He slammed a fist and connected with bone, but something hit him across the back that felt like a club.

The room lights went out.

The suite fell into shadows, but he caught a blur of Violet kicking one of her attackers backwards on his ass. The other one grabbed her by the hair that ... *came off?*

A right hook caught Logan across the jaw. He stepped back, but it took more than that to put him down. Shoving forward, he hammered blows at the one who'd cocked him on the jaw.

Violet had one of hers in a chokehold, but the one on the floor was back up on his feet, a black shape moving fast. He raised his hand and whipped it down in a stabbing motion.

She froze, weaving, then tumbled forward.

Logan shoved his guy aside and went for her.

A sharp stab hit him in the side of his neck.

Adrenaline kept him moving, but when he reached her, he fell forward on top of her with one last thought.

She wasn't breathing.

CHAPTER 8

"Time's up," Nick declared into the lapel mic on his comm set. It reached all his men covering exits from the hotel and garage. "Dingo, you and Ryder get inside the garage and down to the private parking. Check the trunks first. Tanner, go into the hotel and create the disturbance."

"Ten four."

Men were calling back to Nick after each order, confirming their positions and next moves.

Tanner broke in. "I hear sirens coming this way. Might be nothing, but..."

Nick heard something else. A helicopter. Who had called the cops? That might be good news.

Sabrina *could* get Margaux out of jail.

Sirens screamed and strobe lights flashed from police cruisers racing up to the hotel.

"Pull back," Nick called to the entire team.

The beat of the helicopter blades picked up volume, getting louder as it approached.

What were they hunting for? Nick dove into his rental and snagged a set of binoculars. He focused in on the helicopter hovering over the roof, but Josh had called back with a structural breakdown of the significant parts of the building.

No way a helo could land.

Nick couldn't see anything that indicated there was a problem at the roof that would bring the cops in by air.

More police cars poured into the scene. Two fire trucks blew their horns to clear the way.

Guests poured out the front doors to the hotel. People on the street were crowding into the area to see what was going on.

Dingo spoke into Nick's ear, "There's a fire in the basement and someone's dead."

Nick didn't say a word, too focused on the chopper that came into view moving slowly around the roof. Orange-yellow lights from the hotel's interior illuminated the jagged spikes that capped the building. The helicopter lifted and moved away at the same time. A shape dangled from a cable beneath the bird, silhouetted against the roof and rising in sync with the chopper.

The long, black shape just the right size to be a container for a body.

Nick would bet his Ferrari that Margaux was in that container.

CHAPTER 9

Screeching that would irritate the dead hurt her head. Margaux jerked awake and moaned. Pain clawed her body.

More shrieking sounds. *Monkeys.*

She sniffed. Rotting vegetation and mildew stench.

And the noxious smell of her body sucking into itself, dehydrating.

Oh, yes. Memory was booting up. Slowly.

She was in a jungle. Naked, lying on the dirty floor of a hut. Locked inside. She blinked her dry eyes. Been here for one day? Two? Head hurt. Body hurt. So tired ...

Her eyes drifted shut. Blurred images of men came at her, shouting in some language that wasn't English. They dragged her naked body through the mud to a building. Tied her to a chair. Fists came again and again. Then the skin on her arm burned.

She jerked awake, gasping. The world was spinning.

Someone coughed close by.

Turning her head took effort. She dropped her cheek back down on the filthy floor. She focused on a hole at the base of the wall.

That hole was her connection to ...

More coughing. A hoarse voice called out, "You there, Sugar?"

Sugar? Dragan.

Relief flooded her. She wasn't alone. Now she remembered. Dragan had been captured, too. He was still alive. He'd used his fingers to tear a small hole in the rotting base of the boards in the wall between them.

She tried to lick her lips that were parched and cracked. No saliva. "I'm here."

His lips had to be right against the hole. His sigh shuddered hard. "Good."

"How long have we been here?"

"Two days."

"Got any plan?" She was struggling to stay awake. Her body wanted to shut down and quit, but they had to escape.

Dragan coughed and whispered, "Working on it, Sugar."

"What's with the Sugar?"

He chuckled then grunted. Must have hurt to laugh. He said, "The name Violet ... doesn't fit you."

She started to ask why not then heard someone approaching.

Her mind raced, remembering who that would be.

Were Lurch and Tattoo coming for her?

She'd named the tall guard with the square head, hair shaved on the side and thick curly mat of black on top, Lurch. He always arrived with a short, sturdy guy whose eyes hit her chest high. She called him Tattoo after the guy who played on *Fantasy Island* years ago, which wasn't fair since the real Tattoo had only been two-foot-eight and was a lot more entertaining in those old reruns.

The Tattoo in her living nightmare was a bit of a neat freak, constantly knocking dirt off his shoes and wiping at insects that landed on his clothes. Both guards wore jungle cammies and boots, but Tattoo kept his arms covered in long sleeves. Lurch had a dull look in his black eyes and a cigarette dangled perpetually from his dark brown fingers. Tattoo's narrow Latin eyes tilted up with a constant smirk.

If Margaux had to guess her location based on those two being locals and speaking Spanish, she'd say South America.

She started breathing fast, anticipating.

Dragan said, "Rest. Not your turn."

The sound of a door banged open on his side.

Her stomach twisted. She wanted to call out words of encouragement, but they'd figure out that Dragan had dug a hole through the rotting boards so she could talk to him.

Tattoo's annoying voice shouted at Lurch.

Lurch's nicotine rasp snarled something back then the sound of a fist or foot hitting a body followed. Dragan was making them expend energy to move him and Lurch was kicking him.

Don't, Dragan, you have to live ...

The door slapped shut and the silence threatened to destroy her.

Please come back.

She had to think about something other than being left alone. More alone than she'd ever been in her life.

She turned her head again and the throbbing almost blinded her.

Light struggled to sneak through the narrow horizontal window above her.

Not a window.

A slot cut into a metal door. Too high for anything except observation. Another slot at the bottom *should* be for shoving food through.

When was the last time she'd eaten? No idea. What about her last drink of water? A lifetime ago. Who had captured her? She searched her lethargic mind and came up with the Trophy Room.

She'd gone upstairs with the bodyguard. He turned out to be Dragan. Or so he said.

Four men attacked from two directions. She'd held her own even with no weapon and bound up in that damn dress.

Then what?

A hypodermic needle was shoved into her neck.

Everything blurred again. *Think dammit.*

There was more. She had to dredge it up but thinking hurt like a mother. Her brain had never liked many drugs beyond aspirin or Tylenol. She did recall throwing up on her guards here when they'd dragged her to her feet. Bonus.

The attackers could have killed them at the hotel, but she and Dragan had been brought here for interrogation. Questions about the Banker spewed at her over and over again.

Did the kidnappers work for him or were *they* trying to find the Banker too?

She'd asked. Got burned on her hand for that one.

Way in the back of her mind, thoughts of her Slye team huddled, biding their time to get in her face and tell her how badly she'd fucked up. But that would have to wait. She didn't have the energy to push her mind beyond this moment and survival.

She *and* Dragan would survive.

They needed water. She wasn't sweating.

Her hair stuck to her shoulders and back from when she'd been soaked with sweat, but it wasn't wet now. She hated the smell of her hot skin baking in this hut. Not a breath of air. But the little bit of light outside was dimming, which meant night would come soon.

Events from last night—or had it been during the day?—slammed into her thoughts, jumbled up, but a warning came through clearly.

Relief wouldn't come with nightfall.

The guards would.

Dragan was right. They took him first. Then her.

Her headache turned into a dull pulse. Her eyes fluttered. She forced them open. They fluttered again. Darkness closed in.

Lurch tossed her against a wall, scraping her skin as she slid down. Her hands were tied behind her. He unzipped his pants...

She snapped awake, shouting, "No!" But the word had been a harsh sound too quiet to scare a rat. She looked toward the slit in the door. The room was fully dark except for a thin stream of moonlight.

Where was Dragan?

She turned back to the hole, a lifeline she couldn't lose. "Hey?" She waited. "You there?" *Don't panic.* He might not be dead. "Sugar?"

She quieted her breathing and listened.

No sound. He was still being interrogated. Still alive. *Keep believing.*

Her head still pounded, but she was more lucid than last time she was awake.

Their captors had begun with simple beatings, which were nothing more than a starting point for breaking a prisoner to gain information.

Tonight would be different.

The bastards would kick their game up a notch.

By tomorrow neither she nor Dragan would be able to fight back. They had to get out now.

Just like six years ago when she'd escaped on the run from another mess.

One that had involved another sexy man on the wrong side of the law. *Starting to see a pattern here.* She hadn't thought of Pierre in a long time. He'd been the one she'd fallen hard for, the one she'd been sure was not a criminal. She'd missed that one by a mile.

Had he escaped capture in France?

The last time she'd seen him, he'd left her in their tousled bed after taking a phone call that had ended hours of the best sex she'd ever had before or since. He'd hurriedly dressed, promising to call later, and rushed out.

Oh, he'd called all right.

Two hours later, she'd answered the phone, prepared to tell him she was still nude, when he told her to get as far away as she could. Men were coming for him and would go through her.

Leave the apartment? she'd asked.

The country. Get out of France. Hide.

But she'd gone *to* France to hide.

That was her life. Always looking over her shoulder and trying to stay one step ahead of capture. She'd missed a step that time and it almost proved to be her last.

A noise outside the hut triggered a spike in her heart rate.

Not outside her door, but Dragan's.

She held her breath, her spirits spiked at the sign that he was still alive. They wouldn't carry his body back here, right? What little Margaux had seen of the camp looked like an abandoned location for drug runners.

The slap of a door bouncing open next door came first, then the sound of something being dragged and dropped with a thud.

Were they coming for her now?

Her heart thudded in her ears while she waited. That was

part of torture. Anticipation. *Don't feed into it.* She closed her eyes and calmed herself to retain all the energy she could.

Ten minutes passed slowly while she waited for the two guards to come for her, but the next sound she heard was Dragan sliding across the floor of his hut.

Not dead. Still capable of walking?

If he couldn't walk or run, how would they escape?

"Sugar," came out on a hoarse voice.

She smiled at the silly term but grimaced at how thin his voice sounded. "How bad?"

"Shitheads are amateurs." It came out "shithads ur emters."

She swallowed and it hurt. She had no saliva to soothe her raw throat. "Why are they late tonight?"

"I kept 'em longer."

What? "Explain."

"Figured ... wear them out on me. Too tired for you."

You dumb fuck. Why would he take more beatings—or whatever they did to him—for her? "That was stupid."

"No. Strategic." He was silent a moment and she waited while he had to be drawing enough saliva to keep talking. "They bragged about ... plans for you. For tonight." More silence. "Get out. Know you can do it. Go."

He was telling her to escape without him, and that he recognized her skills. He'd taken their abuse to give her an edge. Damn him. She needed him strong enough to go with her. That was assuming she could even figure a way to escape. Her heart was having a throw down with her conscience.

"Sugar."

She wanted to yell but kept her voice low. "No. I'm not leaving without you. Stop taking my beatings. You have to be able to walk." She paused, hoping he'd boast about being able to leap tall buildings in a single bound. Nothing. She asked, "You can still walk, right?"

"I'm good."

Liar. She dropped her forehead down to the floor.

CHAPTER 10

"Sugar."

Margaux lifted her head and turned to the hole Logan spoke through. "*What?*" came out loaded with frustration.

He chuckled, a raspy sound. "Wish we'd met ... some other time."

"Why?" She knew why she wished they'd met under different circumstances but couldn't imagine why he would after she'd blown his meeting with the Banker. Had that been why they were captured? She'd been interrogated about who she worked for and who told her about the Banker. She'd given them nothing and they'd given her more beating.

Margaux squeezed her eyes against the flood of anger. Anger at these assholes, at the Banker, but more than anything? At herself. She should have brought Sabrina and the team in on this back in the beginning when she'd first gone after the Banker. Indulging her vendetta for so long might end up costing the lives she went to San Francisco to save.

She'd blown her only shot at meeting the Banker and finding out where he planned to attack.

She'd let a lot of people down and had no way to gain Sabrina's trust again, but she had bigger concerns than thinking about everything she'd lost.

Dragan had to get out of here soon. He wouldn't last another round.

He hadn't answered her. She repeated, "Why do you wish we'd met some other time?"

Dry cough then, "Because ... you're one hell of a woman ... and a mystery."

His compliment shouldn't mean so much, but it did. He had every reason to hate her, but instead his words had warmed her, stroking her battered ego. But she was a mystery she had no intention of allowing anyone to solve.

Speaking of puzzles, if they were going to die, she wanted

answers. "Are you really Dragan?"

"Yes."

She waited for him to ask how she knew him and why she'd been in the Trophy Room, but he didn't. Instead, he told her, "Don't ask anything else. Less we know about each other ... the better."

Was he worried that she'd break or that he would? She heard footsteps crunching the ground outside. "Shh. Someone's coming."

Dragan whispered with more power than before. "Get out if you can."

"*We* will escape together."

"No, too dangerous to ... "

"Just shut up, okay?" She had no plan, but she didn't want to be distracted by Dragan while she made it up as she went.

"Listen, Sugar," his voice was scratchy, coming fast. "They're going to gang rape you then they ... " The dry cough that interrupted him sounded painful.

He didn't have to explain. Their captors had something even more heinous planned for tonight's torture.

After the gang rape.

She'd counted six men in the camp so far, all disgusting examples of the lowest level of humanity. Her clammy skin chilled at the visual of being dropped in the middle of them.

She'd survived that once.

Didn't mean she wanted to again and she wouldn't be the only one suffering if they gave her an opening.

Dragan's voice faded, but she heard, "Go ... before you can't."

She was done talking. It would only waste what strength they both still had. At least, she was praying that he still had some. No one had answered her prayers in the past, but the Big Guy might answer one for Dragan.

Margaux crawled across the floor, grinding her teeth at the new raw spots being rubbed on her knees. She sucked in air to appease her lungs then lay down and forced her body to relax.

The scrape of a board as it was removed from across the

outside of the door shoved everything out of her mind except concentrating on her next move. Find a way out of here. She'd only get one chance. After that, she'd be in no shape to try again because they would punish her.

She curled into a fetal position, turned so that she could peek between her lashes, feigning sleep.

There was a heavy bump against the hut. Lurch had dropped the board and Tattoo would be opening the door ... now.

Nighttime seeped into her hut. More hot air to drag through her painful lungs, but she felt the first burn of adrenaline pump through her and pleaded with her body to give her one solid push.

Lurch walked in and set down a kerosene lantern. His weapon belt drooped on one side with a machete stuck through a leather loop and a Vektor SP1 9mm automatic in his holster.

Oddly, Tattoo was the one in charge each time, which might account for his carrying the radio in addition to his arsenal that also included a Vektor pistol. But Tattoo had a fixation with knives. One was in a leather sheath hooked to his belt and hung half the length of his thigh. He had a shorter K-bar knife that he wore on a lanyard. He currently used that blade to pick at his teeth.

Tattoo paused long enough from his dental hygiene to order Lurch, "Get her."

Lurch lumbered over to Margaux and clamped meaty fingers around her arm, yanking her up.

She hung like dead weight, eyes half open. "Wh... what ..." She groaned.

"Get up," Lurch yelled at her.

She slid a knee up and tried, then flopped down, shaking. She sniffled and made incomprehensible noises between pleading, "No. Please."

"También, puta." Rough fingers grabbed one of her breasts and squeezed.

You think I'll beg, huh? Tears would have come naturally at that moment if she weren't dehydrated. She wanted to reach up and drive his eyes deep into his head, but that wouldn't get her out of here. Keeping up the show, she keened a pitiful sound and trembled harder.

Lurch let go and she slumped to the floor. He rattled something in Spanish that sounded like he complained that she was too big.

Never capture something you can't handle, Lurch.

Tattoo's Spanish flew even faster in reply.

All she caught was that the little man was pissed. He shoved his knife into the sheath, spitting words out the whole time he strutted over to her. He reached under one arm and Lurch caught her beneath the other one. They struggled together to lift her to her knees.

Tattoo wrinkled his nose.

Hooray for stinking. The little prick didn't like getting her stench on his clothes. The jungle was not the place for an OCD personality. When she made a sloppy effort to get her feet under her, Lurch must have been happy, because he loosened his hold. That allowed her to lean into Tattoo, who recoiled from her.

This had to be fast and quiet. No bullets.

Had to take Lurch out first.

Her only advantage was the element of surprise.

Margaux reached deep inside for all the power she could wield and swung an underhanded fist with everything she had, slamming Lurch in the groin. That threw her weight forward. She landed on one foot and shoved off, spinning around to force all her weight behind a fist to Tattoo's jaw.

His head snapped back. He hit the floor.

She stumbled sideways.

Lurch was making a sick gargle noise and heaved backwards. His head banged the wall with a solid crack before he slid down into a crumpled pile.

The whole thing happened in seconds.

She lunged to her feet, moving faster in her mind than in reality. Lurch was down. She turned to Tattoo. He was coming to his feet, shaking his head and blinking as he reached for his weapon.

Hate raged in his black eyes.

Kicking again would send her off balance. She dove at him, knocking him backwards and landing on top of his body. The pistol flew from his grip. The impact stunned him. She shoved up above to free her hands, gasping for air, and reached for his head. He yanked a knife out with quicker reflexes than she'd expected and swung the blade at her as she wrenched his head hard, snapping his neck.

The blade sliced her upper arm, then dropped from his hands.

Dead eyes stared up at her in shock.

She fell over to the side in a heap, sucking in air.

Get up.

Not happening.

"*Sugar.* You okay?"

She couldn't answer Dragan. *Get up. Never stay down.* Had to go.

Lurch groaned. He was too big to take down a second time.

Hearing him rally was the motivation she needed to force her body to move again.

Going on automatic pilot, she struggled to her knees once more, shaking for real this time. She picked up Tattoo's K-bar knife and crawled over to Lurch. He had one hand cupping his balls and tears streaming down his face. His other hand struggled to withdraw his pistol that was pinned between his body and the ground.

He was snarling unintelligible words as he rocked to one side to yank his weapon free. She didn't need a translator to know how many ways he planned to abuse her.

You're never touching another woman.

He gripped the pistol, finger moving toward the trigger as he pulled the weapon out.

She drove the blade tip into his throat.

He dropped the gun to grab at his neck. Those dull eyes finally lit with realization.

Die, you miserable piece of shit. And he did.

She pulled the knife out, wiped it on the ground then

dragged his pistol close. She checked to make sure a round was chambered, then laid it beside her to keep handy as she started removing his boots and clothes. The real possibility of escape gave her a surge of energy. Her fingers fumbled with boot strings and buttons, but she kept moving, the pistol next to her foot where she could reach it without looking. She listened for a sound, expecting to have company any minute.

It felt like it took an eternity to strip Lurch and Tattoo of their shirts, pants, boots, and weapon belts.

"Sugar!"

"Shut. Up," she hissed back toward the hole. If Dragan alerted one of the other guards right now, she'd kill him herself. Anger was good. It fed more power into her movements. She yanked off the wife-beater undershirt Tattoo wore. That had to be the cleanest piece of clothing here. She used it to wrap her arm.

Hurry. Every second counted.

Sure, she had a pistol, but there were at least four more men who had more firepower. She was waning physically by the time she managed to get Tattoo's clothes on. They stank with body odor. You'd have thought someone with OCD would use deodorant. But she thanked him for the long sleeves he'd worn that covered her bandaged arm even if the sleeves did stop halfway down her forearms.

When she had his size-too-small boots on, belt around her waist and every weapon tucked back into place, she gathered Lurch's clothes and boots in one armload and inched her way up the rough wood wall to stand.

God, she needed water. Her head spun. When her vision cleared, she kept putting one foot in front of the next.

She eased out into the night, leaving the lantern in the hut and the door open in case someone in the Quonset hut ninety yards away was watching to see when the light would move. So long as the lantern stayed in her hut, they might think Lurch and Tattoo were taking their time, toying with her.

When she reached Logan's door, her hand shook as she struggled to ease the board up from where it had been cupped to lock in Dragan. She laid it gently on the ground, lifted Lurch's possessions and moved inside silently.

"Where are you?" she whispered.

"Holy shit ... you ... did it." His voice was full of pain.

She followed the sound and dropped down beside him. "I brought clothes and boots from the big guard."

Dragan's hand fumbled against her until his fingers wrapped her forearm. "You won't make it ... with me. Go, but call ... someone for me." He took a labored breath. "When you get back."

Margaux didn't have the strength to physically drag someone his size from here and she wouldn't walk away.

CHAPTER 11

Logan fought past the pain draining his body to think of a way to make Violet—like hell that was her real name—leave the hut and escape while she could. But if she didn't get moving, she wasn't going to make it out of here.

Might not survive anyhow if she didn't know anything about the jungle.

Her voice was close to him and shook when she said, "Fuck. That. Don't make me waste my breath arguing. Get up and get dressed. You're leaving if I have to drag you."

What woman wouldn't take the opening he'd given her? His admiration flared even though he growled. If he had the strength, he'd toss her over his shoulder and get the hell out of here.

He'd fall on his face in two steps.

Sounding like a wounded beast caught in a trap, he muttered, "So we both die here?"

Her fingers touched his face. She might be just as hardheaded, but her words were softer this time. "I'm not leaving alone no matter what you say. Whatever we face, we do it together."

Where had she come from?

Women in the covert business were normally cutthroat and came with a natural survival defense mechanism. They weren't selfless when it came to a choice of walking away alive or not. The last woman he'd known who had skills even close to this one had been his first introduction to this business. Babette had seduced him when he'd been twenty, then handed him over to the gun runner she worked for, who'd taught Logan the mistake of trusting any female he didn't have a full dossier on.

Even then, he hadn't handed over trust easily.

He gave in. "Okay, help me up."

Violet moved her hand down and reached around him, lifting. The pain that shot through his chest, back and head almost sent him to the ground again. Bile rushed up his throat, but he'd be damned if he was going to hurl on her while she was trying to save his ass. She had to be hurting, too, but all he heard were grunts of effort. Between the two of them, Logan managed a sitting position against the wall.

She got busy first putting a shirt on him, then she worked the pants on one leg at a time. He was doing nothing and panting hard. How she was managing was beyond him.

When she'd gone as far as she could with the pants, she straddled him, squatting over his thighs. He kept forcing his thoughts away from the pain. Like why couldn't they be in a plush hotel room with her straddling him for round one hundred of amazing sex?

And he bet it would be. A woman like this would be unforgettable.

He could feel her lean forward in the darkness. She had to be propping her hands against the wall behind him.

She rasped, "Hook your arms around me and we'll stand together."

He outweighed her by at least a lot, but she walked her hands up the wall and he pushed his bruised, aching muscles until he was standing.

They were both panting and struggling not to cough.

Whatever she'd done next door had kept the other guards content, but for how long? It seemed to take forever to get him to this point, but in truth the guards had only come for her ten to fifteen minutes ago.

Dragan leaned his shoulder against the wall while she finished dressing him and hooked a belt around his waist, but it couldn't be the one the big guard had worn. Too light. "Where's the machete and pistol?"

"I've got them. I just want you to stay upright as long as you can." She slipped under his arm. "Ready?"

Shutting his mind against the agony, he locked out all doubt. "Let's go."

He sagged into her as soon as he moved away from the wall, but by the time they were out of the hut his legs functioned enough for him to keep moving forward.

There was something about drawing a breath of free air that rejuvenated a person. Hard to explain to someone who had never been at the mercy of others, but that first deep breath gave him a fresh push of energy.

He'd been beaten, burned, and cut. He hadn't slept in days, and he needed water more than food, but damn it felt good to be on the move.

Even a slow move.

A partial moon offered specks of light from time to time. Violet didn't say anything as they used streaks of moonlight to pick their way through a trodden path. They had to get off this route soon. It would be the easiest place to get caught, but she couldn't swing a machete and hold him up at the same time.

Time stretched from one breath to the next, seeming like hours when he was sure only a few minutes had passed since they'd left the camp. That's when he heard voices shouting in the distance back where they'd come from. He was getting sluggish, barely putting one foot in front of the other. If they had to fight, he would be more liability than help, but arguing with her about leaving him somewhere hidden would be fruitless.

He whispered, "We have to find water and hide."

She stopped. "Where?"

If they weren't in dire straits he'd tease Superwoman about not having this figured out. "The terrain drops off to our right. Head that way and see if we find a river."

"I hate fucking snakes," she muttered and angled them off the trail, moving more carefully.

"If we're in South America, this is the dry season. They don't move around as much."

"Really?" She sounded like a kid who just heard that spinach tasted like chocolate ice cream.

No, not really, but she had enough to worry about. If they walked up on a snake, they'd deal with it then. "Really."

The voices had died down back at the camp. They might be waiting on daylight, or they could be mobilizing to look for him and Violet.

A palm branch swatted him in the face. He cursed.

"My bad. Missed that one."

Logan started reaching ahead to feel for branches before they hit her. They bumbled along for a while having to stop when the underbrush got too thick and alter their course to find an easy path. The vegetation finally thinned, and they entered an open area. He could hear the water rushing.

She croaked out, "I'd say I'm salivating, but I couldn't call up enough spit to wet a stamp. Come on, I want that."

"We can't drink it."

"What?"

He limped along with her, careful not to slip when the land turned rocky and dropped off steeply for three feet. "Are you trained for the jungle?"

"I'm more of an urban jungle survivor."

"You can't drink this water unless it's treated or boiled." But he was licking his lips at the sound, too.

She sighed. "Dammit. Parasites."

"Right. So you do have some training."

"Oh, yeah, I'm certified by National-fucking-Geographic."

He smiled. She'd left her Violet-of-the-Trophy-Room voice back in San Francisco at the hotel.

This was the real woman. Now if he could just weasel a name out of her and find out what she was doing at the Trophy Room. Had she been trying to sign on with the Banker, too?

He hoped not.

When they reached the river, the moonlight offered more help in making out the terrain. "Let's go to that boulder at ten o'clock."

She guided him there and eased him down. No recliner had ever felt so good. "Check your belt for tablets. I'll check mine."

"We don't have a canteen." But she was hunting through the pouches on her belt. "Bingo."

"The tablets?"

"No." She waved something in her hand. "A Ziploc bag full of his tobacco. I'll dump that—"

"Hell, no. Keep the tobacco in case we need it for a spider bite."

"Gotcha, Tarzan." She dumped the tobacco into one of her pouches and kept digging around then paused. "Oh, thank God."

"What? Tablets?"

"No-o." She opened a small tin the size of his thumb. "Lip balm. Another gift from Lurch and Tattoo." She reached over and smeared some on his lips then covered hers.

"Lurch and Tattoo?" He opened another pouch on his belt.

"I named them. Did you notice how Tattoo kept his icky lips moist?"

"Not really. Guy creeped me out." Logan's fingers touched a bottle that rattled. Could they be that lucky? "I found something."

"The tablets?"

He was tempted to say no just to tease her. "Maybe."

She turned toward him and flicked a lighter close enough for him to read the label, but she kept the flame cupped behind her hand.

He grunted. "That's it."

She cut the lighter off. "Sit tight and I'll get water."

Good thing. He'd hate to collapse on his face at this point, and water would go a long way toward reviving them both. She returned with the quart bag plump with river water. He dumped the tablet in.

"Now?" she asked and licked her lips.

"Need about a half hour."

"*Fuck!*"

"You've really never camped or did any survival training?"

"No, screw that shit. I'm thirsty now."

He smiled, wishing he could do something about her thirst. "We've made it to this point. Thirty minutes isn't that long." He was enjoying the *real* her and wanted to hear what she'd say if he poked at her. "Patience is a virtue."

She glared at him. "Why can't *hurry-the-fuck-up* be a virtue?"

He chuckled. It hurt, but it felt good, too. If he was going to be stuck in the middle of jungle-nowhere with a woman, he was glad as hell it was this one. She had more grit than came with most pairs of balls and was a fighter all the way. But who was she? Now that they weren't around their captors, he should try to pull some details out of her.

But this one wouldn't drop her shields easily. It would take time to chisel away one layer at a time. He said, "Give me the bag and sit down. Save your energy every chance you get."

"You're right." She climbed up on the rock and leaned back, but didn't settle down. She squirmed and wiggled.

Logan offered, "Want to lean against me?"

"No."

Blunt, but honest. Strangely refreshing even if it did bruise his ego that she wouldn't lean on him for comfort. "We can't stay here. Try to relax until we can drink the water then we're moving again."

Her sigh ended in a groan. "You sleep. I'll keep watch."

Damn stubborn woman. "Look, you got us out of there. Think you could give up control long enough to rest? We need each other right now, so just relax."

"Fine. You keep watch."

Relax must have been the magic word.

Damn if she didn't soften enough to slump against his shoulder, murmuring about how they both needed a bath. Just that little bit of trust lifted his spirits.

Now that they were still, he could swear he smelled fresh blood.

Was she injured? He'd ask her when she woke up, because her breathing was slowing down, and she needed the rest.

Once her breathing evened out with deep sleep, he eased his arm away from her head and adjusted her until she slept against his chest, held close by his arm.

Argue now, woman-who-is-not-Violet.

He propped the water on top of his thigh and listened to the sounds of the night. The terrain had pretty much funneled them down to this spot at the river. That meant animals probably traveled the same path. If the monkeys he'd heard were indeed howlers then they were in Central or South America, which meant the potential danger of meeting more threats besides their captors who had to be regrouping right now.

If it was daylight, the kidnappers would have gone to the river first to hike in two directions, figuring on their prisoners heading to water. That's what he'd have his men do, but it was dangerous to split up in the jungle at night, even when there were eight men left.

Logan spoke the language and had discerned that they'd started with a team of ten and had a time frame of five days once he and Violet were in the base camp.

Whose base camp, who had set that deadline and what did the person in charge want? What happened in five days?

His mind was wandering.

Back to the most immediate problem.

He had to find a place to hide the both of them, somewhere to rest while they were being hunted. One down day and plenty of water should revive them enough to start hiking, and to fight if need be.

Decent plan if not for one snag—what if whoever was behind the kidnapping sent in reinforcements with night vision gear and heavy artillery?

CHAPTER 12

Near Mainz, Germany. 9:00 am

Chatton leaned back against the aging stone wall of a castle built into the cliffs overhanging the Rhine River.

She had no cellular service here, but Wayan would not miss this meeting. He was arrogant. Not stupid.

She turned her face to the early morning sun that was trying its best to warm the frigid air still whipping through Germany in April. She preferred the cold for wearing her Burberry trench coat as a cover garment to conceal the HK USP Compact in her shoulder holster.

Not that she felt the need for a weapon when confronting Wayan, but they both had enemies.

Thus, the reason for choosing this tower perched two-thousand feet above the river. Built in early 1100 CE, it offered an unhindered view for miles in every direction. Even with all the safeguards in place for this meeting, one could never be too careful.

Two men emerged from the stairwell, both in suits, but with distinct differences in size. The tall one carved of muscle wore no overcoat and moved with the powerful stride of a man who expected danger and faced it without hesitation.

The bodyguard.

Then there was the diminutive Wayan.

For a man who held a position of influence within the coveted circle of China's party chief and whose opinion carried weight with the president of China, Wayan was disappointing physically. He had the easy mannerisms of a powerful businessman, sure of his place in life, but at only five feet tall and slender, he gave the impression of being too young for his position. He was forty-five.

Not very impressive overall until the first time you gazed into his predatory eyes. That was the moment an adversary realized Wayan was far more dangerous than his bodyguard, because Wayan could kill one—or a thousand—with a whispered word.

"I hope you have not wasted my time, Chatton," Wayan warned in his soft voice as he reached her. The bodyguard hung back at a discreet distance. Close enough to react quickly to a threat, but far enough to prevent hearing sensitive information.

She quoted, "An inch of time is worth an inch of gold, but you cannot buy that inch of time with an inch of gold."

"Exactly."

"If you thought I was wasting your time you wouldn't be here right now, Wayan."

"Keep in mind, I have not agreed to keep knowledge of this meeting from the General."

"Telling him won't be a problem for *me*, Wayan."

The General was the third player in their secret, three-member club called Czarion. He was not a general, but he held a high position in the United States Pentagon. He influenced decision making in the US just as Wayan did in his country.

Neither of the two liked having Chatton in the mix, because she'd manipulated her way into the Czarion by possessing a rare artifact they both wanted. Wayan was convinced that once five specific artifacts were located and brought together, those rare pieces would reveal the bloody destiny laid out in Orion's Legacy, a foretelling of the Final Conflict, the throw down of all throw downs by international superpowers.

Yeah, right. Chatton had stumbled across a lead on these two men while hunting for whoever was trying to wipe out her family line.

The General acted as though he believed in Orion's Legacy, but, in her opinion, his eyes never backed his words. Maybe he'd tossed his Kool-Aid aside when Wayan wasn't looking.

As for her? She didn't go for mumbo jumbo, but the potential for world conflict instigated by men with skewed beliefs had kept her invested in remaining a Czarion while she hunted for answers on her family's killers.

"I will decide what to tell the General once I hear what you have to say," Wayan told her. He angled his chin with the arrogance of a man accustomed to all but his president bowing down to him.

The only time she'd bow to a man would be if she thought the position would give her an advantage in slamming him with a head butt. "The General is going after the Amber Room panel without your knowledge. *The* artifact that holds the majority of the message, if my research on Orion's Legacy is accurate."

He maintained an unconcerned expression, his words unhurried. "It is accurate. And you have learned about this how?"

Because my father taught me all he knew about being an MI6 agent and I surpassed his highest expectations. She lifted away from the wall, rising to her full height of five-feet-eight when you included two inches of boot heel.

Shoving her hands in her coat pockets, she mentally cracked her knuckles, preparing to sell this. "One of the General's *families* is trying to obtain the panel that slipped through our fingers last year. Or, I should say, slipped through the General's fingers."

Wait for it.

Wayan was not a man who liked to be surprised. His hesitation meant he either didn't know about the General's association with a specific group of notable families, or he didn't know that one of them was after a specific panel from the Amber Room, considered the eighth wonder of the world that was believed lost during World War II.

This particular panel wasn't even supposed to exist.

Choosing each word as carefully as one would decide which wire to clip on a bomb, Wayan asked, "Tell me about these families."

"The General has strong connections to five families, some of whom control much of the world's wealth. On occasion, these groups play nicely together when cooperation is needed to manipulate a political or financial outcome."

"We all have associations of significance. Why would the General's hold importance for me?"

"You and the General have known each other longer than I've known the two of you, and you may be convinced that he's sincere about revealing Orion's Legacy, but I'm not so sure. I, however, am dedicated to seeing this through. For that reason, I've kept an ear to the ground on the Amber Room panel and discovered that one of these families has taken a serious interest in gaining the specific panel we need."

His eye twitched a tiny bit. Not much of a reaction on anyone else, but on Wayan that was equivalent to an angry outburst. "The German rumored to possess this panel will trade *only* for the St. Gaudens coins. Those coins are supposed to be unavailable."

"Right. Don't you think everything the General told us about what happened to those coins last year was just a bit curious? They were stolen then recovered by the FBI. But with all the General's resources in his own country, he claimed he couldn't get his hands on those coins before they were locked away in a vault?"

Wayan pursed his thin lips, thinking.

She pressed her advantage. "The General said he could get his hands on the set of coins once things quieted down, but the set has been split up. Two coins are in a museum in New York, one is on display in Seattle and the rest have supposedly been moved to a new vault. If the General was going to produce them, he would have gotten them before that happened."

"And you believe the General is negotiating for the panel without the coins?"

"Yes, but he's not working directly with the German."

"I see."

No you don't, but you will when I get through. "I think the family trying to gain the Amber Room panel needs something from the General, and he's agreed to make a trade of some sort that involves the panel. It's a safe bet that one of the world's power families can come up with something *else* the German will accept."

"You have located this German?"

"No," she admitted. "That's what makes this even more

suspicious. Any lead to him has vanished. I think the General has been working behind our backs and gaining that artifact might not be his only goal."

"What commitment has the General made?"

She had Wayan hooked and kept pulling him in. "That I don't know, yet, but I have to wonder why he has held this from you, in particular, unless he's making a deal that would affect your country. The family involved possesses the ability to influence more than one country economically in a positive, or negative, way."

"Who is the family?"

"I'll keep that to myself for now."

"I could find out myself."

She'd thought about that and had sealed the information leak to keep it out of Wayan's hands. "If that were so, you'd have already known this information before now."

While he digested that, she added, "Once the General gains the panel, he'll have the German killed. The minute that happens, the General will show up to our next meeting ready to boast of an unexpected opportunity which resulted in his getting his hands on the panel. That means *he* will control whether we learn about Orion's Legacy or not."

Wayan turned that black gaze up at her. "You have shown your value."

She gave a tilt of her head in acknowledgment, letting him think she appreciated that he finally noticed. Right.

He asked, "What do you want?"

To drive a wedge between you and the General. But that wasn't the only goal in today's meeting. She was after whoever had been systematically eliminating the entire Macintosh lineage over a period of six centuries. *Her* family, though no one knew it.

She'd uncovered a connection between three deceased Macintoshes and Orion's Legacy, which led her to uncovering Czarion, the secret boy's club which, at the time, had only two members—Wayan and the General.

And in finding them, she'd unearthed the very real potential for World War III if this Orion's Legacy wasn't kept in check.

She was ready to wrap this up. "What do I want? The General has been using the services of the Banker, who has interfered with a pet project of mine." She'd found the person who killed an uncle in Chatton's Mactinosh family, a diplomat. The assassin admitted being paid by a man dealing arms to a terrorist, but she'd since found out the Banker had actually paid the arms dealer for that hit. "I want information on the Banker."

"What makes you think I can provide that?"

"Because I know that you two were behind the failed attack on the Vatican last year, and the Banker was involved."

Not a blink. Wayan had ice water running through his veins.

She laid it out for him. "Here's my offer. I need to get inside the Banker's operations. You have associates who work under the radar, much as I do." Such as the Triads, and the heads of organized crime syndicates in China. "Have them find a weakness I can exploit and I'll keep the General from gaining the Amber Room panel, plus I'll find out if whatever he's up to will put your country, or its economy, at risk."

And when she got her fingers into the Banker, he would tell her why he'd ordered her uncle's death. Step by step, she'd eventually find the person or group who had murdered her mother and her father.

Wayan observed her with the same respect one gave an insect even though he had to look up to do it. "If I provide this information and you are unsuccessful, you will owe me."

Deals with Wayan never came without a catch and she'd rather owe the devil, but she still said, "Agreed."

CHAPTER 13

Margaux opened her eyes to find the half-moon lower in the sky.

She was leaned against a chest bulging with muscle that two days of starvation hadn't softened. He had his arm around her, too.

Did Dragan think she needed coddling?

She'd needed the catnap, but he was delusional if he thought she was going to turn soft on him at this point.

He was in no shape to play hero.

"The water's ready," Dragan murmured.

She sat up then slid off the boulder to stretch. *Shit.* Not so fast next time. Her body ached everywhere, the burns on her right hand and forearm stung like a mother, and a deep lash of pain streaked along her arm. How had she let that little prick cut her? She gritted her teeth against the throb and felt the makeshift bandage to see if it still bled. It was damp. She needed stitches but wasn't going to get them any time soon.

"Drink."

Margaux turned in the direction of Dragan's voice. Waning moonlight dusted across him, but he was so still he'd melded with the boulder. She kept her voice as soft as his. "Did you drink yet?"

"No."

"What were you waiting on?" She would hurt him if he said, 'ladies first.'

"You to get up so I could use both hands."

She stepped over and reached for the water, but when she lifted it, she put the side of the plastic bag to his lips. He drank without arguing. She tilted it a little at a time, feeding it to him slowly. When he'd finished half the bag, he lifted a hand to stop her. She turned it to her mouth, greedy for every drop that slid down her parched throat.

She could drink ten of these right now, but so could he.

When she had the bag refilled with a tablet dropped inside, she tucked the bag down inside her shirt, hoping a stick didn't hit her in the chest and burst it.

She could feel Dragan staring at her and through her. What was bothering him?

He asked, "Are you bleeding?"

How had he figured that out? Her arm had been on the other side of where she'd leaned into him. "Why? You got a Band-Aid in your pack?"

"How badly are you hurt?"

"Tattoo nicked my arm with his K-bar. Are we moving or not?"

Dragan took his time getting off the boulder, but he did it under his own power. Good sign, that.

He said, "We have to find somewhere to hide out until we've rehydrated. We'll move along the river unless we hear someone coming. If we can find a place close to it, we rest a few hours, then we move again."

No point in arguing with him, because Dragan clearly had jungle training. Smart money said to let him call the shots.

Margaux stepped over to him. "Lean on me, Tarzan. We'll get farther faster."

When he hesitated, she turned his words on him. "We need each other. Get used to it."

She was doing her best to accept needing someone else. So could he.

"Fine, Jane." A big arm looped over her shoulders, but when they started moving, he wasn't struggling as much as before.

She fell into a rhythm, moving with him. That little bit of sleep and some water had revitalized her belief that they would get out of this alive.

After what they figured was an hour of walking— and another two shared bags of water— sweat rolled down the side of her face for the first time in days. Dragan was right about finding a place to hide out. Otherwise, they'd lose all the hydration the water was offering. "What time do you think it is?"

"Got somewhere to be?"

Wiseass. "No. Trying to figure out how soon the sun'll be up."

"I'm guessing it's about two in the morning."

"Daylight is around what? Six?"

"Five or six."

That meant they only had about three or four hours to find a place to hide before daylight.

They took water breaks but kept hiking along the rocky banks of the river. When a thicket of trees or boulders too tall blocked the way, they had to crawl up a slope and work back down.

An hour later, Dragan called a halt.

Margaux took that opportunity to refill their plastic bag again. She stood up and turned to him with the bag open for the tablet. "You need a break?"

"That's not why we stopped." He dropped the tablet in and stored the bottle. "We've found our hideout."

She hadn't seen anything except more humongous rocks, dirt and water. "Where?"

"Over there." He pointed past her on the uphill side where a stand of trees grew around boulders that had piled there so long ago vines crisscrossed them. One thick tree had fallen halfway to the ground, stopped by the rocks.

When she squinted, she could see a dark cubbyhole.

That looked like snake central.

If she refused to go, he'd think she was a wimp. Hell, even Indiana Jones hated snakes.

"Ready?" His voice whispered close to her ear.

She turned and knew without asking that he was waiting on her to decide if she could do that. "Neither one of us is petite. Think we'll fit?"

"Without a doubt."

Cocky bastard would say that. She nodded. "Let's go."

Once they'd made it up the incline, he told her, "Wait here for a minute while I make a set of tracks leading into the water and clear ours when I backtrack."

She put a hand on his chest. "I'm faster. Why don't you climb in there and clear a good place to lie down? You know, brush away pebbles and whatever."

He gave her a long look. One that said he knew exactly what she was doing by sending him into the hideaway first to make sure nothing slithered around. "Fine. You handle the tracks. I'll check out the sleeping quarters."

She stomped all over the ground so it would appear that more than one set of boots had walked into the river. While she was there, she rolled up her sleeve and removed the bandage to wash it out in a small eddy where water swirled. Once she'd wrung out her bandage, the idea of running a wet cloth over her upper body was more than she could resist. She took a look around, determined Dragan was too far to see anything, and pulled off her shirt. She dunked her head and threw wet hair back over her shoulders, then gave her arms a good scrubbing.

The knife wound started bleeding again and aching even more, but cleaning it out had to be better than leaving it dirty.

Not a pristine bath, but just that quick wipe down and rinsing her hair refreshed her. She ripped the white undershirt in half, wrapped her arm as best she could and soaked the other half to take back to Dragan.

Halfway back to the hideout, she paused when a dark figure came towards her. "What are you doing down here?"

"What took so long?"

Was he worried? "I was getting a mani-pedi. What do you think I was doing? I washed up a little. It refreshed me. Here's a wet rag for you."

"You should have told me so I could watch your back."

"I watched my back. You want this rag or not?"

He stuck out his hand and she dropped the sopping rag in it. Then he held out his other hand. "Let's get back up there before something four footed comes along and likes the cave I've cleaned out."

Too tired to argue, she took his hand and let him lead her back to the spot, because to be honest she'd lost sight of which hole it was now that the moon had dropped so low it wasn't much use for light.

When he stopped in front of the shadowy outline of rocks and a tree, Margaux suggested, "Use that rag. You'll feel better."

She wasn't stalling. Not really, but if he thought she was climbing into that sad excuse for a cave first, he was crazy.

Dragan leaned a hip against one of the boulders and dropped the rag down next to him. He unbuttoned his short-sleeve shirt and let it fall open while he wiped his face and arms, then his chest. Just enough light brushed his skin for Margaux to see that they'd worked him over good.

And that Dragan was beefcake quality.

Where was a full moon when she wanted to see his skin glisten where he washed?

And what was she doing thinking about skin glistening? Especially his?

Dragan pulled his shirt back together, buttoned it and laid the rag over the rock where it could only be seen from overhead. "Thanks. That does feel better."

"You're welcome." She looked around.

"Let's unclip our belts. I cleared enough room to stash them near our heads on this end of the cave."

She didn't want to give up her weapons, but she couldn't sleep on her side with all this wrapped around her waist. She compromised by removing her belt but kept a knife and left her boots on. Something that crawled would end up sleeping in them if she didn't.

After Dragan bunched their belts and pouches at the head of that hole he was calling a cave, he asked, "How's your arm?"

She turned back to find him right next to her. "It's fine."

His fingers touched her face. The first gentle touch she'd had in so long she closed her eyes, soaking up the way that simple contact soothed her. Every bit of her body hurt, but his fingers were a balm that dulled the ache. She stood like that for a long moment, then he kissed her.

His beard tickled her face. She didn't like beards. Hadn't until now. But this was wrong for some reason. She murmured against his lips, "What're you doing?"

He stopped long enough to say, "It's called a kiss." Then his lips were back to learning hers, brushing softly.

She shouldn't be kissing him. Not this man.

Her good arm didn't get the memo. She reached up to hook her hand on his shoulder. His hands moved down to wrap her waist and pull her close to him until they were chest to chest. She could feel each breath he took. Each beat of his heart. He felt so solid and warm.

She was tired of fighting and running and always alone.

His hand slid up her back, fingers gently massaging her muscles.

Her eyes closed. She soaked up his comfort. So nice ...

She blinked and realized she'd fallen asleep against him.

"Ready to check out the accommodations?" he asked in a weary voice.

"This is the spot, huh?" She pushed away from him and acted as if she hadn't just crashed in his arms.

"This is it. Let's get some rest." His fingers slid down her arm to her hand, giving her a little tug. "You first."

"No."

"I checked it out. There's nothing in there."

"You just want to be last so you can be between me and any threat. That's bullshit since I'm in better shape than you."

He sounded whipped when he sighed. "I know you're a badass. Do we have to keep battling for who's the baddest badass? 'Cause I'll go ahead and forfeit."

Why did she feel foolish when he put it like that? "I just ... don't want to be closed in. Okay?"

Would he argue or badger to get what he wanted? Badgering someone usually worked for her.

But he didn't. Dragan just said, "Okay," and lowered himself to his knees then rolled into the hole. "I'm in."

She could do this. *Don't think about being stuffed in a dark closet where things crawled on you while you screamed until you had no voice.*

Margaux took a couple deep breaths, expecting him to bark

at her to hurry up, but he didn't. She dropped down on her knees, then to her side and scooted back a little at a time until Dragan's big arm wrapped around her waist and slid her smoothly up against his chest.

Spooning in the jungle. Scratch that off the bucket list.

When he pulled her to him, her head ended up on his shoulder and his arms closed around her. She realized then that he'd gotten his way after all. He had her tucked deep in the recess and surrounded her. Her stubborn pride wanted to say something, to let him know she didn't need to be protected.

But for the first time in a long time, she gave in.

She even liked feeling protected, but she would never admit it.

He didn't move his hands, didn't say a word or push any boundaries. Did he know that his stillness was alluring? That the slower he breathed, the more content she was to just lie here and accept the peaceful feeling of being held against his warm body, caught in the luxury of his arms.

She should be hot in the jungle, right? Why did his heat feel so good? She hadn't felt cold in the hut, but maybe the temperature dropped in the jungle at night. She'd have to ask Tarzan tomorrow. He hugged her closer against him and she decided to let him have his way.

With a few hours of rest, she'd be ready to hike across whatever country they were in. She shivered. Had to be warmer once the sun came up. Maybe Tarzan knew a plant to put on her arm and stop the throbbing.

Sweat trickled down her neck and she shivered again. That made no sense. *Figure it out tomorrow.*

Exhaustion claimed her.

CHAPTER 14

Logan came awake at the sound of something—or someone—moving around nearby. He shouldn't have nodded off for so long, but there was only so much a body could take.

From the soft light outside, he guessed it was barely dawn.

The sound of dry grass being stepped on and pushed aside rustled softly.

He remained perfectly still, hoping Violet, aka Jane of the Jungle, stayed asleep until he determined what was out there.

She slept on her side, spooned close to his chest. He slipped his fingers around the stock of the pistol he'd placed on the ground in front of her, keeping it within easy reach. She should be sleeping behind him where he could shield her, but the hardheaded woman wouldn't hear of it, so he had her wrapped as securely as he could in his arms.

Not that he was complaining at the moment.

Asleep, she was soft and pliant, fitting perfectly along his body. Dark hair fell across her face and over her shoulders. He'd finally get a good look at her when the sun showed up.

But he wouldn't disturb her yet just to see her face. She was conked out.

Another whisper of noise reached his ears. Whatever was out there kept coming closer.

Logan gripped the weapon, his senses alert and sharp again.

An animal moved slowly into view, walking past the front of their hideout.

He let out the breath he'd been holding when he realized the wild cat wasn't a jaguar or puma. It weighed around twenty pounds and had a dark, grayish-brown coat. A jaguarundi that preyed on small animals and stayed around water. Logan had bedded down in its hunting grounds.

Pausing, the animal sniffed the air in Logan's direction, eyes narrowed, considering what it scented, then the cat faced the river again.

No problem.

Not until the warm body in Logan's arms moved and let out a groan.

The jaguarundi froze, ears pointing up, tufts of fur lifting on its back.

Logan covered Violet's mouth with his hand. She went rigid, now fully awake.

It might not be a large cat, but it was still dangerous, and Logan didn't want to risk the sound of a gunshot or to kill the animal unnecessarily. Several tense seconds passed before the cat relaxed its stance and moved down the slope to the river.

Logan released a sigh filled with relief. He placed the pistol back down in front of Violet again. Her muscles eased as the threat passed. He moved his hand from her mouth but paused to brush his thumb across her cheek. She didn't say a word or react. That just made him want to run his hands all over her and feel every inch of that Amazon body. Hell, he wanted to do a lot more than feel the curves of her body.

It was surprising what a little sleep, water and even that cool wash down last night could do to revive him.

She adjusted her position, which bumped her butt against his dick.

Heat pooled in his groin, and he couldn't think past the urge to touch her.

Just what she needed. Some horndog panting after her.

Hell of a time to feel something for a woman. In fairness to his deprived body, when was the last time he'd just slept with a woman in his arms? He couldn't recall, because lazing around with a female equated to being involved and that did not happen on an op, *wouldn't* happen again at this point in his life anyhow.

Not after he'd left one in danger years ago.

He'd been sure she was safe from any threat. He'd been in Paris only to do surveillance, and her apartment turned out to be the perfect place for observation. She'd made it clear she was not a woman to get serious about so he'd planned to kiss her goodbye when his job was done and forget about her.

But she'd turned out to be so much more than a casual affair.

And he'd almost gotten her killed when he was called to extract a Russian diplomat wanting to defect.

He'd never met another woman who'd reached inside and cupped his heart and didn't intend to make that mistake again. He had another ten, maybe fifteen years, of fieldwork in him. He wasn't tossing that aside for any woman or hooking up with one just to leave her alone at home always waiting for him and wondering if he'd make it back.

So why did this woman have him on edge?

She had secrets and he hated secrets.

That had to be it. He had to know everything about anyone he encountered, especially on a mission.

Didn't take much to figure out that she was someone who kept her secrets locked in one hell of a protective fort and, damn him, he couldn't stand it. He wanted to slip inside when she wasn't looking and find out who lived behind those walls. To unmask her for real and discover everything about her, like why she wanted to meet the Banker, who she worked for and ... to be honest, what it was about her that had him rock hard even in *this* situation.

He could admit to himself that he wanted her, but that didn't mean anything would come of it even if his dick didn't care what side of the law she lived on.

That wasn't going to happen.

Besides, this was nothing more than a residual effect of getting himself just as turned on as she'd been when he'd had her in the hotel suite, telling her how he had to *prepare* her for Nitro, the man she'd *thought* was Dragan.

Had Nitro made it out of the Trophy Room alive?

God, he hoped so.

Logan's team was exceptional, and Nitro was one creative son of a gun when it came to exit strategies on the fly. Still, leaving any of his men alone ate a hole in his gut. Going upstairs with Violet had been a gamble he'd lost, and Nitro had better not have ended up paying for Logan's mistake.

Logan would make a lot of people pay if anything happened

to one of his men.

Violet shifted her legs, and her bottom brushed him again. Just a simple touch, but she might as well have grabbed him. He knew without a doubt that hadn't been intentional, but that didn't stop him from clenching his jaw at the ache that spiraled through his groin.

He had to get out of this hole and move around. Do some adjusting so he could walk. When he could draw a breath and speak in a normal voice, he said, "Morning, Jane."

He was not calling her Violet anymore.

She mumbled something that started with "f" and ended with Tarzan. She stretched slowly then shuddered as if she was cold. He had a memory of her shaking like that during the night and he'd tried to cover her better with his body each time. He'd assumed it was the lack of body fat and extra weight loss causing her to be chilled.

But now that he noticed, the back of her shirt was damp with sweat.

Cold in this heat *and* sweating?

When she moved the arm that had rested on her hip, he saw the stained sleeve where she'd bled through.

Son of a bitch. She wasn't chilled from the temperature, but from an infected cut. She'd downplayed it by saying she got nicked. How bad was it? He gently grasped her elbow and she tensed again. "Why didn't you tell me this was a deep cut, Sugar?"

She spoke with a rasp and irritation. "Like you have a needle and thread handy?"

Ah, fuck. The cut was bad enough to need stitches and she'd been losing blood. It had probably clotted since last night so he wouldn't pull off the wrapping yet, but they had to get to a first aid kit. He hadn't found any antibiotic in his pouches and if she'd run across any meds in hers, she'd have used them.

He lowered her arm gently back to her side.

Muscles flinched in her face and her jaw was rigid. She was gritting her teeth. Had to hurt like hell. But she hadn't said a word. Damn, what a woman and he couldn't stand to see her in pain.

When he touched her forehead, she swatted his hand away. Didn't matter. He'd felt enough heat to confirm her fever. This changed everything.

He hadn't wanted to move during the day and had planned to cross the river a couple of times tonight to slow down any tracking, but waiting to reach civilization or someone with meds meant her infection would only be worse by then.

He put some steel in his voice. "Drink up what's left of the water, and we'll refill before we get moving."

"Thought you wanted to stay here a while," she said with a grogginess he didn't like.

"I did. We rested, now it's time to move unless you're not up for it." That should raise her hackles enough to get her moving.

"Screw you. I'm fine."

There was that brawler's ego he hoped would keep her going until he could find a way to get her out of this place alive. He might have to piss her off nonstop to make that happen. Not a problem if that was what it took to keep her on her feet so they could cover ground more quickly. He'd rather leave her here to rest and hunt down what he needed on his own, but she couldn't be trusted to stay put. And if she fell asleep, she'd be vulnerable to any human or animal who found her.

He let out a disgruntled sigh. "If you're so ready, move out of here, but slowly so we don't draw the cat's attention. Stay under these trees until I'm out, too."

Drawing the attention of the cat didn't worry him so much once they were out of the hole, but her stepping out into view did. Last night she'd been as sharp as any agent he'd worked with, but right now she was not on her game.

She wriggled her way out and got to her feet.

He followed her, feeling every one of his thirty-four years when he pushed up to his knees and stood. She had her back to him, staring out toward the river where the jaguarundi moved with stealth along the bank. The cat was far enough away to not be an issue.

"Strange cat," she muttered then she took a step.

"Where're you going, Sugar?"

She lifted her good hand and waved him off without turning around. "Don't panic. I've finally hydrated enough that I need to give some back. Just turn around. I'm not going far."

He started to argue until she disappeared between the stand of trees and more boulders that fronted them on the high side of the hill. That allowed him a chance for the same nature break.

He'd just returned to the front of their hideaway when she came walking quietly back toward him. The little guard's pants hit mid-calf on her and she picked at the long sleeves that stopped short of her wrists. Logan would never forget seeing her strut into the Trophy Room on that pair of legs. She'd moved smoothly with confident posture, comfortable with her height where some women that tall tried to downplay it.

Not Jane. She'd swept through the Trophy Room, dragging tongues to the floor and not wasting the time of day on any of them.

Logan had caught her attention when he'd described bending her over that sofa. Damn, he'd love to see her face when he drove into her.

Dream on, buddy.

Speaking of seeing her face, he was finally going to get a look at this woman.

Sunlight leaked across the horizon and brightened the shadows beneath the trees. Jane stepped into better view, swiping a handful of hair over her shoulder. The sun gave life to the red streaks in dark auburn hair that fell past her shoulders. A half-assed smile tilted one side of her mouth.

She had a sweet mouth, a wide one that reminded him of Julia Roberts. Her bottom lip was cracked from more than being dry. Those assholes had worked her over. She had an ugly bruise across one cheek and another on her forehead.

But that mouth was special. It nudged a memory.

Logan's gaze traveled up to take in the rest of her face. Narrow nose and high cheeks. And a mass of auburn hair. She sure seemed familiar.

A lot of women had those features, but not arranged exactly like that.

The skin tingled along Logan's arms when he finally met her gaze.

He stared at eyes too deep a shade of green to be forgotten.

No fucking way.

CHAPTER 15

Dragan's face had been pounded to the point it was painful to look at him, but what Margaux could make out about his eyes looked shocked. They were brown or maybe a dark hazel color. Hard to say with him squinting and her throbbing arm demanding her attention.

She couldn't stop the constant pain thrumming in her arm. Instead, she focused harder on Dragan.

Why did he seem so surprised? Granted, she didn't look like the bombshell who'd walked into the Trophy Room, but he didn't have to gawk.

She cocked an eyebrow and planted her feet. "Disappointed I'm not the blond you were panting after or surprised to find out I really don't have purple eyes?" She rubbed her tired eyes, muttering, "They washed my contacts out with the first bucket of saltwater in my face, but they were only cosmetic."

When her vision cleared, he was frowning, still hung up on something.

"Your bruises look worse than mine, Tarzan." She stared at the middle of his face. "Is your nose broken?"

"It was. I fixed it."

The bruised nose dropped him a point on the attractive scale but fixing it himself raised his badass level by ten so he was still in beefcake range. Especially if lethal men turned you on. She had bad wiring somewhere, because spooning with this one had been more comfortable than she'd like to admit.

He'd been an intimidating personal protector back at the Trophy Room, but out here he was downright deadly.

The black beard that had been thick, but neatly trimmed when they'd first met was now a wild, bushy thing. And he did have some ugly ass bruises. A yellow-and-blue one peeked out from the black hair falling over his forehead. One eye still had plenty of swelling. So much that she questioned if he'd have decent peripheral vision. That nose had a nasty gash over the top, but it did look straight.

That had to hurt like a bitch when he fixed it.

"You got the plastic bag?" he asked, moving on past their rough appearance.

Water. Her throat was dry as old socks. She reached inside her shirt and pulled it free. There was maybe a cup left. She took a good swallow and handed the balance over to him.

After he drained it, he kept the bag. "I'll get more water. You stay here—"

"No. Someone's got to watch your back."

He closed his eyes and did a little headshake over something then opened his eyes and crossed his arms. "Today will go much better if we don't argue every point."

"You mean if I don't argue with your *orders*." She was tired, hot, thirsty and miserable. Someone should warn him against pushing her right now.

"I'm the one familiar with this terrain," he pointed out, angling his head in a way that said he waited for her to top that.

"Yes, you are, but you can't just make decisions for both of us. If we stay together, we have a better chance of defending ourselves as a team."

"But if I go down there alone, I'm less noticeable."

Her head and arm throbbed in tandem. She rubbed her neck. "Then we'll have to be less noticeable together. After that, we'll start working our way down the river like you were talking about yesterday."

He glanced away. "That's changed."

"Why?"

"I've had some rest and time to think through a better plan." He lifted a hand to scratch his beard and spoke in a low volume, just loud enough for her to hear. "They'll be out hunting us by now. They're better rested and fed so it won't take long to catch up to us once they pick up our trail. Way I see it, the leader is staying in camp and sending out the other three in the most likely directions, which would be down to this river unless ..."

Her head wanted to explode. Or she wanted it to explode. Anything to unleash the pressure. Sweat dripped into her eyes.

His deep voice rumbled on. Her mind wandered. She wiped the sweat out of her eyes and shook with a hard chill.

Her arm burned with infection.

She'd be a liability if she didn't keep a grip on reality.

He paused. "You okay?"

What had he been saying? She snapped, "Fine, just stop boring the shit out of me and tell me what you want to do."

"Backtrack to the kidnappers' camp."

"What?" She had to be delusional from the fever setting in, because she couldn't have heard him right. "How is *that* a good plan?"

"I can keep us alive for a long time in a jungle, but we don't have any idea where we're headed. We could end up going deeper into the jungle instead of toward civilization. Their leader had a sat phone. We get our hands on that, and I can get us out of here."

She had to admit it was a decent plan *if* they were in better shape and had more weapons. But she didn't have any idea where they were going or how long they'd survive out on their own. This was not her scene, and she was ready to do whatever it took to get the hell back to her pavement and exhaust fumes.

If Dragan had people who could extract them, she was all in for going after that sat phone.

Then all she'd have to do was escape him and his people.

Had to be easier than this once she had food, more water and sleep. She nodded. "Okay, good plan. I still want to watch your back."

"Keep your pistol out and stay close." He shoved the plastic bag inside his shirt, leaving his hands free when he turned and started down the hill. When he dropped into a crouch, moving through the tall grass, she followed suit, carrying her pistol and dogging his steps.

It took a while moving so slowly, but they finally reached a spot where the two of them could slip into a shadowy area between stacks of rocks and boulders. It was a tight fit in the narrow passage, but Margaux turned her back on Dragan to watch the jungle while he filled their water bag.

She held the pistol in her non-dominant left hand since her right one was worthless.

The ache in her head kept up a steady thumping. She could be more miserable, but it would take too much effort to figure out how. As bad as it had been back in Atlanta where she'd been stuck in her apartment facing an unknown future, Margaux would gladly take that right now in a heartbeat.

She'd screwed up so much. Lost the only contact to the Banker. Got caught. Put this guy Dragan in a jam with her.

The scenery blurred and her head dropped forward. Her arm felt twice the normal size and her body had turned into a human furnace.

"I've got the water. You through catnapping?" Dragan asked right next to her ear.

Margaux snapped her head up so quickly she bumped Dragan who cursed in two languages. Had she hit his nose? Damn. "Sorry."

His hand clamped down on the shoulder of her good arm. "No big deal. Let's wash out that cut."

"I did it last night. Scrubbed the hell out of it. Nothing else we can do unless one of us has some antibiotic ointment."

"No. Are you drowsy?"

That was concern in his voice. Why was he being so understanding when she'd ruined his opportunity to meet with the Banker? It might even be her fault they'd been captured. That weasel Snake Eyes had screwed her.

She stretched her neck. "I'm wide awake and ready to roll. Now what do we do, Tarzan?"

"Jane moves her ass out of the way so I can take the lead."

Still squatted, she moved out of the narrow gap. Dragan swept past, low to the ground, almost bent over enough to touch the ground with his hands, but he didn't. She tried that and fell forward twice so she finally stayed on all fours.

By the time they reached the tree line, her back muscles cried from being bowed over.

Outdoor enthusiasts could have this. She had no desire to do anything close to camping ever again. When Dragan slowed then pushed up to stand, she tried to do the same and started to fall over.

His hands gripped each side of her waist and raised her up until her feet hit the ground.

"I had it," she groused at him. Why couldn't she just be gracious and say thanks? Because she'd learned a painful lesson many years ago about being weak.

It was a simple lesson. Never be vulnerable around a man.

The second lesson? Never let one close enough to expose her identity.

But Dragan didn't know who she was. He was here from Russia, probably traveling on a fake passport. He was focused on getting to the Banker, not turning in some unknown woman to Homeland Security or the FBI.

Or INTERPOL.

She stepped out of his grasp and the world moved around too fast for a moment. She put her hand on the closest tree and leaned in. A bird took flight above her, squawking as it flew and flashing colorful feathers that blurred in her vision. She lifted her knee, bending it in and out, rather than letting on that the fever was getting to her.

"Drink some water." Dragan pulled the bag out of his shirt, which meant she had to stand on her own.

Margaux tightened her muscles and pushed away from the tree so she could take the bag in her good hand.

Dragan stepped over close and held up a corner for her to drink. She didn't care. She was thirsty already and any movement of her right arm sent pain streaking down to her fingers. As she drank, Dragan stared down into her eyes and this time she could see gold flecks in brown eyes.

Brown eyes and a big build had been her favorite for a long time. Since, uh, since she left France and Pierre. He'd had brown eyes, too, and with such thick lashes it had almost looked like kohl around his eyes.

Now that she looked close, Dragan had thick lashes.

But Pierre had brown wavy hair, not straight black locks.

She must be getting delirious, trying to see a resemblance

between the brooding Dragan and Pierre who had laughed and loved ... until he'd done something very bad.

Dragan zipped the water bag closed and stowed it back inside his shirt.

She wiped her mouth with the back of her hand. "Aren't you going to drink?"

"I drank first." His gaze bypassed her and studied everything around them. From the way he cocked his head, she could tell he was listening for something.

Had he actually drunk water this time?

She tried to think back to when they'd first stopped. He sounded sure. She wouldn't argue because she couldn't remember exactly what had just happened. Once he realized the fever was getting to her, he'd suggest leaving her somewhere safe.

She was not staying out in this place alone.

Facing down those men in the camp was preferable to that.

Her gaze wandered over the deep sweat stains on his chest to the machete hanging at his side. When had he taken that?

Did she really want to hack anything today?

No, he could keep the blade and hack away.

His attention came back to her with that frown again. "We've got a couple of hours before we get back, and that's if we don't run into one of the patrols out looking for us. We can't return the same way we came. If you need to stop, tug on my shirt. The less we talk, the better."

"Don't expect me to give you a reason to slow down. I've had all I want of paradise."

Dragan was still standing all over her personal space. They had plenty of jungle. *Back up already.*

He lowered his face to hers and said, "Do you ever let go?"

"Of what?" She knew what he was talking about, but she wasn't going to admit to anything.

"The need to always be in control, to always be one step better."

Her arm had swollen tight as a stuffed sausage all the way to her fingers. She was alternately cold and hot, and sick of being in this heat. He should consider his timing for psychobabble, especially when she had a pistol within reach. "Do you want to spend today analyzing something you'll never understand or getting out of here?"

The sucker smiled. Straight teeth that glared white. "I'll tell you what I want."

She was not up for this crap. "World peace? A razor? Is it a long list? Because——"

"To hell with that."

"What?"

"Telling you anything." He caught her to him and closed the short distance between their mouths. He had a really nice mouth. There was his beard again. She could get used to it on a man who kissed like this one. He was taking care not to hurt her lips that were just starting to heal from being dry. How did he manage to kiss her so tenderly and still turn her insides into a bunch of wobbling Jell-O?

Margaux had never understood why Jane gave up everything to stay in the jungle with Tarzan, but she was starting to get a clue.

She reached up to grab his head with both hands, and when she did, her right arm exploded with pain. She jerked away and gritted her teeth to keep from crying out.

"Ah, shit, Sugar." He cupped her good elbow, keeping her steady. "Hold on a minute." He reached around behind him and pulled out the other half of Tattoo's undershirt that Margaux had turned into a giant washrag, then he fitted two points together. "Can you bend your arm in front of you?"

Yes. The question was if she could do it without throwing up the water she'd just guzzled. She swallowed against the pain coming and used her other hand to guide her injured arm. Lifting it slowly, she breathed in and out fast.

Don't pass out.

"Hold it there." Dragan slipped the cloth carefully into position to make a sling and tied the two ends around her neck. By the time he'd finished, her face was covered in sweat that streamed down to drip off her chin.

She had to hold her arm still for a moment, so she slung her head to one side, trying to get wet hair off her face. If she ever landed in anything remotely close to the woods again, even a park, she'd shoot the person responsible.

Gentle hands cupped her face. She looked up into worried brown eyes.

Déjà vu hit her for a moment. She'd stared into a gaze like his before. Silly brain trying to dredge up old emotions that were better off left locked away.

His fingers moved over her face, wiping away the streaks of perspiration. He smoothed her hair back behind her ears. "Want your hair pulled back?"

Of all the things she might have expected him to say, that hadn't been one, but she'd love to put her hair in a ponytail to get it off her neck and take one aggravation away. "You got a hair bob in those pouches?"

Humor lit his gaze.

He found her funny? Any other man would have probably pushed her off a cliff by now.

She managed to keep her tongue under control while he reached into a pouch and pulled out a small bag that was held closed with a rubber band. He muttered, "The bag smells like Lurch had a sweet tooth. Probably a rock candy stash."

"But the pig didn't leave us any."

Dragan looked up again, rubber band in hand. Margaux turned and couldn't stop the sigh that escaped when he lifted her hair high on the crown of her head. He did something that felt like a ponytail then let go.

She didn't care if she looked like a troll doll.

Dragan stepped in front of her. "Stay close behind and let me know if you need to stop."

Waspish words sat on the tip of her tongue where she kept them, ready to shut down any man who tried to control her or insinuate she was weak, but she swallowed them this time and nodded. "Don't slow down until I tell you. Deal?"

"Deal." He leaned down and kissed her.

"Where did you get the ridiculous idea that it was okay to

kiss me whenever you wanted?" Okay, so some snarky comments just couldn't be contained.

"When I realized you like it as much as I do." He turned away, moving out before she had a chance to say a word.

Damn him, he was right.

Which was beyond stupid because he had been at the Trophy Room to meet with a man who brokered terrorist deals.

She started walking, following Dragan's exact path. With each step, she reminded herself that she couldn't allow this attraction to continue, because if she survived this and got out of here, she'd have to hand Dragan over to the FBI.

Right now, she couldn't conceive of doing that.

When had he stopped being the enemy?

CHAPTER 16

"What do you want, Tigger?" Sabrina asked in the general direction of her cell phone that was on speaker and reached for an oversized Atlanta Braves T-shirt she pulled over her head. It hit just below her underwear.

"Didn't you open the box of ammo I sent you?"

She paused in dressing. "Why are you sending me ammo?"

"To try it out in the field for me."

"The last ammo I tested for you disintegrated upon impact."

His squeaky voice got higher when he was defensive. "I told you what caused that."

"If I'd used that in the field, I would've gotten my ass kicked by the scumbag I'd just shot."

"This is different. I sent you two versions. One to try out on the range and one to use under real time conditions."

This was the first night she'd been home before midnight and just wanted to sit down and eat, even if all she had was leftover pizza. From two days ago. "I'll look at it when I'm back in the office."

"Be sure to read all the information before you—"

She snatched up the phone, "Good night, Tigger," and punched the end call button. When she stepped toward her chest of drawers to get a pair of sweatpants, two red LEDs lit up the bedroom control panel for her alarm system. There was an identical panel in every room and live web cam feeds to her computer downstairs. Someone had crossed the north boundary line of her property. Her fifty-year-old house sat in the middle of a single acre in East Point, an older suburb of Atlanta.

She'd outfitted this simple, ranch-style house with a security system required by someone with a past like hers.

Lifting her Sig Sauer P226 from the nightstand, she left the lights on in the bathroom and stalked slowly through her dark house.

The lights had been left off on purpose.

Habit of nature. She'd learned as a child running the streets in the Bronx that the safest place was often the darkest.

When she reached the living room, she eased up beside the picture window that faced the front yard and moved the blinds just enough to peer at her front porch. No one there. Every window in the house had been replaced with ballistic glass that wouldn't stop a heavy artillery attack, but it would slow down the first rounds to give her a chance to escape through an underground tunnel.

She removed a painting from the wall and placed it on her sofa, then focused a camera lens mounted in the wall that gave her a quick view of her front yard. Faster than booting up her computer feed. Trees within fifty feet of the house had been removed and her landscaping would only hide a rabbit.

A man stood in the middle of her yard with his arms on top of his head and a white bag on the ground next to his feet. He wore a shirt and pants, but no jacket even though the temperatures were in the low forties.

Not surprising. He'd once braved snow with almost no clothes for a CIA op.

Gage Laughton.

She dropped her head against the wall. *Not now.*

When she looked up, he was still standing there. Gage would stay that way for hours if he was determined to speak to her.

She put the painting back in place, disarmed the alarm and opened her front door. "Do you have a death wish?"

"Evidently."

"What do you want, Gage?"

"I brought Thai food. From Surin's."

Her traitorous stomach chose that moment to growl.

"I heard that. Can I take my hands down and come inside?"

The last time she'd let Gage inside her home she'd been living in Virginia, and he'd just returned from being gone for seven weeks undercover for the agency.

She'd spent the happiest weekend of her life with the man she loved.

That was the last weekend she could remember feeling truly

happy.

A week later, someone in the CIA burned her team while they were on an op to bring home a captured CIA agent. Gage was as lethal an operative as they came, and he'd been her handler for the agency. He swore he knew nothing about her team being sent into a trap and he'd tried to regain her trust by helping her out a few times since she'd opened her new operations.

She wouldn't hand over her trust so easily this time.

But he had Thai food. She could always kill him once she was full. "Come in."

She waited for him to enter before she locked the door and reset the alarm. She'd change the code again after he left. The smell of Thai had her close to drooling since she'd only had two protein bars in fifteen hours. Walking past him, she flipped the switch that turned on lights recessed beneath her wall cabinets.

Gage placed the bag on the island that centered her kitchen. His hands moved with fluid efficiency as he pulled out one container after another. He had skilled fingers he'd used with the precision of a maestro when he'd played her body. The sleeves of his dark green shirt were rolled halfway up his forearms. Jeans still looked sexier on him than on any other man. His hair had been short the last time she'd seen him. Now it was two inches longer.

Her favorite look on him because it allowed the natural wave to show.

He once admitted to having his hair trimmed to that length just for when he came home to her after a long mission.

Was she really going there?

Tonight was not the night to open doors to the past. She couldn't stand here and pretend everything was fine when it hadn't been in so long and wouldn't be until she knew who in the agency had screwed her two years ago. "What's up, Gage?"

He continued to unload food on the island space she used for a table as he spoke. "I told you the Banker was in the States."

"Right." That confirmed Margaux had gotten solid intel after all, but she shouldn't have gone off on her own. Sabrina ran her hand through her hair. Still damp. "Any idea what he's gathering mercs for?"

"We're working on it." He put the white bag on the floor then turned to her. The kitchen hadn't seemed small the whole time she'd lived here.

Gage had a way of taking over a room without a word.

He stood three feet from her, drinking her in with his silence.

At one time, that would have been too far away, but now it was too close. She'd had a sniper trained on him the first time they'd met after the blown UK op, but he kept chipping away at her, determined to tear down walls she was just as determined to reinforce.

But being alone with him was testing her engineering skills. Her heart was trying to kick down her walls from the inside.

He took a step toward her. A test to see if she'd balk or back away.

She wouldn't run. Her gaze skipped over the island where he'd placed only one plate. "Aren't you eating?"

"No." He took another step, closing the gap to inches.

"Why not?"

He lifted his hand, reaching out to touch her but it stopped in mid motion.

She tensed, wanting to feel those fingers more than a junkie crashing, wanting a hit, and cursed herself for the weakness.

He dropped his hand. "I can't stay here and not touch you."

Damn him for looking at her as if she were still his world. If he touched her now, she wasn't sure she could tell him no. Time had a way of dulling the righteous fury she'd banked day after day.

He waited for a sign from her. That rigid control he held with an iron grip prevented him from seducing her and risking the fallout. And they both knew he could do it, which was why letting him inside had been a mistake.

She wanted him, too, but if she gave in to her body tonight

would she be able to face herself tomorrow?

His fingers grazed her cheek. To her detriment, she shivered at the contact.

"Are you going to stand there and tell me you don't miss us, Sabrina?"

"No, but neither am I going to put aside what happened and act like nothing has changed."

"Nothing should have changed between us," he argued.

"But it did."

A look of sad resignation crossed his face before it settled into irritation. "Does your stubborn pride keep you warm at night?"

That's all it took to back her away from committing emotional suicide. "I could ask you the same about your conscience unless you're ready to give me the names of everyone who knew about the UK mission." She waited a beat, hoping just once he'd bend his inflexible belief in the agency.

His jaw hardened.

She had her answer. "No? Just as I thought."

"The minute I know who tried to kill you, you'll know. I can't promise he'll still be breathing by the time you get to him. Not after I spent two years wondering if you were alive or dead."

He meant every word. She didn't want to believe him, but her damned heart had trusted him once and wanted to trust him again. And if she was completely honest, she was lonely, but for only one man's touch. Her heart and her loyalty warred. Giving in to Gage would be betraying Josh, Dingo and the others on that team who had barely escaped with their lives that night.

Josh's female contact had bled out in his arms.

Her team, no, her *friends* had placed unquestioned faith in her, and she'd given hers to Gage. She said, "You want me to trust you but you don't trust me."

"That's not true."

"Then why won't you share what you know about the UK op so we can figure it out together? From where I'm standing, it looks like you're protecting someone."

Gage put his fist up against his forehead, eyes closed. "One of these days you're going to realize—"

"What?"

He lowered his hand, sounding worn around the edges. "That you aren't the only one with wounds from that night."

She saw something that she'd never seen in Gage's eyes. Vulnerability. He was tearing her heart apart again. "I can't do this with you right now, Gage."

"I know."

"No, you don't." Sabrina stepped away, anything to break the tension rolling off him. "I have an agent—"

"Who disappeared from the Trophy Room two days ago."

She caught herself before she asked how he knew. His resources trumped hers all over the place. "What else do you know?"

He could have evaded, but he didn't. "That a female agent on your team disappeared after busting a DEA operation. Same agent?"

She had a feeling he already knew the answer to that and wanted to see if she would play straight with him. "Margaux has been after the Banker since he killed our liaison on the FBI case against Ryder last year. She listened to the hit go down on a live cell phone call and took it personally. She got bad intel from a snitch that had been solid for three years. Now the DEA's out for blood."

"They're the least of her problems."

Just the way he said that gave Sabrina a whole new level of worry for Margaux. She asked the question she didn't want to hear the answer to. "Why?"

"We've been after the Banker for three and a half years. No one has gotten close to him and survived."

Sabrina leaned back against the counter next to the sink. Easier to breathe over here without every inhale drawing in Gage's scent. "Margaux's tough to kill, and I'm not ready to give up on her being alive."

"That's not what I'm saying. If she's dead, you'll find out

soon enough because the Banker makes an example of anyone who crosses him. But she entered the Trophy Room alone. No sign of being coerced."

Sabrina stood up straight. "She was after intel. Had to be."

"Who *is* Margaux?"

Sabrina had worked miracles to wipe out Margaux's identity and technically did not owe her anything now that Margaux had walked away, but she'd given her word to protect her. Plus, Margaux was still her friend and Sabrina cared what happened to her. If Sabrina told Gage what she knew about Margaux, would he feel duty bound to share that information?

He sure as hell didn't feel the need to share anything on the UK with her.

When she didn't answer, his chest moved with a sigh of an ill-fated messenger. "We've been working with the FBI on the Banker for a while, because it was only a matter of time before he entered the US. The FBI learned of instructions for a meeting with the Banker being passed off at the Trophy Room. A woman entered dressed as a call girl known as Violet. The real Violet was tied up in her apartment the whole time this was going down. There are witnesses who saw the impersonator walk up to a Russian mercenary called Dragan Stoli who's in this country to meet with the Banker."

This could only be more bad news, but Sabrina asked, "What's this woman's status according to the FBI?"

"The woman who impersonated Violet is suspected of working *for* the Banker."

Sabrina scrambled for an argument. Margaux had been made up so well only Nick had recognized her that night. "There's no evidence that Margaux was the one who—"

He held up his hand. "We both know it was Margaux. Her fingerprints haven't shown up in any database, but a file was delivered anonymously to the FBI. There were photos of Margaux being made up to look like Violet and the makeup artist has already given a statement to the FBI, confirming a photo of Margaux as the woman she did a makeover on four hours before the Trophy Room fire. As of now, Margaux is persona non grata and an enemy of the state."

What the hell, Margaux? How was Sabrina going to be able to help her if she couldn't tap her government resources?

"But if you hear from her, have her contact me. I'll take any lead on the Banker or Dragan. No promises, but if Margaux helps take either one or both down, I'll do what I can in return." Gage stepped up close and put his hand on her cheek. "I know how you are about protecting your people, but you need to distance yourself from her or you'll go down with her."

She stepped back. This was the difference. His people were CIA agents. Hers were her family. "I'll let you know if I hear anything, but I'll bring her in myself before I put her in the crosshairs of the FBI or the CIA."

"She's already in the crosshairs."

CHAPTER 17

Logan watched the Quonset hut his kidnappers used for a headquarters. He didn't have to look over at Margaux—that was the name she'd gone by back in France—to know that she was in trouble. He could hear her trying to keep her breathing shallow and quiet.

Her right hand had swollen until she couldn't close her fingers.

He'd fed her all the water they had and sweat poured out of her.

Once Logan had found the camp, he'd had to make a wide arc to get Margaux to the rear of the Quonset without drawing any attention. Hunkered down this close, he could hear voices through the screened windows.

Their kidnappers now had at least ten men again based on what Logan had translated from the shouting going on in the hut. Most of the men were out hunting for Logan and Margaux, but three had just returned to camp and their leader was stroking out over their returning empty-handed.

They had more men coming soon with dogs that could track.

There was no time to get Margaux away from here and she wouldn't get much farther without antibiotics he hoped like hell were in a First Aid kit in that hut. As it was, she'd never make it to any place he'd consider safe enough to leave her and he'd figured out that she'd rather suffer and stay with him than be left alone. Not much for the outdoors.

He felt a tug on his shirt and turned to where she sat on the ground next to where he squatted. He leaned close to her and whispered, "What, Sugar?"

"We'll wait until night when they're asleep."

"You need antibiotics now."

She cursed. "Is *that* why we came back here ... and risked getting caught?"

He squatted down so he could put his arm around her

shoulders and speak right into her ear. "We're not going to get caught. As soon as those three leave, you're going to cover my back while I take out the leader and get what we need."

She thought on that a minute and turned to him, her voice barely loud enough for him to hear. "I'll walk ... into the yard. Draw him out. You pick him off."

No fucking way. Instead of arguing, he just shook his head. "The leader won't step outside that building."

"How ... do you know?"

He made up something on the fly. "I've been listening to them. I understand the language."

She swallowed hard. Her face was so pale it glowed in this shaded spot. He'd never forget the way that same face had looked when he'd made love to her in Paris. How could you forget a woman who was pure passion? One you lost yourself in every time you were buried deep inside her?

That hadn't been part of the plan back then.

He'd needed her fourth-floor apartment that gave him the perfect location for watching a target. He'd ended up with a woman who made him want to break all his hard-and-fast rules about remaining alone.

Suspicion was a natural part of his being, and for the past hour, he'd been seeing their time together in Paris through different eyes. Had she really been an American on a work visa? Or had she been one hell of a trained operative back then at the age of twenty?

He'd been so sure *he* had seduced her.

Had it been the other way around?

He'd checked on her at her job their first couple of days together, then decided she didn't present a threat. Not to his mission.

His heart had been another story.

Someone inside the Quonset hut let loose with a vicious curse.

Logan turned back to listen. The leader barked out orders in guttural Spanish. He ordered the three men to go back out to search for the escaped prisoners. He warned his men not to forget what would happen if all of them did not make their deadline in two more days.

What the hell was that deadline all about?

The three men cursed and complained but walked out then refilled their canteens from a pump attached to a barrel. Logan licked his lips, craving a drink, and that barrel had to be filled with treated water.

He hadn't told Margaux that he'd used the last tablet two hours ago when he'd found a stream. If he didn't get her meds soon, water wouldn't matter.

Once the men disappeared in different directions, Logan gave it twenty minutes to be sure they were far enough not to hear gunshots through this thick vegetation.

Margaux caught his arm. "Help me up."

Those three words had to be tough for her.

This was the same woman who'd refused to accept any money he offered her in France to help with her expenses. She took nothing that smacked of dependence. She was also the woman who had destroyed him for other women. She'd been so sweet and loving, just as mysterious and secretive back then, but he hadn't cared.

Maybe he should have taken a closer look but being with her had been the only time he'd ever felt alive.

For a short time, he'd begun to think about what it would be like to have someone for more than a few nights. He'd been so sure of himself and his skills that he'd taken all she'd given, never doubting that she was only a bartender, and never expecting to see her again.

She'd been the one to state the no-strings-attached rules.

Nine days was all it had taken to become addicted to her scent, her laugh and the feel of her in his arms.

How the hell had she ended up in this situation?

In spite of suspicions clawing at his mind, he would get her out of here alive or die trying. To do that, he wanted to leave her sitting here where she'd be safe while he went inside to take care of business. But he couldn't trust her to stay back, so he hooked his arm around her waist and lifted her easily to her feet. He was exhausted and losing what physical ground he'd regained by drinking water and sleeping, but she was fading.

This changed his original plan for getting inside the Quonset hut that had included her. He couldn't risk it now. Not in the shape she was in.

When he had her standing, he cupped his hand to her ear. "I'm going in. You stay back and cover me."

"No."

His temper flared but he managed to hold onto it by a thread. "We have one chance to do this before anyone else shows up and having you with me will divide my attention."

He expected her to snarl that she could take care of herself, but she couldn't right now. He should put her out and forfeit traveling faster by carrying her. He could do it, render her unconscious with one quick move to the pressure points in her neck, but she'd given him her trust. That was a commodity he was starting to realize Margaux held more precious than anything else.

Her gaze sharpened and she surprised him by admitting, "You're right. I'd slow you down."

Cupping her chin, he kissed her gently and said, "Wait for my word, okay?"

"I will. Hand me my pistol."

He lifted the pistol out of her holster and put it in her good hand. Her other one had blown up like a red clown hand. He had no idea how she wasn't writhing in pain on the ground.

He eased through the undergrowth and wove his way first to the window where he peeked in to see the leader sitting down to an MRE he'd opened, which meant he'd be distracted eating.

Logan helped Margaux position herself in the ten-foot space between the window and door. Then he moved quietly to the side of the back door the men stepped through to pee outside.

Logan led with the Vektor pistol and eased the door open. The place reeked of body odor and nicotine. He slowly pulled the door wide enough to step inside without making a sound. Until the damn door squeaked.

The leader turned with his gun in hand, firing.

Logan snapped off two shots, hitting the kidnapper center-chest with both shots. He crumpled to the floor.

Margaux stepped inside. "The sat phone's on his hip."

Logan was already reaching for it while Margaux checked to make sure the leader was neutralized, when the base radio crackled. Someone called in that his group was a mile out and would be there in two minutes. Fuck. Reinforcements coming in and had to be in a truck to get here that fast.

He clipped the sat phone on Margaux's hip. "A truck's on the way here with reinforcements. We need to move fast. Go straight that way." He pointed out the back of the hut. "For fifty yards and wait for me."

"What are you going to do?"

"Find the First Aid kit and leave them a gift. Longer I talk, less time I have to get out."

She cursed lividly, turned and headed out.

Logan did a fast visual sweep. One wood chair and a heavy table were off to the side with a lamp and fan run by a generator Logan had seen at the edge of the camp. There was little in the way of electronics or paperwork.

The kidnappers had come here for one reason and hadn't planned on staying long. Crates of ammunition and food supplies were piled around. He grabbed grenades from an open box, stuffing what he could in his pouches and setting one on the desk.

He found a hefty, two-foot-square aluminum First Aid kit he dropped by the back door along with the full canteen that had been on the table.

A sharp male voice burst from the radio, demanding a reply from Felix.

Logan shoved the heavy table until it was in position ten feet from the door. He found a length of rope piled in the corner, a roll of duct tape, and a small propane stove that had a twenty-pound propane tank. Perfect. He took the grenade from the desk and taped it to the thick edge of the wooden table. He tied the rope to the door handle and threaded the other end through the finger hole on the grenade pin.

A truck motor groaned, coming down the dirt road.

Logan pulled the pin on the grenade, keeping his thumb on the spoon—the detonation lever. Then he threaded the straightened pin back into its hole and carefully let go, judging the weight of the rope against the pin. It held with just the right tension, and he stepped away.

Door opens, pulls the pin out of the grenade and the spoon releases.

Boom, baby.

A Jeep rolled into the yard with six men armed with AK-47s. Two men walked over to the water tank with canteens while the others climbed out and stood with their weapons ready.

The driver looked around and shouted for Felix.

He's in here. Come and get him.

Logan cranked open the propane to give his little surprise an extra kick, then grabbed the First Aid kit and canteen on his way out the back.

He slung the straps across his body and ran through the brush, searching for Margaux everywhere.

When he'd reached fifty yards, he slowed. Had she passed out and he missed seeing her?

She pushed aside a palm leaf and hissed. *"Here!"*

He grabbed her and dove behind a tree for cover. She cried out in pain despite his trying to protect her arm.

The explosion shook the ground and sent a burst of fire into the air. Logan had her head tucked up against him. "I'm sorry, Sugar."

She said something he didn't think he wanted repeated, took a couple of hard breaths and said, "I'm good. Let's go."

She wasn't good, but they couldn't stop yet. Not until he got to high ground.

He stood, pulling her up as he did. She sidestepped then got her footing as he dragged her forward.

Gunshots zinged past him.

He yanked her ahead. They were east of the hut and those shots had come from the south, probably a search party returning from the river.

She growled, "Let go, dammit. I can keep up."

Not for long she couldn't. He held tight to her good wrist. More shots were fired, hitting trees near them. At least two men following. When he found a tree four feet thick, he pulled her behind it with him, wrapping her up close with one arm.

"Not far enough away, Tarzan."

"We can't outrun those guns." He could, but she couldn't.

She had a thoughtful look. "Let me take this side. I can use the tree to steady my arm to shoot."

He moved her to where she hugged the tree but out of view from the direction he figured the threat would be coming. "Do not move from that spot unless I tell you."

She mumbled something about not mistaking her for Tarzan's chimpanzee.

"Just wait until they're both close enough."

More grumbling.

Logan moved to his right, hoping he could get off both shots before she had to shoot. She'd turned bone white from all the jostling and banging her arm again when they'd hit the ground.

Every person had a limit. If she had to go through much more, her body would take over. She'd pass out.

He saw the first man sneaking through the bush, gently pushing palms out of his way. His sidekick was thirty feet to the right.

Neither one appeared skilled at hunting in this environment. They were nothing more than common thugs without any real training. No wonder the leader had called in more people.

Logan could get the one on the left first, but he had to wait until the one on the right passed by a tree so that Logan could catch him in the open, too.

When the guy cleared the tree, Logan nailed him at thirty yards, which was saying something for an unknown pistol. The second guy fired at Logan, but a bullet struck the guy in his chest a split second before Logan fired.

Both men were down.

Well, hell, Margaux was a decent shot with her weak hand.

Logan grinned, turning around to tell her she wasn't half bad, and found her on the ground.

CHAPTER 18

Margaux couldn't catch her breath against the pain.

"Are you hit?" Dragan's hands were carefully lifting her shoulders up.

"No. He missed." She was panting. Her arm from her shoulder to her hand felt as if it was the size of her thigh. Hot air burned her lungs. It felt like someone was torching her insides and beating on her arm at the same time.

The First Aid kit dropped into view. Dragan was flipping the catches and rummaging through the supplies.

She still couldn't get past Dragan's going back to get antibiotics. If he hadn't been set on that, he might not have handed off the Sat phone. She'd fought her way to the spot where she'd waited for him and taken that opportunity to call Nick, the only person she knew who wouldn't condemn her for going after the Banker.

Nick had used ten seconds to tell her she was an idiot, but he'd been ordering someone to track the sat phone at the same time.

Sabrina would send in a team.

Ninety-second conversation. Help was on the way.

Margaux had to convince Dragan to go along with her story that he was just another prisoner in the camp here. She couldn't hand him over to Sabrina and the FBI. Not after what they'd been through. Once he was gone, though, he would be back on their radar because Margaux would have to come clean with Sabrina.

Then she'd find out what Sabrina had told the FBI, who weren't supposed to know that Margaux existed, but she'd brought this on herself going after the Banker for months.

She started shivering hard. Hot, cold, hot, cold. She wished her body would make up its damned mind.

"Give me your arm, Sugar."

"All yours. Just cut it off." Did he really think she could command this arm to move?

She kept breathing in gasps, just trying to stay conscious. When she didn't make a move to offer her arm, because she couldn't, Dragan turned her around carefully and leaned her back against the tree. Bile ran up her throat over that small motion.

She squeezed out, "We have to go."

"We're as far as we're going to get until this infection is dealt with."

You'd think he had a First Aid kit just like that one by the efficient way he pulled out everything he needed. He dumped two pills from a brown pharmaceutical bottle into his hand.

Just when she was sure the throbbing couldn't get any worse, her arm would prove her wrong. That limb could be a heat beacon. Her sausage fingers wouldn't close. She had the mother of all headaches and, now that she was drinking water again, sweat poured out of her.

"Take this," Logan ordered.

She opened her mouth, wanting water more than anything. He placed two pills on her tongue then put the canteen to her mouth, pouring slowly.

She ignored the metallic taste, leaning forward for more than two swallows.

He pulled it away and she glared at him.

"Sorry, Sugar, but I'm not sure you're going to hold it all down and it's time to deal with that arm." He slit her sleeve open and started unwrapping the undershirt bandage.

"'K." It couldn't hurt any worse than it did right— *"Fuck!"*

"I hate it, Sugar," he murmured as he pulled the cloth away from where the dried blood had glued it to her skin.

Tears welled up in her eyes. She heaved in and out more deep breaths through clenched teeth.

Dragan soaked a wad of gauze with water from the canteen. He cupped her injured arm in a gentle but firm grip and said, "This is gonna hurt but it'll be better soon."

He scrubbed open the wound.

She lurched away from the pain, straining her neck when she twisted, but he held on and kept cleaning it out. She could smell the nasty infection that had bottled up in her arm, but oh, fuck, that hurt.

Tears ran down her face and that just pissed her off.

She must have blacked out at some point, because the next thing she knew, Dragan was telling her to wake up. She rolled her head against the tree trunk until she faced him.

He used the extra piece of undershirt that had been turned into a washrag to wipe her face and neck with cool water. Worry rolled through his grim gaze. "How you doing?"

She had to think about that. Her arm no longer felt twice its size even though it was still swollen all the way to her fingertips. It continued to throb and burn, but the agonizing just-kill-me-now pressure had eased. "Better." How long had they been sitting there? "I'm ready to go."

"Drink some more water and we'll head out."

She did, again with his help, because even though he'd cleaned out the infection and probably loaded it with some kind of topical antibiotic, she was lightheaded and shaking. Not hard to understand why when you'd been tortured, starved, deprived of water, and let a wound get infected. Of the many things she had on her hate list, being weak was close to the top.

When Dragan had the First Aid kit on his back and the canteen stowed, he got her to her feet. "Can you walk?"

"Do I have a choice?" she smarted back.

"I can carry you."

"Don't take this whole primitive living too far, Tarzan. I'm good to go." Then she almost fell on her face when she took a step, but Dragan had her good elbow and kept her upright.

She managed to walk, but it wasn't fast, and she was losing strength.

She'd told Nick that she couldn't stay at the GPS location he was picking up due to more unfriendlies on the way, but that she'd walk north-northeast to reach a high point. That had been the plan Logan laid out on the way to the Quonset hut.

Sabrina had contacts all over the world and she was fiercely protective of her team, even the ones who did something stupid on occasion. This time tomorrow, Margaux would be eating food, taking a real shower and sleeping in a real bed.

If she never saw another tree up close again, she'd be happy.

"Careful, Sugar." Dragan caught her around the waist and pulled her to him.

Where was her sharp tongue when she needed it to tell him she could stand on her own? But she wasn't standing on her own. She was leaning against his hard chest and, hell, she just wanted to rest here for a moment.

His hand cupped her head. She didn't care. He muttered, "Have to get that fever down."

She was fine so long as she could snuggle up to him and get rid of the chill that she doubted would ever go away. She opened her eyes and saw the sat phone hooked to his waistband. The First Aid kit was cumbersome, but she could at least carry the damn phone.

Did she really care? No. Let macho man carry it all.

"Come on, Sugar. Just a little further."

She could do this. Pushing away from his chest, she looked up in his face and noticed his swollen eye had opened more since this morning. He had nice eyes. Pretty brown eyes for a man. She'd told another man he had pretty brown eyes once.

When?

He kissed her, not crazy wild like before, but just a kiss on her forehead. She let him. Why not? They were stuck here, wherever here was. He kissed her on the lips this time.

She liked the way he kissed. Had always liked that mouth.

That was a dumb thought. It made no sense.

"Can you still walk?" His words came from a distance, but he was right in front of her, still holding her and rubbing circles on her back.

She thought she'd snapped back, "Is the Pope Catholic?" but it sounded slurred. Must be the drugs and that she was so dog-tired.

She clenched her eyes and tried to think. They were running from kidnappers. Check. She called Nick on the sat phone. Check. She had to tell Dragan something before Nick or Sabrina showed up. What was it?

The world came into focus and went out again. One minute, she was walking and the next minute everything blurred then she was hanging over Dragan's shoulder. What the hell?

Every time she almost fell asleep, he'd say, "Wake up, Sugar. I need you to watch my back."

She'd shake her head and look around.

Time stretched forever with that constant drill of waking up and falling out of time until Dragan stopped. He slid her down in front of him and held her head against his chest. She could feel his heart thumping, but she was no small woman and he'd been carrying her awhile.

He sat down on a fallen tree and pulled her onto his lap. "Let's rest."

She should tell him he was a pussy and they had to keep moving with the enemy on their tail, but she was freaking tired and lying here against him felt too good.

"Don't pass out now," he ordered her. His hand cupped her forehead again and he cursed. "Stay alert. We aren't out of here yet."

That perked her up. She lifted her head and looked around, but nothing was in focus. "We need to hide until ..." She swallowed. "Until we can make it further."

"We're good here."

She couldn't push him to keep going when he was stuck dragging or carrying her. "I have to tell you something."

"What?" His hands were massaging her neck and back.

He had nice hands. Not like the two other men she'd been with in past years, but hands that knew her body.

"Sugar?"

"What?"

"You had something to tell me."

"I like your hands."

He chuckled, but it was drowned out by a whomp, whomp, whomp sound. Her brain registered helicopter.

Dragan yelled something. He picked her up and was hugging her to him as he started moving.

A chopper. Sabrina was better than anyone knew. Who had

she called to get someone here so soon? *Sabrina. FBI.* Oh, shit. That's what Margaux had to tell Dragan.

This rescue would suck if he said the wrong thing.

The noise roared as the chopper descended.

She remembered what she had to tell him. She clutched his shirt.

He covered her hand. "It's okay, Sugar. Don't worry. This is our ride outta here."

"You don't understand. Don't tell them your name." She thought she'd shouted that, but she hadn't heard her own voice.

Dragan stood with her in his arms, and she didn't have the fight left in her to bite his head off for carrying her in front of a rescue team. She tugged on his shirt again.

He leaned down. "What?"

"Don't give up your real name," she whispered, the last of her energy draining out with that effort. Her head rolled to the side where she saw men dressed in fatigues, armed to take out a small country and ... not a face she recognized.

Sabrina must have used a marker with her military contacts.

Add that to the debt Margaux owed her.

The men blurred into one big blob of jungle camo, and she gave up the fight to stay lucid.

CHAPTER 19

Voices were whispering again.

Cold cloth moved over her face. Margaux had to climb out of this black hole. She'd been bobbing up and down, living in this half world, listening to sounds in between moments of pain and falling back into the void.

This sucked.

She hated to be still. Add that to her hate list, too. Right along with not being able to find her way out of this stupid darkness. Who was talking around her? Warm lips touched her forehead, then her cheek.

She mumbled something about kicking someone's ass.

Not that those lips hadn't been nice, but no one kissed her unless she decided they could first. Someone was getting ripped a new one, just as soon as she got her stupid eyelids to open.

How hard could that be? *Blink, dammit.*

Time dissolved.

She surfaced again, but this time she opened her eyes.

Why was it *still* so dark? Was she blind?

A flicker of light registered to her right. It wasn't enough to make out anything but dark shapes in the room, and she didn't see a window. A candle had burned down to the point the flame was little more than a suggestion. Anxiety hung at the edge of her consciousness, reminding her of the last time she'd been locked in a dark room. A closet really.

She curled her fingers and touched ... sheets. Thank goodness. She wasn't sure why that was special, but trusted her gut that this was a good thing. Now, to figure out where she was and what was going on. She was lying on her back with her arms at her sides, but not bound. Lying on a bed. She had on a shirt that clung against her hips, but not another stitch of clothing.

Her right arm lay on the bed, and it was sore, but tolerable.

Nothing like before.

That's right. She'd been in the jungle. She'd gotten cut. The back of the other hand, at the edge of the bed, felt pinched. If she started counting aches and pains, she'd need a calculator. Her hair was pulled up in a ponytail. Odd that she wasn't scratching her scalp after going without a bath for so long, but she didn't feel grungy either.

She'd been naked on the floor of a hut in the jungle. She and Dragan had escaped.

They'd been rescued.

Men in cammies. Sabrina had made a call and a military unit had picked them up.

What had happened to Dragan?

Margaux's heart thudded in her chest. She hadn't been cognizant to protect him from Sabrina. Had he ...

The mattress moved.

She looked in the direction of the shift and someone was there, turning to prop up his head on his hand and bent arm. Dragan. She couldn't see his face, but the outline of that large body had to be his. She just knew, could feel him when he was close. How weird was that?

He asked in a ragged sleep voice, "You caught up on your rest, Sugar?"

"Guess I needed it."

"Want some water?"

"Hell, yes." She unconsciously licked her lips, anticipating a swallow while the bed moved. When he returned to her, he lifted her head and put a cup to her mouth. She drank the best tasting water she'd ever had but stopped before she made herself sick. "That's all I want."

He put the cup away and came back, a big hulking shadow hovering over that side of the bed. "Think you can eat?"

That didn't sound so good. "Not yet. How long have we slept?"

"I napped an hour since lying down tonight."

"Is that all? You have to be beat."

"Oh, I slept the first day here."

She didn't like the sound of that. The first day? As in, they had been here longer? Were they locked up together? Couldn't be. She didn't understand and frankly didn't care right now, because she was glad he was still here.

With her.

She could have died out in the jungle, but the two of them had gotten each other through and he'd kept her moving when her body wanted to hole up somewhere and quit. If they were locked away together, why question good fortune when it came her way? "How long have we been here, and *where* is here?"

"We've been here for four days. You've been out most of that time."

"What the hell? Why didn't you wake me up?" She raised her hands to emphasize her words and sucked in a breath when she bent her injured arm at the elbow.

He reached over and put his hand on her shoulder, gently pushing it back down. "Careful. We'll take out the IV in a little while now that you're drinking water."

"How about *right* now? I hate anything attached to me."

"Hold on." He got up and moved around. How he saw in such low light she had no idea, but his fingers seemed to work by rote once he unclipped the IV. He moved around and made a noise searching for something then came back to remove everything from her left hand. He pressed cotton and tape over the puncture.

As soon as she was free, she tried to lift her injured arm again and sucked in air. That hurt.

"Don't make me regret doing that, Sugar." He took her hand and guided it back to the bed then leaned across her, putting his arm down for support. "If you don't eat, the IV goes back in."

"Yes, sir. Sir," she smarted back. That kept her from thinking about how nice he smelled. He'd had a bath. The dog.

His fingers brushed over her cheek and forehead. "You were unconscious longer than I expected. Once the fever was down, I let you sleep because your body needed it."

She'd managed to stay out of hospitals and couldn't recall the last time anyone had cared for her. For four days, no less.

She didn't want to feel anything for this man who had been in San Francisco to meet the Banker but tell that to the warm sensation that spread through her with him so close.

"Where are we?"

"In a secluded location in the mountains."

"What are we doing here?"

"Waiting."

Ah, hell. Sabrina didn't want Margaux back in Atlanta yet, which meant they were locked up in a remote location. Probably an armed guard outside. "Nobody said anything about you taking care of me?"

"No."

"Did they send in a doctor?" Singleton was Sabrina's field medic, but Margaux wouldn't share anyone's name from the team.

"No."

That sucked. Margaux expected a little more consideration out of Sabrina, but now that she thought about it, Nick advised her to do whatever she was told whenever she was told if she didn't want to make things worse.

"Don't worry," Dragan told her. "I cleaned out the infection again, stitched it and gave you heavy antibiotics."

"*You* stitched me?"

"Wasn't my first stitch job."

"Who else have you sewn up?"

"Me. I had a gash in my leg one time."

Of course.

He brushed hair off her face and smoothed his hand along her cheek. "You had me worried there for a while. Thought you were just going to wimp out and let some puny infection win."

The lips she'd felt kissing her at some point must have been his.

Guess she'd have to leave his ass intact. This time.

She made a scoffing sound at his poor attempt to insult her. "If you knew anything about me, you'd know I *never* give in to an opponent, human or bacterial."

"Oh, I know you."

Something poked at the back of her brain when he said that. She needed a day just to recall everything that had happened since the Trophy Room. Spending intense time together in the jungle while trying to survive would make any two people more familiar, but his voice *was* familiar and the way he'd said that bothered her.

She wished he'd turn on the lights so she could see his face better. Look into his eyes and see what emotion had pushed that comment.

Teasing, serious, or sincere?

She went with teasing and returned the favor. "If you know me so well, then you'd realize that I want a bath. Where's the shower?"

"You don't feel clean?"

Now that he mentioned it, she did feel clean. That bothered her because she'd been nasty the last time she'd been awake. "I had a bath?"

"Yep. Not that long ago. I kept thinking you'd wake up and yell at me." He was twirling a lock of her hair around his finger. "I washed your hair, too. That was a trick to pull off, but I had help."

She frowned, trying to decide if she was happy to be clean or pissed off that a man had been handling her body while she was out of it.

Dragan handling her body.

He sighed. "Quiet's not a good sign with you, Sugar. No one saw all of you but me, and I didn't take any liberties, so stop fuming."

That was better. Sort of. "Why did they let you bathe—"

He leaned over and kissed her, taking his time gently studying her mouth by touch. He turned kissing into an art. His tongue explored and tangled with hers.

She really should tell him that he couldn't kiss her every time he had a notion, but no one was around, and he tasted like cinnamon mint.

He deepened the kiss and lust rolled through her. She used her healthy arm to reach his back.

He didn't have a shirt on. Running her hands over his muscles just turned her on even more. Her fingers slid across the smooth skin over cut muscle. Dragan was all male from his powerful body to his deadly skills.

Her mind must be mush, because she no longer cared about being manhandled for a bath, not as long as he was willing to keep kissing her this way. He nipped, teased her lips that felt much improved. She lifted her hand to his cheek. The beard was gone. He had a nicely sculpted face. She pushed her fingers into his hair, smiling at the softness.

That was the *only* thing soft on this man.

Hovering over her, his hand touched her waist. Long fingers spread out, moving across her stomach. She'd forgotten how good being touched by the right man could feel.

Dragan was far from the right man, but she wasn't in a position to judge him considering her own pile of problems with the law. She'd never been much for living in glass houses and judging someone without all the information.

There was a chance that Dragan had been meeting with the Banker for a reason other than to sign on for terrorist work.

Margaux had been out to meet the Banker for what she considered moral reasons.

What if Dragan had, too?

If so, that would make him no more of a criminal than she was.

Bad analogy considering she was wanted by the FBI and INTERPOL, but a lot of story went along with that little complication she'd have to face soon.

If Dragan was willing to trade information on the Banker or if she could determine he wasn't running a team that worked for terrorists, she'd find a way to get him out of here.

Right now, he was the man who had put his life at risk to get her out of that jungle alive.

Dragan's fingers moved up from her waist, pausing at the side of her breast and all thoughts vanished except how close his hand was to really making her feel better.

What was he waiting on? Her breasts were starved for

appreciation. The girls were cranky and letting Margaux know it. Timid had never been part of her makeup.

She kissed Dragan back.

He didn't need much encouragement at that point. His lips were warm and firm, sexy as hell. Kissing him was better than making love to other men.

She hadn't had that thought in years.

And kissing Dragan felt familiar. As if she'd kissed this mouth before. Everyone supposedly had a physical twin somewhere in the world, but could two men kiss the same? The more he kissed her, the more her memory stirred. His hands touched her with a familiarity that she missed.

Was that freaking weird or what?

He must have bathed her more than once so maybe she dreamed about him. About this. Or maybe she was just horny as hell, and he was one hot male.

No. She was sure it was Dragan causing this need that coiled and twisted inside her. Her body tightened in all the right places. Now if she could just get him to connect the dots and spring that tension.

He pulled his lips from hers and lifted his head, breathing as fast as she was. Then he dropped his forehead to hers. "Sorry. I'm just so damned glad to have you awake and better."

Sorry? What the... "Why are you apologizing?"

"Because all I can think about is how much I want you and that wasn't my intention when I kissed you."

"Why not?"

He let out a long breath. "I'm not going to take advantage of the situation."

"Do you really think I'd let any man take advantage of me?" she asked with a grin she knew he couldn't see because she couldn't see his mouth when his body was blocking out what little light they had.

He teased, "You *are* at my mercy right now."

Her grin widened at his light tone. "If that's the case, is that the best you can do to a woman at your mercy?"

His fingers slowly massaged the side of her breast. "I'm not doing anything until your arm is better."

Ah. He clearly *intended* to do something after all, huh? No time like the present. "If you're any good with those fingers, you should be able to keep me from thinking about my arm."

Silence answered her challenge.

Well, hell, she'd never been the flirty female type who played games.

She was direct and went after what she wanted. Life had screwed her over so many times and she'd lived on the run for so long, she'd learned to take what she could when she could and be willing to let go when the time came.

She wanted Dragan.

He ground out a discouraging sound. "You don't know me, Sugar."

"I know enough." She chuckled at him being Mr. Noble all of a sudden. It was, well, she couldn't come up with a better word than sweet, which she was sure he wouldn't want said in public.

"You don't know who I *really* am."

"Then tell me then we can move ahead."

"Not tonight. Tomorrow."

Why then? And was he really going to tell her anything about himself? Hell, no. This was just his way of saying he thought she wasn't physically up to having sex. And that was all she was talking about. Sex.

She couldn't consider anything else. Not with her past. Any man foolish enough to get involved with her risked being dragged into the hell she called a life. She had a scary track record for picking men.

They turned out to be criminals or ended up dead. Or both.

Life had taught her to recognize the limitations of her world. To accept that she would spend every tomorrow alone. She wouldn't apologize for the comfort she found with a sexy man for a few stolen hours.

It was an empty comfort, but it beat giving up that little moment of happiness.

And there was something about Dragan that called to her,

that made her wish for more than one night, but neither one of them would see each other again once Sabrina showed up.

His thumb was brushing back and forth across her cheek. He was treating her the way a man touched a woman when he intended more than a quick ride. When he planned to take his time learning her body. She could practically hear Dragan debating on what to do.

Just the fact that he was hesitating raised a longing in her to hold onto a man like him. That was a dangerous longing that would end in disappointment.

She'd had enough misery in her life.

No emotional ties equaled no broken heart.

She pushed away that rogue longing and beefed up her defenses internally. She'd lay this out in simple terms no man could refuse. She hoped.

"Listen, Dragan. We both have things in our past that we don't need to talk about tonight. Actually, not at all."

"You don't underst—" She put her hand on his lips. "Hear me out. Considering how we met, neither of us is destined to be sainted in this lifetime. We just survived a stint where at least one of us should have died, and more likely both, but we didn't. If we'd died, this moment would never have happened."

He didn't say anything and that was the green light to keep going as far as she was concerned. "Right now, right this second, I don't care what you want to tell me about who you are. I don't care about the past or the future, because my life will not be my own the minute daylight shows up. I don't get a lot of opportunities like ... this. I haven't been with anyone in over a year. Okay, two years. And rarely before that. I won't beg a man for anything, but I'm asking you to not take this away from me."

Her fingers slid down to his bare chest that moved with deep breaths. Running her hands over him gave her a mental picture of what hovered over her.

He was power and danger leashed by a tether of corded steel.

She wanted to snap that leash and see what happened.

Yes, that probably made her certifiable, but she'd given up a lot of things in life and wouldn't forfeit this moment. All she cared about was her next breath, the need to feel alive and cared for, even if it was little more than a fantasy.

She added, "You have to know I'm the kind of woman who means it when I say no regrets ... unless that romp in the jungle was harder on you than I realized, and you just aren't capable of—"

He kissed her again. No, he consumed her. His lips were ferocious, demanding and wild. She loved it and lifted a little, pushing into the kiss. His fingers held her head, then eased the binding out of her hair, clutching the locks that he released. Dragan held his weight off her and moved his other hand carefully along her side, then to her hips.

He stayed there in a holding pattern. Still too careful to suit her.

Then he broke the kiss and started to pull away.

She gripped his shoulder. "Where are you going?"

"As far as I can get from you. With any luck, I'll find cold water at the end of that trip."

"So you're going to get me all worked up and leave me to take care of myself?"

CHAPTER 20

"Shit," Logan ground out. How was he supposed to form a thought with a visual of Margaux touching herself? She knew exactly what that would do to him and he was already hard as a steel spike ready to drive into something.

Her.

And she'd been serious. There wasn't a damn thing coy about her.

Muscles bunched across Logan's back the longer he hung in indecision over what to do. He'd only wanted to kiss Margaux, just feel her close to him again. He'd slept by her the entire time she'd been in and out with the fever, but she was awake and smelled of the lotion he'd rubbed on her chaffed skin.

What kind of man gets an erection while taking care of a woman who's unconscious?

The kind who'd known her body and missed it.

He didn't want to get into that discussion tonight. Too many land mines in their history and he didn't want her stressed now that she was relaxed. She still needed more rest and wouldn't get it if he opened that Pandora's box tonight.

Margaux might be more dangerous than Pandora. She'd want to kick his ass. And he deserved it, but not until she was better.

She lifted her hips, intentionally bumping up against his erection then purred, "Such a shame to waste that ... Sugar."

The hellion was back even if she hadn't fully recovered. He wanted the same thing she did, but not until she had one more night of rest and not until after they had a chance to talk.

If he was going to go, it had to be now.

Like right fucking now, asshole. Logan kissed her again, quickly, and pushed up off the bed. "Get some more sleep. I'll be back."

"Don't come back. By the time you do it'll be all over with," she threatened.

She had grit in her voice, but it couldn't hide that he'd insulted her. Dammit. He couldn't win this one. Should he just tell her everything right now? No. She wasn't as strong as she thought after that infection.

On the other hand, she'd really get some rest if he took her up on her offer.

Leave it to his dick to come up with an end-justifies-the-means argument.

Logan stepped away from the bed, his sight good enough to navigate the dark room.

She muttered a challenge from the bed. "Coward."

The candle finally burned out, pitching the room in total darkness.

His jaw got rock hard from clenching his teeth, but he kept walking to the door. When he got there, he stood hidden in the dark. She wouldn't really back that threat. She was too tired and just screwing with him.

His heartbeat kicked into high gear, because she'd never bluffed when he'd known her before.

He opened the door to more darkness, then closed it just as fast before he could walk out and slowed his breathing to just short of comatose.

Who knew stupidity ran in his genes?

Or maybe that was a natural condition for a man close to testosterone overload.

He should go, but he didn't know a red-blooded male on this planet who would leave right now without finding out if Margaux really meant to play with his mind or her body.

She was still exhausted. Any minute now, she'd settle in and go back to sleep.

Her breathing quickened then it changed to soft gasps.

Sweat beaded along his neck and forehead.

She made a sexy sound deep in her throat and his erection throbbed in response. She panted faster, getting closer.

Shit. He started toward her and stopped. He wasn't even supposed to be in here right now.

"Oh, yes," she moaned. The mattress was moving. "His loss."

He was going to explode.

She started making an mm-mm sound and the bed was making a steady noise.

Logan swallowed, trembling with the need. His fists were so tight his fingers dug into the palms of his hands. *Open the door and go. Just slip out.*

A keening sound shivered in the silent room.

When did you become a voyeur? About thirty seconds ago evidently.

Disgusted, he put his hand on the door and stalled when she whispered, "Come on ... yes ..."

Oh, hell. He knew what came next and turned toward her without another thought beyond needing her to come apart with his hands on her.

He crossed the room in two steps and climbed on the bed, reaching down to lift the edge of the T-shirt she wore. His T-shirt.

She stilled. Passion dissolved into an icy order. "Get out."

But she was still breathless as if she'd been outrunning gunfire. She wasn't getting off that easily. Or maybe she would.

He answered in a quiet voice. "No."

"You had your chance. Go fuck yourself."

He lowered his head and took a nipple between his teeth, biting carefully.

She arched up and shook, still hanging at the edge, close to her orgasm.

He pushed her arm away, ending her self-service program, and suckled her breast. He pressed her back down to the bed and spread his hand across her stomach, then he started grazing his fingers lightly over her skin. He circled lower and lower, pausing before his fingers touched her mound.

Tremors built and shook through her body.

He ran his tongue lightly over the nipple and it beaded into a hard tip.

"Do something, dammit," she growled at him.

He smiled around the smooth breast and slipped his fingers down between her legs, but still not touching the heat churning there.

She moved her hips up, trying to help his fingers find the right place.

Did she really think he couldn't find *that* spot?

She was shaking so hard the bed was trembling.

He released her breast, and she cursed him then ordered, "Either fuck me or get off me."

That's all she expected out of him. To get fucked.

What had happened to the woman who cooed to him to make love to her?

Was that all she expected now? No intimacy? Didn't matter. He wasn't going to do it. Correction. She would ultimately get what she wanted, but he intended to make love to her even if waiting to get inside her was going to bruise his balls from being denied.

He kissed her.

She'd opened her lips before, but not now. She was intentionally keeping this all about sex. He kept kissing her and, while he did, his fingers got busy between her legs, going to the spot she'd been warming up for him.

She opened her mouth on a gasp. He kissed her, his tongue joining hers in a dance. Just like that, he felt the switch in her from hunting a fast release to engaging with him. Wanting more.

He would give her everything she could take.

Pleasure flooded him from head to toe at that small concession.

He kissed his way to her neck and whispered. "You're soft and hot and I want to taste every inch of you."

She muttered, "This is a fast-food menu."

He smiled and kept moving his finger back and forth through her folds. She slowly arched up and slid her hand to his back, holding him to her and kissed him with an intensity that rocked him. He changed the pace, teasing her until her thighs tightened against his arm.

Sharp fingernails curled into his back.

He'd missed that.

Without warning, he drove a finger inside her and pumped. A sharp noise escaped her. He kissed the breast he hadn't touched and nipped her nipple, holding it between his teeth as he ran his tongue back and forth over the tight bud.

She bowed off the bed and cried out. Fingernails scraped his skin, clinging to him as she shook. Her inner muscles clenched around his fingers, and he wanted to smile. He kept stroking her with his thumb until he drained the last shudder from her.

She'd soaked his fingers.

His balls were ready to explode and all it would take was diving into that wet heat. But that was a line he couldn't cross until they talked. If she didn't try to kill him first.

Her chest was still heaving from the exertion.

He dropped down beside her and traced his finger along her shoulder. "Is your arm okay?"

"It's fine," she answered, breathless.

That could mean anything from just sore to aching painfully since she'd rather cut off that same arm than admit a weakness. "Now, will you sleep?"

"Sleep?" She moved fast, cupping his thick erection. "That all you got?"

She'd challenge the devil in his own territory.

"That's enough for now."

"You don't want yours?"

They were back to her trying to distance herself from the intimacy. Turning this into tit for tat on the orgasm scoreboard. What had happened to her? He kissed her forehead and down the side of her face, then her neck where the T-shirt had bunched.

"Don't you have a condom?"

He had them. "I'm saving it."

"For what? Someone else?"

What? She'd said that with a casualness that didn't match the suspicion lying in wait beneath her words. "No. I told you we have to talk first." He couldn't think of another woman when he had Margaux in his arms. He could spend hours enjoying this body, but not tonight.

Stop now or you'll never get your dick under control.

"What's with this talk you want to have?"

He was not going there right now, no matter what. "Tomorrow. Get some sleep this time. I'll be back later." He turned to roll off the bed.

She caught his arm. Not a strong grip yet.

He twisted back around. "What?" How many times could he say no before he caved?

"Stay."

That caught him off guard. That was as close as she got to asking for anything. Of all the things he could have said no to, that wasn't one. He laid back down and scooped her over to him until he had her hugged up against him using his shoulder for a pillow.

She didn't say another word, just breathed in and out slowly until she turned boneless, sated and snoozing.

He whispered, "I hope you remember how much you enjoyed this tomorrow when you're pissed off."

He wouldn't forget.

Worse, he'd never expected to find the woman who had turned his heart upside down in his chest. He'd given up on ever feeling that deeply for a woman again. Now that she was tucked inside his arms, he wanted every second of tonight.

He'd thought back over France and was convinced that she had only been a waitress and nothing more. *Then.*

But somewhere over the last six years, she'd changed. Gone was the happy young woman who lived to love and in her place was a trained operative. Who had trained her and why?

Tomorrow, he'd have to figure out what to do with her because she couldn't stay, but neither could he turn her loose when she knew what he looked like, and he was sure she knew about the Banker.

But what exactly did she know?

CHAPTER 21

Margaux squinted when she opened her eyes. The room did have a window, but the shade had been pulled down. Someone with rustic tastes had decorated this place. But it had air conditioning. She searched for vents. None. Why was it so cool inside?

Was this one of Sabrina's many safehouses?

Where was Dragan?

Had he been taken away? She pushed up on her elbows too fast and the room played whirligig with her brain. Her stomach rumbled.

Good idea. Eat something and get her strength back.

Better idea was to find a bathroom. She swung her feet to the floor and noticed a short wood wall that *could* be a screen. "You have to be kidding me. Where did Sabrina stick us?"

With some effort to maintain her balance, Margaux crossed to the wall and, yes, there was a self-contained toilet with the obligatory roll of paper. "Whatever." Her bladder didn't care so long as it found relief.

She'd just gotten back to the bed to sit down for a moment when someone tapped at the door.

Before she called out, she took in her state of dress, which was still an oversized T-shirt and no underwear. Even this XXL would only hit her at mid-thigh. She leaned back and pulled the sheet up over her legs.

No free show for the Slye team men. "Come in."

Damn, that sounded weak. She cleared her throat and tried again. "Come in."

The door opened and a guy walked in carrying a plate and a canteen.

Not just any guy, but the shorter one she'd originally thought was Dragan at the Trophy Room. Except he'd exchanged his hot Manhattan suit for camo cargo pants and a green T-shirt that stretched across the bulge of muscles making up his chest. Dark gray eyes filled out the face that had been all smiles that night, but there was a sharpness in today's gaze he'd hidden behind dark glasses at the night club. He moved with the grace of a predator that could sneak through the night and kill without a sound.

He worked with Dragan. Not Sabrina.

"Morning," but it sounded like "mahnin" from Boston. He asked, "Ready for some grub?"

His too-chipper attitude ran up against her stony silence.

He placed the plate down on the bed and lifted another plate that had been stuck on top like a lid. Steaming scrambled eggs, sausage, biscuits and hashbrowns. The food smelled amazing. Her body was craving protein and carbs.

But this was the wrong person to be serving her.

What the hell was going on? "Where's Dragan?"

"Right here," called from the doorway. He looked over at the guy who served her and said, "Thanks, Nitro."

"You got it, Cuz." Nitro walked out.

Margaux had lost interest in him, the room, the food, everything except the man standing in the doorway who had just turned her world on its axis.

That sounded like Dragan, but he was not Dragan. His name was Pierre. No last name.

They'd never gotten to that point in Paris.

Her heartbeat thundered in her ears.

They'd spent the best part of two weeks in bed doing far more than they had last night. Back then he hadn't been filled out as much. His voice had gotten deeper and rougher, like everything else about him. This was not the carefree young man she'd laughed with ... and loved.

The one she still woke looking for on some mornings.

No, this one was a man who'd been chiseled into a deadly warrior.

Her mind was determined to connect the dots.

The Pierre in Paris had been nothing more than a man on holiday until the morning he'd gotten a phone call and left her apartment without any explanation. Then he'd called to tell her to run, that dangerous men would come for her if she didn't. She'd found out later that there had been a bombing at a Russian consulate.

If Pierre had been an operative back in Paris, too, then he'd only been with her as part of his mission. He'd only slept with her to use her for a cover or for her apartment. She'd nursed a broken heart for six years, wondering if he'd survived.

He'd been off on another mission, seducing another woman.

"You son of a bitch." She reached for the plate.

He lifted a hand. "Don't. You need to eat, and the cook just left to go out on patrol. If you toss that, you're stuck with eating an MRE."

Decisions, decisions.

She wished the smell wasn't twisting her stomach into fits because it was worried about not getting fed. Her heart was doing a bang-up job of putting dents in her breastbone. The stupid thing was thrilled that Pierre had survived after all.

Her brain brought up all kinds of arguments like the fact that he had to have recognized her at some point in the jungle.

Last night.

He'd known who she was last night. "You bastard."

"Just eat. Please." He rubbed his forehead and walked forward. "You may think you can kick my ass right now, but I've been eating food for the past three days and you've been on a drip."

Now there was motivation to eat. She did want to kick his ass. She picked up the spork. Escaping would depend on being in better physical shape.

That first bite was five-star level to her deprived tastebuds. Swallowing past the lump of hurt in her throat took some effort. She ate slowly. Chowing down hard the first time would end with tossing it back up.

The taste hit her. The food was spiced heavily with black pepper, just the way she peppered her food. Jalapenos were mixed in with the hashbrowns. The sausage was split and crispy on the bottom, and the biscuit was perfectly cooked, not doughy in the middle.

She looked up at him. Did he think fixing her favorite food would smooth over anything right now?

"What's wrong with the food?" He waited. When she didn't reply, he said with the patience of speaking to an invalid, "I had him cook everything I could think of that you liked so you could pick what you wanted."

He was trying to make sure she ate. That sounded considerate, but the same person had spent nine days making love to her then walked out one morning to meet someone and she'd never seen him again.

He'd only called long enough to tell her to run as far and as fast as she could. To disappear and forget about him. Never try to find him again.

She'd tried, but some things were beyond a person's control. She'd never allowed anyone to get that close again though.

He'd pulled a chair up on the far side of the bed.

Wise move. That would give him time to react if he had to, but she had no intention of striking out. Yet. She chewed a little more, determined to be the perfect prisoner until the opportunity came to slip away.

Another moment passed until he said, "You're pushing food around and thinking."

"Sure. How did your men find us so quickly?"

"I had a tracker inside a button. They followed my signal until the kidnappers stripped us then handed us off in Cartagena to their leader. That put them close enough to get to us fast once I called them on the sat phone. Now, you ready to talk?"

"Not really." She raised her gaze to his, daring him to think he mattered as much as her silly heart claimed he did. She'd known those eyes, and she might have put two and two together if he hadn't worn a beard and his face hadn't been swollen so badly.

It was still bruised.

So? She should add a few.

The Pierre she'd known had caramel brown hair, not that thatch of black locks, but the biggest difference was how much he'd changed physically. He'd been muscular before, but in a different way. More athletic and sinewy instead of a body carved up with hard muscle.

He studied her just as silently as she studied him.

The stare down lasted several minutes until he shook his head. "You may not want to talk, but I do."

She shrugged. He wouldn't get anything for free.

Just like years ago, Pierre was not easily put off. He'd chased her for two days until he landed in her bed. Undeterred again, he asked, "What were you doing in the Trophy Room?"

"You show up after six years and that's your opener?" she asked, snorting. "Okay, let's go there. What were you doing in San Francisco?"

"Meeting someone."

She didn't say a word.

"I answered. What were you doing there?" he asked.

"Working as a trophy girl."

He leaned forward with his elbows on his knees and propped his chin on his hands. "I need straight answers. Can you do that, Margaux?"

Hearing her name roll of his lips pinched her heart. She'd dreamed of hearing his voice again. The last time she'd heard it this close, he'd said, "I need you to wait here for me. Can you do that, Margaux?" And she had.

But a lot of things had happened since then and he was the one on the wrong side of the law. Again.

She tilted her chin up in a thoughtful pose and tapped her cheek with her finger. "Let me get this straight. You expect me to just spill my guts and all you're going to say is that you were at the Trophy Room for a meeting. No deal."

"Did you know who I was there to meet?"

"How would I know anything about you? I thought you were dead all this time, Pierre. Or is it Pierre?"

He gave his next reply a lot of thought first. "It's Logan."

"This time."

"I know you thought I was dead," he said, so quietly that she almost didn't catch it. "But even though you didn't know who I was in the Trophy Room you came on to me."

"That was my job."

"Cut the crap. Start talking."

Yeah, that worked like never with her. "You want to talk, tell me what happened in Paris."

"I can't."

"Won't," she argued. "Big difference."

"I still need to know why you were in the Trophy Room."

She leaned back, feeling exhausted even though she'd just woken. Her eyelids wanted to droop, but she forced them open. "Give me one reason why I should tell you anything?"

"Because I'm trying to keep you alive."

That hadn't been what she was expecting to hear. "Thanks for the concern, but you should have realized by now that I can take care of myself. That's what you told me to do. Run and don't look back."

He was up and around the bed so fast he gave her whiplash. Then he was looming over her, hands pressing down on the mattress at each side of her hips. "This isn't a joke, dammit. We were lucky to survive what happened out in the jungle. When they figure out we escaped, they'll come for us. I need to know what they wanted with you."

"Me? What did they want with you?" She'd take responsibility for screwing up whatever *Logan* had in play at the Trophy Room, and she'd messed up the meeting with the Banker, but she hadn't brought the rest of that down on his head.

His head dropped until his face was inches from hers. "They kept you alive. There had to be a reason."

"Not necessarily. I was just in the wrong place at the wrong time."

"Bullshit. You're no hooker."

She fisted the sheets, twisting them and wishing it was his neck. "How would you know? A lot could've happened in the years since you left me in Paris?"

His jaw was rigid. "I. Know. Just tell me what you were doing at the night club."

"Same as you."

"Not possible."

"Why? Did you corner the market cutting deals in this business?"

"*What. Deal!*" he growled between clenched teeth.

Damn him. He didn't get to walk back into her life, accidental or otherwise, and start demanding answers. She didn't care what had crawled up his butt and homesteaded. Having him close and not touching him shredded her.

She would not let him know how much it hurt to see him again. But stupid her, she couldn't take her eyes off his lips.

He'd used her in Paris. She'd been nothing more than a cover.

Keep thinking that. Maybe it would blot out memories of that mouth on hers.

"My deals are none of your fucking business," she told him in an even voice that didn't give away what she hid inside. "Just like your deal in Paris was none of mine. You said to forget you, so I did. Sugar."

Veins pulsed in his neck. His eyes blazed an angry shade of brown. He stayed that way, fixated on her for several seconds, then he seemed to give up on whatever held him back and he kissed her.

She refused to respond. Her pride screamed at her to hit him, hurt him somehow to make him feel a glimmer of what she'd gone through.

His mouth molded to hers, kissing her with a gentle power that was overriding her brain.

She should be pushing him away. Biting his lip. Anything to make him think twice about kissing her ever again.

Years of hurt poured through her. Enough that it should have drowned any feelings she had for him, but he was still kissing her and she couldn't make herself break away. The longer his lips touched hers, the more indecision yanked on her until she thought her body was going to split down the middle.

He whispered, "God, I missed you," against her lips.

Damn him. She finally gave in.

She wrapped her arms around his neck, ignoring the

remaining soreness and the bite of her stitches, and held on, kissing the lips that she'd dreamed about for years. And never replaced, no matter how many other men had tried to sway her with their seduction techniques.

Her mouth fit with the lips of only one man.

His arms wrapped around her, lifting her up on her knees. The bed dipped with the weight of him sitting down and pulling her to him. Her fingers fisted in his hair. He was a fire threatening to rage out of control.

How could she want this man after all he'd done?

She didn't. Her body did.

She'd keep telling herself that.

Margaux grabbed his shoulders and pushed even though she'd have better luck trying to budge a mountain. He slowed the kiss, nipping at her lips. Then broke away to drop his forehead to hers. "I'm sorry for Paris. I would never have put you in danger."

Was that true?

She wanted to rail at him, but she hadn't gotten her bite back yet. It would come out like a terrier instead of a rottweiler. Besides, no matter what had happened between them in Paris, she had a job to do.

This man had still gone to the Trophy Room to hook up with the Banker.

Sabrina needed to know about that and who Logan was.

The eggs in Margaux's stomach started an acid reflux party at the thought of handing him over to Sabrina.

"You're trembling, dammit." He lifted her up and laid her down on the bed.

Her stupid body was shaking. She hated weakness. But that was already on her hater list so she changed it to hating to feel defenseless.

Logan was pulling the sheet up over her. He leaned down with his hand propped next to her head again, but he didn't look as tense as before.

What would he do with her? Lock her in this room? She'd get out. He had to know that. Had last night been about getting some leg before the truth came out?

Not fair, Margaux. He'd tried to make her wait until they talked today because he knew what this morning would bring. And she'd been the only one to benefit last night. She'd tried to convince him to donate his body to sate her lust.

How was last night any worse than using her as a cover back then? It hadn't felt like just sex once he came back to the bed and she now knew why.

She'd thought they had something special in Paris. That she'd found a place she could live a simple life with a man who turned her insides into a butterfly convention every time he looked at her.

That had been the last time she'd allowed herself to dream.

Dreams were for the chosen few who got to walk in the light like normal people, not those who were destined to live in the dark where lost souls belonged. She'd learned the hard way that allowing herself to be vulnerable was dangerous.

Never again.

Logan brushed his hand over her hair, exhaling a long breath. His gaze took in her face, pausing to meet her eyes. He rubbed his knuckles over her cheek. "You may not want to hear it but calling you that morning in Paris was the hardest thing I'd ever had to do. I was insane with worry that you wouldn't escape. I know you think I never cared, but I saw you board the ship you left on. I had people in the States who assured me you were safe, then you disappeared. I ..." He looked away, shutting down.

Her lips parted but nothing came out.

He'd seen her get on that freighter? Why hadn't he come to her then? Why had his people watched over her when she got back to the US?

Why go to that trouble when he said he never wanted to see her or didn't want her to contact him? "Why didn't you have someone tell me you were alive?"

Logan stood up, pulling his hand back. "Get some rest."

"No. You reappear in my life and tell me to just forget about it? What happened that day in Paris?"

"Let it go for now, Margaux."

When he moved to step away, she reached out to catch his hand and gritted at the sudden movement of her injured arm. He stood there for a moment, finally turning to look at her. This time, the anger and frustration slid away from his gaze, leaving only longing, but for what?

He was the one who had played with her in Paris then cast her away. He could have sent word to her.

He turned and gently tucked her arm back against her side. "Keep resting and don't try to leave. You won't succeed and I don't want to have to restrain you."

Note to self to heed that warning. Her skin pebbled at the cold. "Are we still in the jungle?"

"No. It'll warm up some during the day. Water is in a canteen on the bottom shelf. Latrine is—"

She piped up. "Found it."

He kept on as if she hadn't spoken. "—in the corner. I'll bring more food in about an hour."

"This is bullshit," she muttered. *She'd* dragged him from that hut in the jungle and he locked her up? Why? "What do you plan to do with me, Logan?"

He stood with his back to her and his hand on the door. "I haven't decided, but you can't stay here, and I can't risk turning you loose."

"Why?"

"I can't answer that question."

"But you were willing to tell me something when you thought you were going to die in that prison hut." She sounded bitter. Who wouldn't in her place?

He had the decency to look guilty, but not enough to release her. She could see it in his eyes. Whatever he was after was more important than the guilt she'd flung at him. Asking about the future was going nowhere so she let it be. "Where are we?"

"In a forest on a mountain."

"What continent?" she asked dryly.

"We're in the States. There's no threat here now that we're with my team."

He tried to leave again, and she stopped him with one more question. "How many in your team?"

"Enough."

"For what?"

"To protect you." He disappeared out the door.

To contain me.

He just *thought* he could contain her. She gave in to the weariness seeping through her bones and fell back asleep. When she woke, she'd be better rested for an escape.

If he didn't move her before then.

CHAPTER 22

Logan could smell a hint of campfire the closer he came to their base camp on return from his stint at patrolling the outer perimeter. It would be dark in another hour, and he was ready to sleep after spending last night more awake than asleep.

Ty Brander headed toward him, taking the graveyard patrol shift. The team called him Slider because he had a 90+ fastball. A shame that he'd never played pro ball, but he never said a word about regretting his decision to sign on with Logan, who'd needed someone who could fly anything.

If he'd had Ty back in Paris, he'd have flown Margaux out of there.

A yawn took him by surprise. He shook it off.

How was he supposed to get any rest with Margaux so close at hand? He'd close his eyes and drift off to sleep, then she'd step into view with nothing but his shirt and a smile on her face. In his fantasy, she lifted the edge up slowly, dragging it across her breasts and those gorgeous nipples would pucker.

He wiped his mouth with his hand.

Then she'd laugh and he was lost.

She'd haunted him for years. There'd been other women since Paris, but none had imprinted on his brain the way Margaux had. How could they? Margaux wasn't just a woman. She was a living, breathing treasure. A woman who'd asked no questions about his life or tomorrow but had given him her all every minute they were together. She'd lived for the moment.

When he'd been with her, he had, too.

Spending that time with her in France had been a mistake. He'd started thinking about tomorrow and having someone like Margaux in his life.

Not just someone. Her.

He'd been young and ready to do something stupid, then he got a wakeup call in the form of a bombing that killed two. Someone had found out the Russian diplomat was going to defect. Logan had gotten an emergency call to get the diplomat out. He reached the consulate just as the diplomat's office exploded.

Logan called and was told to disappear.

There had been a leak.

He'd done the only thing he could to keep Margaux safe—ordered her to run, sent others to watch her back so she made it, and told her to never look back.

Forget he existed.

If only he'd taken his own advice.

Forget Margaux? Impossible.

Six years should have taken the edge off his desire, but it was as sharp now as the last morning he'd pulled her under him.

For a while in the jungle, he'd considered that Margaux might have known where he was going that morning. He'd reported his location when he'd checked in while surveilling the consulate. Her prints would have been taken from her apartment and sent to INTERPOL as part of standard procedure.

If anything had hit on her back then, he'd have been informed.

He had to decide what he was going to do about discovering her involvement with the Banker.

As the head of the secret HAMR Brotherhood that went deep undercover for months at a time, Logan was responsible to a number of international clients, particularly with regard to his contract with INTERPOL. They required him to share any discovery connected to past and future terrorist events.

But Logan decided *when* he shared that intel.

He wasn't ready to expose Margaux's existence or point to her presence with him during the Paris bombing. The minute he did, INTERPOL would order him to hand her over.

She was going nowhere until he got answers.

That sounded like strategy in his head. In reality, he was putting off the inevitable.

Logan gave tweet whistles as he approached the outer

boundaries of the camp. He stepped over one of the many trip wires set up for security just as he got a turkey call in answer. His team changed up the sounds daily.

When he strolled past a hammock that belonged to Sam "Party Man" Leclair, he found all the guys except Moose in a close circle around the fire, which surprised him. Not that they didn't get along great, but they liked space when they weren't on a job that usually required a lot of time in tight quarters.

Moose leaned against a tree with his M4 carbine at ease, but ready. He glowered at the other four men who had been leaning into a huddle then broke open with a loud round of laughter.

Now Logan could see what entertained them.

Sitting dead center was Margaux, smiling so wide her green eyes sparkled.

Seeing her smile forced a knot in his throat. He'd missed that smile more than everything else about her. She could give the sunshine competition for brightening a day when she was happy.

Her eyes flicked up at him, focused with recognition, then her face locked down so quickly into a blank composure that each of his men turned around. They glared at whatever had ruined her upbeat mood.

Him. He glared right back, letting them know he didn't like her smiling at them.

Why the hell was she out of the shack?

All of them shifted back toward the fire except Nitro who had to push every fucking button he found in life. He asked Logan, "Problem, Cuz?"

"Not unless there's no food left." The last thing he could do was let any of them know this woman turned him inside out.

Nitro grinned like a son-of-a-bitch who had seen right through Logan's answer. "There's plenty. Like always. Grab a seat. Margaux was sharin' a good joke."

Margaux's attention drifted down to a plate of food in her lap that she started picking at. She had on someone's cammie pants and a brown T-shirt instead of Logan's gray one. That just pissed him off all over again, which was stupid because he didn't want her out here in only a T-shirt.

But he didn't want her in any other man's clothes either.

Logan ground his jaw to keep from saying something this group would never let him live down. His stomach growled, reminding him the best way to keep his foot out of his mouth was by shoving food in it right now.

Nitro cooked most of the time because he'd been a chef in another life and refused to eat what the rest of them cooked. He loaded Logan's tray with hefty portions of tonight's entrée of venison steak, potatoes wrapped in foil and tossed in the fire and fat corn on the cob.

"What's your joke?" Logan asked as he lowered his tired bones into a camp chair.

"It's not that funny." Margaux popped up and handed Nitro her plate. "Thanks. Better than I'd have expected out in the woods."

"You're welcome, ma'am."

She looked hard at him. "Margaux, *Cuz*. Not ma'am."

"Yes ma—uh, Margaux."

Cocking her head at Sam "Party Man" Leclair, she asked, "Ready?"

Party Man glanced at Logan who nodded.

Margaux rolled her eyes at Logan. "So now I need permission to be locked up?"

Logan caught the snap in her tone. She was itching to have words with him, but she was too pale to be out of bed as it was and in no condition to be going a verbal round with him. Telling her that would only piss her off and make things worse.

Logan ignored her, focused on cutting his meat. "Yes."

She made a disgusted sound and stepped out of the circle with Party Man right behind her, armed, eyes alert, just as Logan had ordered everyone that morning.

Logan had told them not to harm her, but if there was any question that she would get away to taze her and don't reinjure her arm unless they wanted to face him.

Nitro had been insulted at the idea that she could outmaneuver any of them until Logan shared how after days of no water, no food and torture, Margaux had taken down two armed guards to escape and free him as well.

She had no idea how much respect that had earned her.

Just thinking about how she'd refused to leave him in that hut slugged Logan in the chest with another fist of guilt.

He owed her. That was bad enough if it had been a stranger, but it was Margaux. Having her within reach again turned chaos loose in his brain. He watched her walk away and it cut him to the bone, because he'd never forget her walking down the dock to that ship and out of his life permanently.

She nodded in Moose's direction. "What's his name?"

Party Man answered her in a low voice that belonged to the spawn of Wyatt Earp and Darth Vader. "He goes by Moose."

"Why?"

Nitro called out, "Because he can't spell sasquatch."

Margaux's laughter bubbled and every man paused to listen.

Logan really liked this bunch. He'd hate to have to hurt them. His stomach grumbled, drawing his attention back to his dinner. His guys were unusually quiet. Party Man remained near Margaux's building, standing guard.

Logan finished his meal and handed Nitro the plate that his second in command stacked with the others for someone's turn at KP. "How long was she outside?"

"This time?" Nitro asked.

"What do you mean, this time? I told you she could come out and stretch her legs *once* until she got tired."

Onnjel "Angel" Castell shrugged. "The woman is stir-crazy. Who would not be in that place all day?"

Logan argued, "She's only been awake twenty-four hours. She still needs rest."

Nitro never knew when to let it go. "She looks better now than she did this morning. Think getting out to walk around was good for her." Nitro kept picking up, not even trying to hide his taunting grin. "She *looked* better until you showed up. In fact, she cleaned up nice, was looking downright pretty then—"

"Can it, Nitro."

"You don't think she's pretty?"

Logan snapped, "That's not relevant."

"Then you don't mind that we're drawing straws to see who gets to watch her tomorrow."

Angel growled. "We have decided that tomorrow I will guard."

Party Man called out, "I heard that word tomorrow. *I'm* on for the next twenty-four hours, so don't start no sh and there won't be no it."

Logan snarled, "No one does a damn thing until I give the orders for tomorrow. Understood?"

Moose, who rarely smiled, had a sarcastic grin. He was the only one not vying for a spot in the rotation.

Party Man did a two-finger salute in answer and Angel ran his hands in his thick black hair and stretched back. "Si, señor."

Logan's team functioned better than a well-oiled machine. They thought of each other as family and called each other Cuz, short for cousin. They were tight. They didn't salute him or say si, señor, which was the equivalent of "Yes, sir."

He shoved an acidic glare at Nitro, sure that this was somehow his fault. Nitro wasn't happy unless he was getting under someone's skin. "Where'd she get the clothes?"

"I loaned her some of mine." Nitro picked up what was left of the leftover food that they stored high in the trees to keep it away from bears, but he didn't move. "She wanted a bath. I helped her out."

Logan had sucked in a drink of water from the plastic tube of his backpack hydration bag and choked on it. He lowered it to ask softly, "How *exactly* did you help?"

"Took her a bucket of warm water, soap and change of clothes." Nitro raised his head to face Logan, eyes bulging with mirth. "I unwrapped her bandage, then stepped outside. When she said she was dressed, I went back and bandaged her arm again. Sir."

"Don't be a dick," Logan muttered.

"Excellent advice, but then she doesn't think *I'm* a dick. Sir."

I'm going to kill the best second in command I've ever had.
"Sir me one more time and we eat what I cook tomorrow while you're out on patrol."

Party Man, Angel, and Moose called out, "*No!*" at the same time.

Nitro lost his chipper look and mumbled, "Understood, Cuz."

Logan wanted to see how well her cut was healing for himself, and if she was in such improved health, she could answer questions on what she was doing in the Trophy Room.

He strode over to where Moose stood with his eyes tracking everything. The Swede was built like he had Viking blood somewhere in his ancestry, and he had little patience for anything not related to a mission.

Logan asked, "Got something bugging you, too?"

"She's trouble."

He was probably right, but that had no bearing on any decision Logan made. "So noted. But as long as she's here, she's to be protected at all costs."

Moose nodded. "Understood."

"When Nitro finishes packing the food and picking up, get an inventory of supplies from him. Then you and Angel take one of the ATVs and make a run to town."

"Nitro bitched last time. Said he didn't like what we picked."

"Fine. Let him and Angel go. You and Party Man run a check on the outer perimeter."

"You got it, Cuz."

Logan grunted in response. Everything was back on keel with his men. He strode away as Moose called Party Man over and started directing the team. That would get them out of camp for a bit and give him a chance to deal with Margaux.

There was no telling what she might say and loud enough for everyone to hear.

He faced the door, reminding himself to keep his temper in line. He'd meshed together the Margaux from Paris with the woman he'd met at the Trophy Room as Violet and the

Amazon warrior who escaped the jungle with him. Out of all that, her true nature emerged when put under pressure.

Back her in a corner and she'd fight to the bloody end.

He didn't want her in that corner, but neither could he sugarcoat this.

His need to protect her surged against the need to do his duty. He couldn't imagine any right answers to his questions, but he hoped she had some or he'd have to make the second hardest decision of his life and contact INTERPOL about taking her into protective custody. He had nowhere in this country that would be safe.

CHAPTER 23

The scratching sound of the door latch being moved announced Logan's entrance. None of his men would dare enter without knocking on her hovel-slash-prison.

What spirit had she pissed off to end up in another primitive camp?

She looked over from where she sat cross-legged on the bed.

He closed the door quietly and swung around, arms hanging loose at his sides, watching her. That was no casual pose. Logan only wanted his hands in the best position for moving quickly if she came at him.

He underestimated her ability to plan if he thought she'd hit him straight on when he was expecting it. Now was not the time to expend energy she'd need soon enough.

He turned silence into an adversarial atmosphere, his stare poking at her to say something.

She had nothing to say to him.

Her body had plenty to discuss, starting with who would end up on top. But her body had sent her down wayward paths in the past—Logan Highway being one—and she was done being guided by nothing more than a physical urge.

She'd reduced him to that in her mind today.

Now it was just a basic exercise of mind over lust. The fact that he made her skin feel too tight just by standing in the same room was nothing more than an animal response, and one that she *would* control.

He wasn't the man she'd known all those nights in Paris who made her happy and she'd thought could do no wrong.

That was a memory, nothing more.

This man was *all* wrong.

Logan moved another step forward and leaned against a pair of three-foot-long metal boxes stacked up as high as his waist. Food and supply storage. No ammo or weapons. She'd checked.

He propped a hand on the top of one crate. "How're you feeling?"

"Screwed over." She hated that I'm-in-control monotone of his.

"I didn't drag you into this. You came in on your own."

"So that makes it okay for you to hold me prisoner? Even after what I did to get you out of that hut in the jungle?"

He looked away, taking his time before he met her gaze with a hard one of his own and that flat voice again. "Tell me what you know about my meeting and—"

"Oh, for crying out loud. The Banker is looking for mercs. You were there to meet him. So was I. There. Feel better about your interrogation skills now?"

"What do you want with him?"

"Same thing you do."

"I doubt that."

He hadn't hesitated long, but it had been enough for her to read disappointment flicker in his eyes. Really? "So that's what you were doing in Paris, too? Hiding in my apartment while you scoped out a target? Two actually, now that I remember. I read about the diplomat and his attaché being killed. I never thought you had killed them until now."

She still refused to accept that he would kill in cold blood, but she was channeling Sabrina right now.

"I didn't kill them."

"Oh, so you *weren't* in the business of committing terrorist attacks back then?"

"No."

"But you are now." She waited for him to say the words that would drive a stake through the part of her heart that still cried out for him. Keeping her libido in check was one thing, but stomping on the feelings that rushed to the surface when he was near would take hearing him admit he murdered innocent people for a living.

Or for a pastime. Maybe he didn't need the money, just the sick adrenaline rush.

"We're not terrorists," he finally answered.

"But you hire out for them. You have no political agenda, therefore you're saying you are only a tool?" She smiled, something she hoped bordered on deranged with the mood she was in. "Yep, you're a tool alright. I heard about the bombing in Pakistan. Six died. Did the low head count pay less?"

"I didn't do that. I don't hire out to terrorists."

She studied the sincerity in his eyes. "Why would someone else give you credit for their work?"

"That's a question I've been trying to answer myself."

She kept watching for any sign of lying. Nothing, but he was no prisoner being grilled and was clearly trained well. *Take the facts and flip them over to see if they look different when they land.* Could someone have been giving Logan and his team credit for attacks they hadn't committed? Was that why Logan hunted the Banker? To find out who had spread erroneous intel?

Or was Logan just that skilled—enough to sound convincing when he was lying, even to someone trained to watch for it?

He turned the inquisition back on her. "What else do you know about the Banker?"

Mr. Just-give-me-the-facts was back.

She considered how to play this and what might gain her some usable intel she could give to Sabrina. "Word is he plays broker between terrorists and mercs. What do you know about him?"

"Why did you want to meet him?"

"He owes me."

"How much."

"Why? You willing to pay his debt?" She'd fed enough edge into that to make a cautious person think twice about answering.

"Maybe."

No caution in that body. Anger turned her voice icy cold. "You can't pay this debt with money."

"What did he do to you?"

Not me. Nanci. "It's personal. Something I plan to discuss with him alone."

"That's not going to happen." Logan rubbed his chin, thinking. "You aren't going to meet him. I'm going to send you somewhere safe."

"No way! I admit that I blew your meeting with the Banker and mine, too. I won't share your camp location, but if you don't believe me, have your men blindfold me and take me to a drop off point."

"The Banker would find you."

If wishes came true. "Your point."

"I could keep you safe with me—"

"Does that ego inflate on its own or does it pump up when you give yourself a hand job?"

"—but since that isn't an option, I'm making arrangements."

Like hell. "Are the accommodations there any better than these?"

"Marginally."

She wanted to scream at him for making her wonder if he used his abilities for the wrong side of the law and for twisting her insides into a pretzel. He'd denied being responsible for the terrorist attacks his team had been credited with, but that only mattered if she believed him.

Did she?

What deal are you making with the Banker, Logan?

He wouldn't answer and, if he did, that would be just another reason to keep her. She gave him one more chance to do the right thing. "Turn me loose or pay the consequences."

"Make this easy on yourself. Do as you're told, and you'll be treated fine. Try anything and the men will taze you. Then I'll have to handcuff you."

"I'm not trying anything. We're done talking." *Just go so I don't have to fight my emotions as well as you.*

He nodded, walked over to the bed and sat down then started removing his boots.

"Don't even think about sleeping here tonight," she warned.

"Uh huh."

"I mean it, Logan."

He dropped both boots off to the side and stretched out on the bed with his arm under his head, clothes still on. "Your being here is stretching our man hours too thin. I'm staying in here, so no one else has to guard you tonight. If you're thinking about escaping, don't. I don't want to hurt you."

"You didn't have any problem last time," she muttered and slid down to sleep. She turned her back to him.

"Margaux, it wasn't—"

"Shut. Up. Or I will hurt you and not feel a moment of remorse." She needed one more night of sleep. It wouldn't bring her all the way back up to full power, but she'd have enough strength to take her shot and run once she got away.

Logan had severely underestimated her if he thought she was going to go quietly and do as she was told. She had the skills to escape.

And she would.

CHAPTER 24

The General closed his office door in his Arlington home and locked it. His wife and sons knew never to walk in on him, but he didn't take any chances when it came to getting caught corresponding with international terrorists.

He only needed a few minutes to access the email that should be waiting in an account protected with heavy codes. He and the Banker exchanged one-way emails that couldn't be traced back.

Taking the laptop from his floor vault, he placed it on his desk and booted up. While he waited, he pulled out a bottle of Highland Park Single Malt scotch wrapped in a swirly silver casing designed by a jeweler. Real silver. He had to hide it in the vault, just like he had to keep his offshore savings protected. Live as large as he could and his associates in the Pentagon might take a closer look at his dealings.

The program opened and his email was waiting. He and the Banker had foregone encrypted messages once they'd both confirmed secure communications.

The Banker sent back:

I have located a source to perform the task you require.

That was the right answer with the Duner family breathing down his neck. If the Banker pulled off his part, and there was no reason to doubt that he would, the head of the Duner family would continue to enjoy the results of heavy investments in traditional oil production facilities. Those locations might not be green enough for the eco-militants, but sacrifice was part of progress.

He scanned the email further and stopped at one line.

With regard to your concerns about damaging US/China relations, I do have something in the works for that.

The General chuckled and took a sip of the smoothest single malt he'd ever touched to his lips. This was why he'd told his sons over and over again to never cut corners with money when it mattered. Pay the best to get the best.

The Banker's closing sentence was:

I will of course dust away any refuse to prevent a trail that could be followed.

That's why no one had ever managed to locate someone who had dealt with the Banker. He hired quality mercenaries, paid them well, then hired a new team he sent to handle cleanup, making it all look like part of a contract, so they never caught on.

When this was done, the General would have the key part of Orion's Legacy. He'd hold the most significant piece of the five artifacts.

Wayan had once said that piece would show the way to the other five artifacts, no matter where they were. Once the General had that piece, he and Wayan could find Chatton's artifact.

With that in hand, Wayan would gladly chip in to send the Banker after Chatton.

CHAPTER 25

Logan had slept better sitting under a tree in a driving rain with the enemy hunting him. This shack had been used for storing supplies and as a temporary infirmary until he'd carried Margaux into the camp pale and unconscious. The team had come up with a self-contained toilet to turn this into a patient room fit for a female.

Margaux moved around and grumbled something in her sleep. Again. She kept bumping her injured arm and occasionally grunted in pain.

He could smell her.

No flowery scent, just her warm skin. That wasn't all. Wrapped with her scent was the sensual musk on the bed linens from last night when he'd brought her to orgasm.

Damn. Wrong thing to think about with a hard dick and no relief in sight.

She muttered something.

He reached over to stroke her hair and soothe her but pulled back.

She thought he'd used her in Paris.

He *had* needed her apartment, but sleeping with her hadn't been a requirement. It was an expected gift. He'd planned on accessing her apartment while she was gone bartending so that he could study the main road the apartment was located on— two blocks away from the consulate. The area was so tightly built that he could work street level for only so long without becoming obvious. The street running in front of her apartment was the simplest route in and out from the rear entrance to the consulate and her apartment afforded Logan a birds-eye view of who traveled there and back.

He'd told her he was traveling Europe for six months.

The plan had been simple. Find a woman with an apartment situated in the right spot. Cozy up to her and steal her key long enough to make a copy, then slip it back into her possession before she left work. Somewhere in the following week to ten days, Logan would get a call with extraction plans for a Russian diplomat wanting to defect.

Logan would deliver him to the French intelligence.

He should have found a nearby dump to hunker down in, but he'd been on back-to-back missions for over two years and Margaux's smile had triggered a thaw inside him.

She'd made it clear that she was not looking for anything serious and would never be marriage material. Neither was he, but after two days with her, he missed her when she left and wanted her even more when she returned. He started believing he could talk her into an arrangement that she'd have gone for. Something that was a win-win for both of them.

A life on the side he could maintain that no one would know about. That way she'd never be in danger.

Looking back, it was lunacy, but he was younger then and she'd seduced him with that crazy laugh of hers and the way she made him feel. Alive and connected.

He'd never felt anything like that again and had missed her every day since he'd watched her walk away from him, and away from danger.

Now? He had too many unanswered questions.

What did she want with the Banker? Logan latched on to her claim that the Banker owed her a debt, wanting to believe that she'd been wronged. But she could just as easily mean he welshed on a deal.

But she'd refused money.

Maybe she was only a snitch who got screwed on some deal involving the Banker?

He kept denying that she could have been an operative in Paris, but finally admitted that was his ego talking. He just couldn't believe she'd been playing him, but he'd sent her fingerprints to a contact here in the States that should shed some light on her answer. He hoped she was nothing more than an informant. He could accept that better than believing she had tipped off someone the morning he went for the diplomat and gotten two people killed.

She rolled over on her good side, facing him and mumbling something incoherent. Then her arm landed on his bare chest.

His shirt and pants were piled on a crate. He normally slept in the buff, but had left his boxers on just to remind him there would be no touching tonight.

That rule pretty much exploded in his head when her fingers started grazing his chest. He held his breath, waiting for her to move away or touch more of him.

His dick was voting hard for the latter.

His skin was on fire, and she was the only thing that would soothe that heat. She laughed softly then her fingers stroked his skin. He flinched.

He should get up, get dressed and sit outside in the cold. That would cure the aching hardon tenting his boxers.

But he'd have to give up this time with her. He'd told her he was here to let his men sleep and let her think it was to prevent her trying to escape. A part of him did expect her to make an attempt to leave, but in truth, that was a small concern.

Staying with her tonight was selfish and masochistic at the same time. He wanted to be close enough to watch her as she slept, but not touching her was killing him.

Her hand moved down his chest.

His stomach muscles tightened. Just a little lower. His dick was drawing all the blood from his brain. Had to be why he couldn't make himself get up and leave.

Her fingers curled, clutching at his skin.

Sweat broke out on his forehead. Enough was enough. He'd move her arm, roll her onto her back and leave.

She curled up closer to him and hugged her arm around his waist, killing that idea.

His heart thumped so hard it should wake her. He could wait a little longer to leave.

She muttered, "Idiot."

He smiled. She must be dreaming about him. He leaned over and kissed the top of her head, but she lifted her head at the same moment and stared at him with soft eyes.

Don't kiss her. There was no coming back from that.

She blinked slowly.

Heat churned in her gaze. He'd seen that look time and again in Paris in the middle of the night. She'd wake ready and wanting. One move toward him and he'd be all over her. *Go back to sleep, Sugar.*

She leaned even closer.

Just a tiny move, but his hands itched to pull her to him. Bad idea. Almost as bad as the one he'd had when he climbed back in bed with her last night.

She moved her hand up on his chest and his skin quivered under her touch. She leaned in and he couldn't let it go. He cupped her head and kissed her. Her fingers were in his hair, pulling him closer. Then her hands were all over him.

He couldn't get enough of her. He lifted her to straddle him and never broke the kiss. Her tongue invaded his mouth and challenged his to match her hunger.

She moved her hips up and down, rubbing against his hardon. Up and down, up and down. She was clearly in a hurry again.

What had happened to the woman who'd challenge him to see who could take the longest on each other's body?

She'd always been passionate. Never one to rush things. She'd loved the way he took his time with her, but she was in a hurry now and letting him know it.

He was going to come any minute if she didn't stop. He wanted her too much. She broke the kiss and whispered in a husky voice. "I want to feel you come all over me."

She might as well have set the hair trigger on his cock.

His brain was beating on his consciousness, warning him something was off. He couldn't hear it over the roar in his ears. She reached down and shoved her hand inside his boxers and gripped him. His chest and leg muscles locked up, fighting against the orgasm. "Whoa, Sugar."

She rubbed her hot folds over the tip, stroking him at the same time and his grip on reality slipped. No condom. He grabbed her at the waist and moved her, just enough that when she stroked him the next time he came hard, shooting on his chest instead of inside her. The force was so powerful it left him dizzy for a moment.

She started to move away.

His brain fought through the haze of post orgasm blur.

Where was she going? She was sliding off the bed on his side. The sink was on the other side.

Everything clicked into place.

He lunged for the gun sitting next to his clothes at the same second she went for it. His forward momentum knocked her off balance, but she got her hands on the gun first. She lost her footing and rocked backwards off her feet. He grabbed for her arm to catch her before her head slammed into a wooden crate of MREs.

She shouted in pain.

He'd wrenched her injured arm, dammit.

She came up swinging the gun. He ducked and barely missed getting clocked upside the head. He clamped his hand on her wrist and banged it down against his arm to break her hold. The weapon clanged against the floor.

Logan snarled, "Stop it before you get hurt any worse."

She got her feet under her and pulled away.

He only let go so he wouldn't do more damage. They stood facing off, both breathing hard.

She had to be in pain, but she'd never say so. He pointed at the bed. "Sit so I can see if you pulled your stitches loose."

"Fuck you."

"You just did." That's when it dawned on him what had felt off. She'd used sex to get the drop on him and he'd let her. That wouldn't happen a second time.

He put more power into his order this time. "Sit. Down."

She backed across the room, balking.

Logan picked up his gun and placed it on the bed close enough to reach first if she made another dive for it. He doubted that she'd try by the way she cupped her injured arm to her chest. He kept his eyes on her while he pulled on his pants and shirt again. Stepping back, he lit the gas lantern that brightened the room enough to show the dark red stain on her bandage.

They'd broken the damn stitches loose. He took a deep breath and told her, "I'm going to look at your arm."

"I want Nitro to redress it."

Just when he thought he'd gotten his temper leashed down, she had to say that. "He isn't fucking touching you again. No one is but me."

"Then this arm can rot and fall off."

"You have one of two choices. Sit quietly and let me redress that arm or I'll tie you to the bed and do it. Your choice and right now I'm leaning toward tying you down."

She must have believed him. She buttoned her bottom lip up tight but sat down.

When he got close and lifted his hand to her arm, she looked away from him. Thank God, because his hand was shaking. He'd rather cut his own arm off than harm her and it might not have been his fault entirely, but he should never have dropped his guard. She wouldn't be in pain right now if he hadn't let his dick influence his decisions.

The wound hadn't bled much, just in one spot. He wouldn't put her through sewing it again, so he just taped that spot closed and applied a new bandage.

He put a finger on her chin, ready to face her anger. She hated him. He got it. But when she turned to him, he saw remorse and shame.

He'd pushed her to make a move by telling her he was going to ship her off. How could he blame her when he might have done the same thing if he'd been standing in her shoes? He offered his hand. "Let's get you back to bed."

Fire flashed, burning away any remorse. She scooted past his hand and stood then stepped around the end of the bed. By the time she lay down, she had her arm tucked against her chest like it had been in the jungle when the infection had been at its worst. She was hurting again, and he couldn't do a thing about it, because she wouldn't take Tylenol from him right now.

He walked over and lifted his weapon, shoving it into the waist of his cargo pants. He reached the door when he heard her say, "When?"

She wanted to know when he'd send her away.

"Tomorrow." He wanted to turn around and tell her he was sorry for what happened, but that would only blur the lines between them even more right now. He'd put her somewhere safe until he could either clear her of being tied to the Banker or he had indisputable evidence that would force him to do his duty and hand her over to the proper authorities.

Question was *which* authorities, since every country wanted those associated with the Banker.

But that was the best he could do given the situation.

He walked out and closed the door on the woman he'd never get out of his system. That, he could deal with, but forcing his heart to give her up wouldn't happen.

CHAPTER 26

"We got word."

Logan stopped shaving and turned at the quiet announcement from Nitro who strode up to him wearing a heavy jacket. Temperatures had dropped into the thirties turning his shaving water icy. "Word on the Banker?"

"Yes. I just checked in with our contact. Someone finally answered his inquiries and claims to have a message from the Banker specifically for you." Relief hit Logan in the chest. He'd been sweating the possibility that getting snatched from the hotel by men wanting information on the Banker had been the end of any chance he had to meet again. His last hope for saving Yuri.

Maybe the Banker had been waiting to find out he was still alive after disappearing. "What's the message?"

"Don't know. Our man said he got a phone call from someone who would only tell you the message and only in person."

"Shit."

"Yep. It stinks of a trap."

But Logan would be walking in alone this time. He leaned close to the mirror hung on a post and finished shaving. "I know. That's why you'll be covering me."

"Our man said he might have a report on Margaux's prints by this evening."

That should be good news, not something that turned Logan's breakfast into a stone in his stomach. "Good. Tell Angel and Party Man that they're coming with us. Ty covers the outer perimeter."

"Moose is our best long range shot if distance is an issue."

Logan had considered that. "I'm leaving him with Margaux."

Nitro scratched his chin. "Hate to say this, Cuz, but Moose doesn't like your girl."

She wasn't *his* girl, but Logan let that pass. "That's why Moose is perfect."

Understanding dawned and Nitro scowled. "You saying you think she could manipulate the rest of us into letting her escape?"

"No, but she won't waste her time with Moose, because she sized up everyone last night and would know he won't listen to a word she says. If she doesn't have a play, she can't hurt herself."

"Okay, I'll get word to our contact to set the meeting for one this afternoon. That'll give us time to scout the area first. We'll ride the ATVs until we're a half mile out and leave you then hike in. Once I radio back that we're set, you take an ATV the rest of the way."

"Sounds like a plan." Logan wouldn't insult his men by trying to go alone, but dealing with the Banker was like mesmerizing a Cobra. One wrong note and you could end up dead. He packed up his shaving bag then found Moose, who was going through his molle vest, moving ammo around and repacking pockets.

Moose paused but said nothing.

Logan told him that they had word from the Banker and explained that Moose would be watching Margaux. Logan wanted one thing clear. "She can wait until I'm back to get any exercise. Nitro will feed her before we leave."

Nitro walked up. "Done. I left her some power bars to keep her content while we're gone. Don't go all scary on her, Moose, now that we're getting her healed up."

Moose snorted a sound of disgust. "That woman's not afraid of anything."

Logan considered something he'd forgotten. "Actually, she is."

Nitro's eyebrows lifted. "No shit?"

A frown creased Moose's wide forehead. "What's she afraid of?"

"Snakes. If she gives you a hard time, tell her you've got a pet snake you're going to turn loose in her room if she doesn't quiet down."

Nitro muttered, "Might give her a heart attack."

Logan argued, "Not Margaux. She's got no outdoor training, but she'll probably argue that it's too cold for a snake to move."

"Tell that to Party Man who found one in his sleeping bag the other night," Nitro reminded him.

Moose almost grinned again. Twice in two days. Had to be a record for the Swede. Logan cautioned Moose, "But I better come back and find her safe and not a scratch on her."

That wiped any pleasure off his face. "Got it, Cuz."

Now to see if he could convince Margaux to be on her best behavior.

Logan knocked on the door. When he didn't hear anything, he called out, "Margaux, I'm coming in."

Still no answer. He opened the door and found her sitting on the bed, propped against the wall, looking away from him. The dejection in her face turned him inside out. "I just wanted to let you know I'll be gone for a while today. Until this afternoon."

She didn't acknowledge his presence.

He stepped inside and shut the door.

She slid off the bed and stood to face him, wiping everything from his mind to leave room for the lust that sucked his brains out. She was wearing his T-shirt again and nothing else. Not unless Victoria's Secret had made an air drop of underwear.

Just that T-shirt and miles of leg.

"Eyes up here, Logan," she snapped, pointing two fingers at her fiery green ones. When he raised his gaze, she asked, "Well? What do you want?"

For you to forgive me and smile at me like I'm the only man in the world again. Stupid wish. He'd never have what he and Margaux had shared, not with another woman. That took the kind of chemistry that had exploded between them the first time and a connection he hadn't experienced since.

But she was waiting on an answer, and he had to leave.

"I want you to not try anything that will reinjure your arm. Moose will be outside while I'm gone. Stay put and you'll be fine. Take any chance and he has orders to contain you for your own safety."

She made a chuff sound. "Keep telling yourself that you're holding me for my own good." Crossing her arms under her breasts caused the shirt tail to ride up. "I want a bucket of water."

"What for?"

"So I can bathe when I know there's no chance of you getting a free peep show."

She'd shot that dig with the force of a warhead, determined to demolish any feelings he had for her. If it were only that easy to purge what he felt. He told her, "You'll get your water."

Back outside, the men had two of the ATVs warmed up and they were ready to move out. Logan sent Ty to patrol the outer perimeter and had Moose deliver the bucket to Margaux and secure her shack before he climbed on his ATV and drove away.

The woman had used sex to get to his gun last night. She'd screwed up his meeting with the Banker. She had a secret agenda. How many more reasons did he need to think of her as a suspicious interloper instead of Margaux, the woman of his dreams?

Evidently more than that because his gut was kinked over leaving and knowing he could spend a few more hours with her if he didn't have this meeting.

CHAPTER 27

Margaux leaned her ear against the wall, listening for the ATV's engine noise to fade into silence. Logan hadn't said how long he'd be gone, but if he was taking his team, she hoped it would be at least an hour each way.

She couldn't risk miscalculating.

Stripping out of the shirt that she'd worn again because she could smell him ingrained in every fiber, she walked over and lifted the bucket of water with her strong arm. Her injured one hadn't let up on complaining since she'd struggled with Logan and ripped a stitch.

Heat flamed her face.

She'd used sexual advances in a mission before, but only to the point of distracting an enemy or a target. Never had she slept with anyone to accomplish a mission. But she still felt dirty after using Logan's body to outmaneuver him. And she'd have made it if she'd hadn't paused to appreciate the sound of him coming.

She'd reveled in seeing him let go so long ago and had missed that. But her hesitation had cost her.

Not this time.

She placed the bucket next to the side of the bed that faced the door and soaked a towel in it, then she started dribbling water on the floor around the bucket.

She'd almost screwed up last night after waiting hours for Logan to relax. She'd fallen asleep and had been pleasantly surprised to wake up snuggled to him and with him wearing only his boxers.

Talk about the perfect set up.

Then he'd looked into her eyes and kissed her.

She'd forgotten about escaping and indulged in kissing him back. Nothing had mattered more than climbing into his arms and forgetting about everything else.

She might have stayed right there if she hadn't tweaked her

stitches when he lifted her on top of him. That pain had been enough to shake her out of the moment and shove her survival instincts back into place.

She stopped dripping water to survey her work.

There was a nice pattern of water on the floor that appeared as if she'd jumped up and splashed some out while washing. That should work. She climbed on top of the crate that served as a nightstand.

Lifting the wet towel, she squeezed the cold water over her shoulders and body, shivering at the quick chill.

She had one chance to make this work. Gripping the towel so that it was between her breasts and dangling down to just cover the essentials between her legs, she shouted, "*Logan! Godammit get in here. Logan!*"

Moose was at the door, banging. "What's wrong?"

"*A fucking snake.*" She kicked the lantern so that it crashed on the floor. "Get in here and kill it!"

The door flew open, and a blond Rambo Jr. stood there looking both capable of taking on a terrorist cell alone and afraid to take a step inside.

Now was the time to show true terror. She used the memory of thinking the kidnappers might have killed Logan and shouted, "*Kill it you son-of-a-bitch!*"

"Where is it?" Moose moved in, a Glock 21 in one hand and a Taser in his other.

She was shaking hard to sell her fear, but he wasn't coming in fast enough.

She shrieked and dropped the towel, pointing.

His jaw fell open.

Perfect. She snarled at Moose, "*Stop looking at me and kill the fucking snake!*"

He jerked at being caught staring and got serious. "Where is he?"

She pointed at the bucket. "Right there. He's curled up behind the bucket. Oh shit, he's coiling. He'll bite me." She punched a lot of fear in that last shout. "Do something, dammit."

The best view of behind the bucket forced Moose to take two steps in a hurry and stop next to her then lean to his left to look around the bucket.

She cupped her hands together and came down hard on his head, knocking him to the floor. In the half-second it took him to hit the ground, she jumped and snatched the Taser away, stunning him.

He jerked and shouted in pain, then nothing.

She'd feel bad about tazing him if not for the fact that he'd have done it to her in a minute without an ounce of remorse.

He hadn't liked her for no reason before.

Now at least he had a reason.

Grabbing his arm, she dragged him to the bed where she propped him up. First, she had to secure him, then get dressed and, if the universe was feeling generous, she'd find an ATV outside with the keys in it.

CHAPTER 28

Nick hated playing the messenger, especially taking bad news to Sabrina.

Sabrina hit her desk with her fist. "Margaux calls from a Columbian jungle and isn't there when her extraction team arrives. Nobody has seen her or heard a word since? *Not a word?* She didn't just disappear."

"She might have. She didn't mention Dragan, but there was evidence of two prisoners in the camp. They found two huts where someone had bled recently."

"Someone has to know something on her or Dragan."

Nick scratched his neck, then ran his hand over his two-day-old beard. He was saved from taking another verbal hit by Josh walking in.

Josh announced, "I got the final report from the extraction team. Two bodies found in one of the prison huts, which probably happened when Margaux and Dragan escaped. Three charred bodies and parts of at least one or two more were found near a fire or explosion that destroyed whatever they were using for a supply building. Two more bodies were found on the route between the camp and where Margaux told Nick she would be headed. The team located fresh vegetation wind damage that leads them to believe another helicopter landed closer in than we'd anticipated. I'm guessing whoever was picked up couldn't make it any further."

Nick interjected. "Probably Dragan's team. Margaux sounded kind of sick when she called. If Dragan got his hands on the sat phone, he brought in his people. They might have been closer if they had a way to track him to a point. That would have given them a jump on our extraction team."

Sabrina stood. "If the Banker is here and Dragan survived, then Dragan is probably trying to connect with the Banker again."

"Right," Josh agreed. "One more thing about the

kidnapper's camp in Columbia. They reported finding six more bodies staked in the middle of the camp. Based on their bodies being on top of debris from the fire, those men were tortured and gutted *after* the fire."

"Sounds like a message," Sabrina stated. "I want her found and brought in."

"No parameters?" Nick clarified.

Sabrina and Josh exchanged a look.

Afraid of what I'll do without guidelines? Nick waited patiently.

"Do whatever it takes, but find her," Sabrina said, ending the meeting.

Nick would do whatever he thought needed to be done, but now the safety was off on this mission.

CHAPTER 29

The sun had bailed out early this morning, shoved aside by a front that couldn't make up its mind whether to snow or rain.

Logan cut the engine on his ATV, stuck his helmet on the backseat and climbed off. Rain spit in his face, but after that ride the jacket he had on was heating up. He unzipped it, taking in the building covered in tin and patched with wood in some spots. A rusty sign claimed this was the home of Charlie's Garage and Towing, the local auto repair for anyone who didn't want to drive eighty miles to Idaho Springs, Colorado.

Logan had put a bounty out for information on the Banker, but only to a select number of resources. He had to hand it to the person called "Charlie" who chose this location. It was a decent place to meet. No one would question a strange vehicle coming here. He waited by the ATV, sure that he was being watched closely.

Charlie called out from the window, "Come on in. Got coffee."

Logan smiled and waved. "No time."

That was the signal Charlie wanted for identifying each other. The screen door opened and a lanky guy in blue overalls and steel-toed boots came walking out, in no hurry. He was wiping his hands on a rag as he approached. Frizzy brown hair sprang out from his head before he stuck a ballcap on it and his beard would give ZZ Top competition. He reminded Logan of an ungroomed Airedale Terrier.

When Charlie reached him, he squatted down and started tinkering with the ATV as he spoke. "Got a hit on feelers I put out. Bounty's ten, right?"

Ten as in thousand. Logan crossed his arms and watched Charlie just like he would if something was wrong. "Right."

Charlie lifted a spark plug and held it up, squinting at the part, then lowered his head back down and kept working.

Logan caught sight of a motorcycle parked on the side of

the building with a license plate too muddy to read. It fit the grungy, broken-down appearance of a rat bike.

But this person wasn't from Podunk, Colorado and that bike could very likely do two hundred miles an hour. The real Charlie was probably sleeping in the garage, lightly sedated.

This Charlie acted perfectly at home in the cold weather as he ducked to look closer at the ATV engine. "Here's what you're paying for. You're to give me a phone number that can be called."

"Who's calling?"

"My contact said it was your banker." Charlie looked up. "I'm thinking you know which bank. Said he was still interested in what you had to offer, but time was of the essence. If you two didn't work out the terms soon, he would no longer require anything from you."

The Banker wouldn't lift a finger to meet if he didn't want Logan's team—or—and this was the worse alternative—he was laying a serious trap for all of them. If that was the case, the Banker could have been behind Logan getting snatched in San Francisco, but the jungle interrogation had been clumsy and all about how to find the Banker.

If the Banker had been behind that, why not send in skilled mercs for the jungle operation since he had a reputation for hiring the best?

Logic said the Banker needed him. There were other mercs, but no one that Logan knew of who had the skill level of his team.

Still, this was a gamble.

Logan's camp location could be triangulated through a sat phone call if it ran too long. The Banker wouldn't be in the US now unless this was a significant job and it was happening soon, which was just confirmed by Charlie's message.

Logan wiped rainwater off his face while he thought. "I'll give you a number and a message to send back with it."

"I need time to get the message through my channels."

"Tell him to call at nine Pacific time tomorrow morning and to give me instructions on where to meet. He has one minute to talk and when I hang up, that number will no longer be active."

The minute that call was finished, Logan would destroy the link. He had a sat phone he kept just for backup. Logan gave him the number.

Charlie's furry head dipped with a nod. "Got it. Now about my money."

"You have anything on the prints I sent out?"

"Yes."

"Then you'll find your money inside the garage." Nitro would have already entered, dropped the payment and would be watching to exit as soon as Logan drove off.

Pushing to his feet, Charlie grinned. "I've got news on the prints, but you may not like what it is."

Logan steeled himself to hear that Margaux was a criminal. "That's my problem."

"Those prints don't show up anywhere in an American database. That person doesn't exist except for the FBI looking for a woman reported to have left those prints in San Francisco at the scene of a terrorist attack on a nightclub."

Logan was still trying to process that Margaux didn't exist. Like a spook didn't exist. "Anything else on her?"

"Only that I hear she's got a banker, too. One she works for who's looking for her."

The pressure in Logan's chest that had started to ease at finally making contact with the Banker just squeezed tight again.

He couldn't wait to get his hands on Margaux. There would be no rolling in the sheets this time. Had he been the biggest fool on earth to believe she was just some innocent woman back in Paris?

Or was he being an even bigger fool now to have left her in his camp and let her get to know his men?

He shoved on his helmet, zipped his jacket up and shoved the accelerator lever hard, spewing gravel behind him.

She wouldn't try anything with Moose.

If she did, she'd regret it.

CHAPTER 30

Margaux accelerated the ATV every time she had a stretch of decent path in front of her.

Key word being path.

How did Logan and his men come and go from the camp? There were no roads. Not a beaten down strip. She kept winding her way back and forth, reasoning that downhill would lead to some civilization. She kept her eyes peeled for a cabin, a trailer, a tent. Anyone who might have a way out of here or a cell phone.

Of course, the weather was too nasty to expect anyone out during the middle of the week.

She'd at least found out today was Wednesday by listening to Nitro and Moose talk outside her prisoner shack. But no one had mentioned what mountain range she'd been sleeping on.

First miserable heat and now frigid weather. She was lucky she'd found a pair of insulated overalls, gloves and a full-face helmet or the sleet would be even worse to suffer.

After zigzagging her way down for three hours, she found a dirt road that looked more like a motocross trail and took that for a bit as long as it kept angling downhill.

Another ninety minutes later, she'd found a gravel road that went back uphill.

Someone had spent money to build that road.

Should she turn downhill and hunt a highway?

Or uphill and maybe find a residence with utilities and phone line?

She took a right and her ATV growled its way up, curving around a bend. This might be nothing more than a road to an abandoned hunting camp. Maybe it was a construction road for cutting wood. Did people cut trees for wood here?

Taking it easy on the tight curves, she pulled up to a plateaued area with a log cabin and waited to turn off her ATV in case a dog attacked. None came. She cut the engine and listened. No dog barking in the house or anyone looking out a window.

No poles with wires running.

Buried cables?

She walked over to the porch and climbed the steps then looked in.

This was one of those nice log cabins built to look rustic but everything about the furnishings screamed money. She checked the windows for alarm wires. None. That meant this place was too far out to be reached in any reasonable time by law enforcement or a fire department.

The sky was losing light by the minute.

She hurried back down and drove the ATV to the side of the house, pointing it at an opening in the woods in case she had to make a fast getaway.

Picking the lock would be ideal, if she had a pick set and any real skill at that. Nope. She'd kept telling Nick she was going to take him up on his offer to teach her, but she'd put it off.

At the rear of the house there was another deck that spread out to accommodate a gas grill, outside fireplace and sauna. Snow was still around in pockets, but the sleet was beating it down. The house had a wood door with glass panes on the top half. Much less damage than breaking in the front door. She used a log off the stack next to the house to break one window and chip away the loose glass so she could open the deadbolt on the door.

Inside, she found the wall phone and ... yes, a dial tone.

She started to punch buttons then paused. What reception would she get from Sabrina? Or the team? Margaux had a feeling that Nick wouldn't judge. He had his own set of rules and understood that she did, too.

But she had to inform Sabrina about the Banker being stateside.

Margaux squelched the nerves churning her stomach and punched the numbers for Nick's secret number she figured was one of his burner phones.

He picked up on the second ring. "Yes?"

"It's me." She waited. "Nick?"

"You're alive?"

"Yes, but it was too close to call at one point. I am so ready to come back to civilization."

"What happened in Colombia?"

"Is that where I was?"

Nick ground out a sigh. "Where are you now?"

"I found a vacation house with no one home. I'm not sure where it is yet."

"You need a GPS mounted on your ass."

"Very funny." She had yanked a drawer open and bent down to pillage the contents. Every normal house had a drawer, usually in the kitchen, that was filled with expired coupons, notepads, pens and emergency numbers. "Looks like the area code is 303."

"You're in Colorado."

"Give me a minute and I'll find an address then Sabrina can—"

"No."

Margaux stopped digging and stood up. "What's going on?"

"I'm at the office, but I haven't told Sabrina you're on my phone yet. She can't shield you if you come back. You're on the FBI's wanted list."

"How do they know who I am?" She leaned her forehead against the wood cabinets, suddenly too tired to think of her next move.

"There's footage of you entering the Trophy Room voluntarily and witnesses rolling right and left on the owners. A bartender and one of the women on the floor said you approached Dragan Stoli's bodyguard voluntarily and left the room to go upstairs with him voluntarily. But they received a tip that the bodyguard was really Dragan."

True and true. Dammit. She pushed off from the cabinets, turned around and leaned a hip on the counter. "Wait a minute. How can they be sure it was me? I was incognito."

"I know. I saw you."

"Where were—"

"I was there with Tanner when you walked in dressed as Violet. More of the team arrived after you went in. We were coming for you when all hell broke loose."

"You couldn't have gotten to me." She swallowed. Last Wednesday seemed like such a long time ago. Eight days ago, she'd thought she'd hit her lowest point when she'd busted an undercover DEA agent.

Nope. There was a basement level to her misery. "So how bad is it?"

"The Feds were all over the Trophy Room and that hotel so fast we barely got out of there. It's like someone had them sitting, waiting to pounce. I saw the chopper lift a container that looked like a metal body bag off a patio and disappear before anyone could have followed it." Nick paused. "Knew you were gone and thought you were dead until you called, then you disappeared again. Sabrina got a friend in the military to send an extraction team in and they found the torched camp and bodies. But not you. What happened?"

She told him about her infection. "The kidnappers wanted to know what I knew about the Banker and why I was trying to find him. Who I worked with, on and on. I didn't give them squat."

"How'd you get out?"

This was not going to help her case. "Dragan and I escaped together. I've got intel to share and need to get out of here."

"Sabrina can't send anyone for you. She's trying to convince the Feds that you're one of her snitches and that you've never been involved in a terrorist plot that she knows about. She sold them hard on the possibility that you were captured with Dragan while trying to get the meet point for the Banker."

"That's exactly what happened."

"The Feds aren't buying it. They've sent your fingerprints to INTERPOL."

Shit. If INTERPOL had her prints from the room in Paris, she was screwed. No one had a photo of her from back then.

She hadn't needed an ID at that time to work nights for tips and she'd avoided getting chummy ... until Logan, aka Dragan, aka Pierre.

The only reasons she thought they might have prints from when she was in Paris was if the French law enforcement had tracked Logan back to the apartment and dusted for prints.

But Logan acted as if he had been trying to help the Russian diplomat. If that was true, he'd been worried that someone other than law enforcement would have been coming after her. Like killers.

Criminals didn't dust for fingerprints.

Maybe she'd worried all this time about INTERPOL for no reason, but Sabrina had kept Margaux on domestic missions only just in case.

Margaux thought out loud. "I may be okay, Nick. The FBI has prints but no positive ID of my face."

"Wrong."

"What? Spit it out."

"Someone delivered an anonymous envelope to the FBI with photos of you being made over by a woman called Andrea and she rolled first. She didn't have your name, but she *did* identify a photo from that envelope as you being the woman she made over four hours before you entered the Trophy Room."

Walls were closing in from every direction. This was way more screwed than even Margaux imagined. The only person who could have had photos of her was Snake Eyes.

He was a dead man.

Nick asked, "Why'd you take off from the apartment?"

She needed all of them to know she hadn't snuck out over a selfish whim to avoid whatever Sabrina had planned to do with her. "I had to do this. I know no one will believe me, but I got word the Banker was hunting for the person who was trying to find him that night in Atlanta. And once he found out who it was, he'd kill that person first then come after everyone connected. The Banker had my contact set up with bad intel just to catch me, and my contact would squeal in a minute."

"Where's your snitch?"

"He's probably having a dirt nap by now. I would never have walked out on Sabrina, but if I'd stayed you would have all ended up as targets." But the Banker would have known about her for the past week if Snake Eyes had squealed, so had anything happened? "Has anyone been attacked, Nick?"

"No. Maybe your snitch sold you out to someone else."

"Like who?" She had her share of enemies like anyone in this business, but who wanted her bad enough to frame her as a terrorist working for the Banker?

"The DEA agent with the cracked skull has those kind of contacts."

She hadn't really forgotten about the agent whose operation she'd blown, but he hadn't been in the forefront of her concerns for the past week. "Maybe, but I'm telling you the truth about the Banker's threat."

"I believe you, Duke, but the FBI has marked you as working with Dragan, the Banker, or both."

"No fucking way. I need to come see Sabrina."

"Sabrina has Feds climbing all over her and the phone lines. Hang on a minute while I flag her." Nick covered his phone.

All Margaux heard for the next thirty seconds was muffled voices then Nick was back on the phone, and it sounded like he was outside in the wind. "I'm leaving so there's no chance of this being heard. She gave me a message for you."

The lump in Margaux's throat was the size of a golf ball. Was this when Sabrina cut all ties? "I'm listening."

"Is Dragan a danger to you?"

Only to my sanity. "No. He got me out of Colombia and kept an infection from killing me."

"Good, because here's what Sabrina wants you to do. Stay with Dragan for now and pull as much intel as you can on him and the Banker. She has one shot at keeping you out of prison and it depends on your value as a snitch right now."

Margaux closed her eyes. That was not going to happen. "That's not a good idea."

"It's the only idea. Sabrina is going to tell the FBI that she's gotten word from you that you're insinuated with Dragan Stoli and that you have a lead on the Banker. She wants them to put an order out not to kill you."

"I don't have shit on the Banker."

"Then get some," Nick barked right back at her. "You haven't lost Dragan have you?"

That would be one way of looking at it, but no, she'd managed to lose *herself* by escaping. She must not have answered fast enough. Nick continued, "The only right answer to that is 'no, Nick, of course I haven't lost a lead on the man everyone is looking for right now who put my neck in a noose.'"

"I know where he is." *That doesn't mean Logan is going to welcome me back with open arms.* Then there was Moose. Margaux rubbed her eyes until she saw stars.

"Then your job is to do whatever it takes to stay close to him and send intel any chance you can. If you can find out what the Banker is here for, Sabrina thinks she can parlay that into a deal."

"Banker is definitely pulling together mercs for something and it only makes sense that the attack will be in this country."

"We've got that figured. When will Dragan meet up with him?"

Logan had to locate the Banker first.

She'd have to get close to Logan again to find out if he could. But Sabrina was working for her, and Margaux would not let her down. And this was her only hope to avoid getting brought in by the FBI to face charges of terrorism.

Nick told her, "Sabrina's letting me run on my own. I'll check my leads and see what I can come up with."

Margaux smiled. This would be a perfect time for one of Nick's crazy plans. She'd help him clean up any mess he made if he got her a break on *her* mess. He wanted to know when Dragan and the Banker would meet. She told him what she hoped would be true.

"Dragan and the Banker should have a meeting soon. I don't know how I'll get details to you on that, but I'll find a way to contact you if I learn what the Banker is planning."

"Not if, when." Then Nick gave her a new number to use the next time.

She hung up and realized her new problem was going to be hunting her way back to the camp.

If Logan hadn't packed up and left by the time she returned.

She wasn't going back into the woods until she had a meal and shower. She nuked a lasagna TV dinner while she showered and dried her hair. Looked like the home was owned by a couple in their forties. Attractive pair.

Digging around in the closets, she found a half-filled bag marked for donation. The woman was short and plump, but there were male clothes in the bag. A pair of jeans with a worn knee, a faded Broncos sweatshirt and wool socks with thin heels fit Margaux better than she'd expected. His hiking boots were a half size too big, perfect with the socks.

By the time she'd finished eating and cleaned up behind herself, including taping plastic over the window in the door and wiping everything down so she left no prints, she'd also written in a backhanded style that was not hers a thank you note for allowing a desperate person to borrow their shower and food. She added that although they probably wouldn't believe her, she intended to send them money to repair the window and to replace everything she took, including the donated clothes.

Shrugging back into the heavy outdoor gear, she fired up her ATV and started back toward Camp Penance.

She had until then to come up with a perfectly sound reason for tazing Moose, stealing an ATV, running away and coming back, plus a way to convince Logan he should keep her around.

She was so dead.

CHAPTER 31

Logan stepped inside Margaux's shack and stopped short. "I'm going to kill her!"

Nitro stepped up beside him. "You may have to stand in line behind Moose."

"Cut him free." Logan took in the bucket of water on the floor. A wet towel hung half off the crate and a shattered lantern spread glass across the floor. Moose's hands and ankles were tied with a rope, then a section was used as a tether between them. Another piece of rope had been looped around his legs in a complicated figure eight crossover that prevented him from bending his knees to reach his feet and untie himself. Or to reach anything else.

She'd hobbled Moose and used a shirt to tie him to one of the metal legs on her bed.

Logan had ordered the bed bolted down while Margaux was unconscious so she wouldn't dismantle the structure when she woke up and use a leg as a weapon.

While scouting the outer perimeter, Ty had picked up an alert from a trip wire—Margaux exiting the camp—and radioed Nitro that he couldn't reach Moose. Nitro had told Ty to wait for backup in case the camp was compromised.

Sweat had poured down Logan's back from worry that someone had killed Margaux and Moose.

Nitro cut the ropes on Moose then got busy cleaning up the mess. Offering the big guy a hand up wouldn't be appreciated right now.

Moose picked up his Taser and Glock that had been left sitting next to him, then lumbered over to Logan. "There's no excuse for this."

Logan scrubbed a hand over his face. "What happened?"

"Remember you told me she was afraid of snakes?"

"You found one to put in here?"

"No." Moose couldn't look any more humiliated. "She

started yelling about a snake in the room. I opened the door with both my Glock and Taser in hand. She was jumping up and down on the crate by the bed and kept ordering me to shoot the fucking snake. She didn't have a thing on and was holding a wet towel in front of her, so I thought it was for real, because she was more worried about the snake than me seeing her naked."

Margaux had played that perfectly.

If she'd pretended to be afraid instead of pissed off, Moose would never have bought it. She'd stripped down to look as vulnerable as possible to convince him she really was panicked, but instead of crying, she'd yelled and cursed.

"I'll track her down," Moose offered, enthusiasm gleaming in his eyes.

"No. She took an ATV so there's no telling where she is." Logan called over to Nitro. "We need to pack up and move to our alternate location."

"You want to roll tonight?"

"Yes." Logan could take the sat call from the Banker anywhere. His gut was telling him she wanted out, not that she'd gone to bring someone back. But he'd err on the side of being overcautious this time. If he really thought she'd send someone in he'd have the men grab their go bags and head out now. Once Party Man and Angel finished checking out the satellite camp that provided another exit plan, Logan would know if anything important was missing or disturbed, like the sat phone.

Party Man came around the corner. "Got a problem, Cuz."

Lack of sleep over two days turned Logan's question into a snarl. "What?"

"The transport truck won't start."

That truck was hidden under camo tarps a half mile from the camp. "How could she have found it?"

"It looks like she went in a big loop when she left and got to the truck by accident. She probably would have taken it if we hadn't left a tree blocking the path. I can fix it, but it's going to take a while. Wires have been rerun all over the place and that's just what I can tell at first glance."

Margaux couldn't just humiliate one of his men and steal an ATV. No, she had to fubar his best exit strategy. "How long?"

"I could get lucky and figure out where everything goes in an hour, or it could take all night. Or I might get it fixed and find out we're still missing a part."

"What about the sat phone? Did she find either one?"

Party Man shook his head. "Nope. Doesn't look like she tried to find the phones or take anything else. All the ammo and weapons are accounted for. Only thing I can tell is she took one of the heavy overalls."

Logan shouldn't be glad the little thief was going to be dressed warm for the weather, but he was.

She was right. He was an idiot.

Nitro had the bucket full of glass in one hand and the lantern base in his other. "Still want to pack up tonight, Cuz?"

"No." Logan gave the room another glance, and declared, "Besides, she isn't sending anyone."

Party Man, Moose and Nitro exchanged looks loaded with doubt.

Logan explained, "If she was going to send someone in, she wouldn't have done anything but leave without touching any of the camp or she would have taken this place apart looking for the sat phone to make the call and bring someone in immediately. Dismantling the truck was to prevent us from using it to overtake her if Moose freed himself or we returned before she made it to the highway. If she wanted to give away our location, she would have taken the truck *and* a phone."

Nitro brought up a problem. "She's seen all of us."

"I know." Logan had made the grave mistake of underestimating her. "Moose and I'll take the first watch, me on the outer perimeter and Moose in the camp." He had to give his man the more significant of the two positions so he could earn his pride back.

Nitro shouldered past. "I'll get dinner going, then Angel and I'll take second watch."

Party Man followed him, muttering, "I'm going to need Ty

with me and a spotlight so I can see."

By the time Logan walked the outer security zone for eight hours, he was feeling more like a seventy-four-year-old man instead of thirty-four. He was fatigued and his body was still aching from his fun little vacation in the jungle. He trudged back through the woods, ready to climb in his sleeping bag and crash hard for four hours. Give him that and he'd make another week on his feet.

Nitro came up to Logan, who expected his man to lift his chin in acknowledgement on the way to take his shift, not for Nitro to say, "Cuz, your sleeping bag's gone."

Logan didn't have the energy to get pissed. "She *took* my bag."

"Looks like."

"Screw it. I'll sleep in the shack." Logan and his men slept outside where they could better hear an approach.

Angel strolled up to them with an M4 carbine cradled in his arm. "Everything set?"

Logan kept his voice low. "I just double checked the perimeter. You both know what to do if we get an intruder tonight."

"Oh, yes," Nitro assured him. Built with compact muscle, his easygoing smile had caused more than one enemy to underestimate him. Nitro had gone to school in Boston and college in the UK when his parents divorced. He was former SBS, or Special Boat Service, an arm of the UK Special Forces and considered the UK equivalent of the US Navy SEALs.

"Ten four, Cuz." Angel wore a skull cap over his ears and had three days of beard growth. His eyes took on a hard glint that too many missed because of the black, curly lashes.

You only crossed him once.

Logan dismissed them and walked on to the infirmary shack. Moose was already snoring in his bag. The last time Logan had checked on Party Man, his resident Mr. Fix It was neck deep in the truck's engine compartment. Ty had crashed on the front seat.

A replacement lantern lit the room when Logan stepped into

the building. He peeled down to his boxers, turned off the lantern and landed face down on the bed.

That smelled like Margaux. Son-of-a-bitch.

Just that one whiff and his cock stirred.

But not enough to deny him the sleep his body was demanding. He just needed a couple of hours to ...

Margaux danced through the dark mist, smiling and laughing. He was back in Paris with her spread across the soft white sheets of the bed they'd spent hours frolicking in. The setting sun cast a glow over her nude body.

She called to him to bring her some wine.

Everything replayed perfectly. He strolled over to open another bottle of wine, his mind tinkering with the idea of keeping her.

She tossed a pair of silk underwear and hit him in the head, laughing. "You're too fucking slow."

"You liked that a little while ago."

More of her throaty laugh.

He chuckled and poured her a glass of something special she'd brought home from work, but when he turned to take the wine to her, Margaux wasn't smiling. Or breathing. Her eyes stared unseeing. Blood poured from the slit across her throat.

He roared, "No!"

Someone touched his arm.

He whipped around and launched himself at the dark shadow, both of them crashing to the floor.

"Stop, you fucking idiot."

Logan blinked awake. He knew that F bomb. Ten strong fingers clutched at his wrist, pushing his arm toward him as hard as he was forcing his hand to stay where it was.

"Logan, don't."

It wasn't the order, but the hitch in Margaux's voice that brought him to full consciousness. He had her pinned to the floor with a knife at her throat. Shit.

He stopped pressing the knife toward her throat, but he didn't relax a muscle, not with the skill and ability she possessed. "You should have kept running, Margaux."

CHAPTER 32

Sabrina looked up to see the only other agent still in the Slye office besides her at 2:15 in the morning.

White Hawk had an HK 416 slung over her shoulder and was picking up a file she'd been handed in an earlier briefing.

"Heading home?" Sabrina asked.

"Soon."

The twenty-two-year-old woman had come to her via a friend on the White House Council for Native American Affairs. He'd told Sabrina that White Hawk was an unusual case, but a natural the CIA or FBI would snag if they had a chance.

Sabrina had interviewed her.

White Hawk had some fair requirements. She did not want to leave the continental US and she had to have the freedom to go home if someone needed her.

She'd gained her skills through a family member who was part Cherokee and part Caucasian, and who'd been a Ranger in the US Army. But she had serious trust issues. She'd work with a team but would not partner with one man or woman.

Sabrina liked to give her encouragement when she could. "I may need you if we go wheels up on short notice."

"I don't need much notice." White Hawk carried the file she had with her into Sabrina's office. She wore her dark brown hair in a chic cut and no makeup. You didn't need it when the genetics gods smacked you with a beauty wand.

"But you need rest." Sabrina sat back in her office chair and her muscles squawked at having been bent over her computer for so long. "Exhaustion is part of our business, but that means we have to take advantage of downtime when we can. You aren't doing that."

"I will perform as required."

"I don't doubt that for a moment, but I also won't use anyone on a mission who isn't taking care of herself. Are you having problems sleeping?"

"No."

She didn't even hesitate with that lie.

Sabrina remembered being twenty-two and so full of herself that she knew better than anyone else. But her agents were adults, and she wasn't their keeper. She would pull someone not ready for action, but she couldn't tell a woman who was the epitome of robust health that she wasn't ready.

Instead, Sabrina asked, "Why that HK? Thought you were working on your handgun skills?" Because White Hawk was one hell of a shot with a rifle.

White Hawk's eyes twinkled. Her voice was as soft as her movements. "I haven't shot this one yet and I read that this is what they used when they inserted to get Osama. I want to know it better."

"Take plenty of ammo."

"I did." White Hawk had made it to the doorway when she turned back.

"Yes?"

"I have personal limitations, but they will never interfere with my job."

"I understand." Sabrina sensed that White Hawk might have doubts about her standing on the team. "You're a strong addition to my team, White Hawk. You have exceptional skills, especially when it comes to tailing someone alone."

"But we still lost Margaux."

"We'll find her. When we do, I'll need you again."

"I'm ready." She stood a little taller with that one compliment and walked out.

Sabrina yawned and closed her computer, ready to call it a day since it was almost twenty-four hours since she'd walked in. She should take her own advice.

Her cell phone buzzed with an unknown number. Phone calls didn't make her heart jump, but Gage's calls were from unknown numbers. It buzzed again. He was making it tough for her to hang on to her anger, but she didn't forget when someone betrayed her and he was standing in the way of getting answers.

She picked up the phone. "Yes?"

"Hello, beautiful."

Her heart flipped at those two words. That used to be the first words Gage would say as soon as he called to tell her he was on his way home after a long mission.

Every time either one of them came home it had been as though they both celebrated being alive. They'd meet somewhere and make the most of every minute.

Until the UK job.

Gage kept chipping away, sure that he'd find a toehold and convince her to let him back in.

But all he had to do was tell her who in the agency had known about the UK op. She wouldn't climb over the baggage piled between them to make this work.

He had to do his part to clear it out of the way first.

His sigh rumbled. "We have reason to believe the Russian from the Trophy Room is still alive and back in the states."

She debated on admitting what she knew. She might have called Gage after Nick heard from Margaux if Sabrina could trust Gage not to tell the agency. But he'd made his loyalty clear. "If the Russian is alive that means Margaux—"

"—might or might not be alive," he finished.

She'd let him think that. "What can you tell me about the Russian?"

Gage growled something under his breath. "I'm already telling you more than I should."

"And not as much as I deserve," she countered, sure that he'd get her meaning about the blown op.

"Do we have to do that tonight, Sabrina?"

"No."

The silence became a living thing, stretching and morphing into a challenge to see who would fold first. Gage finally said, "You can't go running your own op on this one."

"How do you know one of the agencies hasn't contacted me to run one?"

"I know."

She ignored that. "Are you *involved* in this stateside?"

"No. Even if I could do it without ruffling feathers, I'm tied up on the other side of the pond. I just don't want you going in dark and no one knowing it's you. Anything connected to the Banker ends bloody. We've never been able to find anyone alive who has contracted for him and I'm starting to wonder if he does repeat business with any merc."

"I'll govern myself accordingly."

"Not going to let this go, are you?"

She smiled at the capitulation in his voice. "No."

"I better be gaining major points for this."

"You are. I just can't guarantee how you'll get to cash them in," she joked, enjoying this little moment.

"The Russian surfaces from time to time then disappears. We thought he was dead then he surfaced again eleven months ago and started taking heavy contracts with different factions. He was putting a resume out for the Banker. If you get between him and his goal, Dragan Stoli will mow you down."

"If he gets between me and one of my people, I'll mow him down."

"Just be careful. Okay?"

She gave the empty room a give-me-a-break look. "I have a better team now than I did back when you called me your ace-in-the-hole."

"You were more than that and you know it."

She'd thought so at one time. How did he expect her to hang up and sleep alone tonight when he said things like that? He didn't. He wanted her to miss him as much as he missed her.

She had for so long she didn't want to think about it. And neither did she want to argue any more tonight so she didn't remind him yet again that he could fix this. "Thanks for the intel. I'm sure my team can handle anything I take on."

"There's never been a question of that, but whoever burned you in the UK is still around. If I knew who it was, I swear I'd bring you his head. Until that happens, stay safe for me."

Those last four words clutched her heart and squeezed.

The click ending his call echoed in her head with finality.

Was she making a mistake by keeping them apart? Punishing both of them when she no longer believed he had any part in burning her team?

She didn't know, but once this mess with Margaux was cleaned up, Sabrina had to make a decision to either put their differences aside and be with Gage or end all personal contact until she had answers on the UK.

CHAPTER 33

This might not have been her best plan.

That happened when you only had one play.

Margaux could just make out Logan's face by the wisp of light coming off a tiny candle across the room, but that was plenty. Enough to see that he was not going to be easy to convert into a Margaux fan. "Let me up and I'll explain."

"Really? You think you're just going to stroll back into camp after popping Moose with a Taser, dismantling my truck, and stealing an ATV, give me some bullshit and that's all it takes?"

"I *am* sorry about Moose, but you left me the hardest one to take down." Margaux lost her thought when Logan's hardon nudged her between her legs. Not to be left out, her breasts perked in response, wanting to rub against the heat coming off his chest.

What had she been saying? Moose. "I tried not to hurt him."

"Where'd you go?" Nothing soft in that tone. His body might be happy to see her but having her beneath him didn't seem to bother him at all.

"Margaux."

"What was the question?" She knew, but his superior attitude was getting on her nerves. She hadn't had the best day.

"Where. Did. You. Go?"

"For. A. Joy. Ride. Played Goldilocks. Found a house, got a real shower. Ate a meal I nuked and put on some clothes that fit me better."

"Who'd you talk to?"

"No one. It was a vacation home. I had to break a window to get in." She stopped short of telling him she intended to pay for that when she got out of this mess.

Hardass mercs did not leave apology notes.

How could Logan act unaffected by his reaction to her? She could feel his dick getting thicker.

Heat pooled between her legs. She had to be crazy to want a man who looked ready to string her up by her thumbs. But Logan wouldn't hurt her. She knew that all the way to her bones. And the minute she'd driven away today she'd felt a hollow place open up in her chest at leaving him.

She'd missed him.

No matter how many times she tried to tell her body that he was the wrong man to trigger her hormones, it changed nothing about the way she felt when he was close.

Too close.

Logan wasn't moving. He had her sandwiched between the hard wood floor and over two hundred pounds of cut muscle. Not a give anywhere she looked, definitely not in his face. This whole intimidation routine was wasted on her.

"Come on, Logan. If I wanted to hurt you, I could have."

"No, you couldn't have."

Her ego had taken enough hits lately. "Think not? I disarmed Hulk Jr, took your truck out of action, found my way out, then made my way back and hiked around until I could sneak in here without anyone knowing. Not bad for Jane."

"My men knew you were here."

"Prove it."

Logan lifted up and spoke in a normal voice. "Angel?"

The door flew open and an automatic weapon was pointed at Margaux's head. The flirty Angel was nowhere to be seen. If Logan said the word, he'd unload his magazine.

Logan really had been expecting her and opened his security so that she'd just walk right in.

That realization destroyed the false confidence that had convinced her this would work.

"I've got this," Logan told Angel who backed out and closed the door. His gaze returned to her, and she read trouble. He explained in a very matter-of-fact voice, "The minute you entered our outer perimeter, you were located and observed to determine if you were carrying a weapon before you were allowed to proceed."

"I could have had one in my boot." Had she really said that?

The point was to downplay herself as a threat, not rise to his baiting.

"You wouldn't have entered this room without something in hand if you had a weapon on you. You came unarmed to convince me you're no threat."

Point to Logan. He'd read that one right.

In one lithe move, Logan was up standing over her, the knife still in his hand. "Get up."

She pushed up on her elbows, gritting at the sharp pain in her arm, but she'd be damned if she was going to complain. When she got to her feet, she kept her hands in view. "I only wanted to make a point."

He crossed his arms, knife still clutched in his fingers, expression flagged "no sale."

This had sounded like such a clever idea in her head, but right now she was questioning her sanity for even trying. She smiled, trying for unconcerned. "I don't like being held against my will so I wanted to show you that I could come and go as I pleased. That's all."

"Why'd you come back?"

"I told you I want to meet the Banker, too. I don't have your resources, but I'm a merc and you know I've got skills. Some skills even *you* don't have. Now that you know a few more of them, and how effective I am, I'm back to talk about working together, but as peers. Not your prisoner."

Logan's face didn't so much as twitch with a reaction. He kept studying her, letting the silence build. She wouldn't break and be the first to talk. She'd laid out a logical reason for coming back and with the universe on her side this time he'd accept it. Plus, she'd helped him escape the jungle prison.

Didn't that count for something?

He flipped the knife over in his hand then threw it at a crate where the tip stuck deep into the wood. "I don't take on people I can't trust."

Yes, she had an ulterior motive for coming back, but he was one to talk about trust. "You can't trust me after I refused to leave you to die in that jungle hell, leave your man safe here, leave your truck pretty much intact and walk back into your camp unarmed?" Getting pissed wasn't the right tactic with Logan, but he was the one she had to watch out for in this partnership. "I'm clearly willing to trust you in spite of getting shafted in Paris."

"I didn't shaft you."

"No? You mean to say you weren't screwing me for my apartment?" She hadn't realized just how much that hurt until the words were out.

"That's not the way it was."

"Like hell. I finally put it all together after I woke up here as your prisoner." She let the word prisoner hang there between them. "You got a call that last morning and left immediately. The diplomat and his assistant died two blocks away. For years, I convinced myself that you had only been in the wrong place at the wrong time, but that's not true. You were in the perfect position to reach the kill zone within minutes."

"I already told you I didn't kill them."

"Why should I believe you?"

"I was there to save the diplomat."

"So you were in the saving business?" she smarted back.

"He was my aunt's only son. With some time, I can prove that."

His admission drowned her anger. "Why didn't you tell me?"

Logan turned away. "I couldn't."

Because she hadn't been more than a means to an end. "All those days together, all the sweet words, you telling me about the places you wanted to take me *one day* and the whole time I thought—" ... *you cared about me.* She caught herself before the words slid past her tongue and gave him a weapon to turn on her.

Her fingers were clenched, dead giveaway that she'd let him get to her.

His granite face softened when he turned to her. "I did mean everything I said. At the time."

"Stop lying to me." She rolled all that anger and pain into a tight wad and shoved it deep, no plan to revisit it. "I came back to talk business. Make up your mind if we're going to be able to work together or not."

"You tell me the truth, Margaux. Your prints don't show up in the law enforcement database in this country. You don't exist. And you were in Paris when my cousin died."

She deflated at that. "You ran my prints?"

"Why shouldn't I if you have nothing to hide? Why were you in Paris? What *are* you hiding?"

Her world was imploding and every step she took risked another land mine. "I went there to hide from someone who wanted to kill me because I'd called in his plans for a bombing here. Things went bad and his son died. A friend helped me get to Paris. I knew enough French to get a job bartending. I was safe. Until you came along."

Emotions shifted in his eyes. "You didn't know about the diplomat?"

"Not until I read about it. I came back here, and a friend taught me how to defend myself." Sabrina had given Margaux far more than self-defense training. She'd given Margaux skills and a sense of value when she'd most needed it.

"How'd you end up looking for the Banker in the Trophy Room?"

Who did Logan work for? CIA? MI6? Some other covert group? "Which side are you on, Logan?"

"Mine right now."

"Just give me a straight answer for once. Are you trying to hook up with the Banker to execute an attack or to stop one?"

"It's complicated." He looked away. "You shouldn't have come back."

That hurt.

Oh, shit. He still had the power to hurt her, even after all this time. She still loved him. She might lie to everyone else, but not to herself. Her heart was doing a jam-up impression of a stress ball being squeezed by a gorilla, but that didn't mean Logan had ever felt the same way about her.

He thought she was a criminal, and that was how she was

playing it, so it shouldn't hurt.

Why couldn't she get her head straight when it came to him? She let anger wash over her to drown out the sound of her heart breaking. "You're right. I shouldn't have walked into the Trophy Room. I shouldn't have dragged your ass out of that hut, and I shouldn't have believed that it mattered to you if I lived or died. Does *anything* matter to you, Logan?"

Logan grabbed his hair, gripping it and growling. He let go of his wild locks. "Nothing is fucking easy with you."

Like his aggravation was all her fault? "Then let's make it easy. I'm done with you."

She swept past him, headed for the door with no plan beyond that.

She opened it halfway and the door slammed shut.

Logan yanked her around.

She punched him in the chest.

He stood there and took it then dropped his forehead against hers. "I can't fucking live this way. I need to know the truth."

"You *know* the truth. I've never harmed innocent people, Logan. How could you think that of me?"

He took a deep breath and exhaled a sigh filled with anguish. "This life fucks with your head until you can't see up from down some days. I don't kill innocent people either. I'm done doubting you. I believe you. Now I need you to believe me."

The pain in his voice reached her when nothing else would have. There was no hope for her because this man was her emotional kryptonite.

She kissed him, hoping she was right to go with her heart on this one. He kissed like he made love, completely, leaving nothing on the table. He lifted her up and she wrapped her legs around him. She clutched his head and his neck, pulling him in harder.

He shoved up against her and she could feel her own damp heat. They ended up against a wall, freeing his hands. One went under her flannel shirt and cupped her breast. The relief at being touched switched to an ache to be touched everywhere.

His fingers played with her nipples, sending heat spiraling

down to her core.

She tightened her legs, riding hard against his thick ridge.

He started making that deep growling sound she used to love, the one he made when he was beyond stopping. She'd gloried in pushing him to that no-return point every time he tried to slow things down.

There was no slowing down this freight train.

He licked her neck, just under her jaw and she clenched against him. His mouth kissed and nipped, then dove in again for more of her.

He yanked down the waist of her jeans until he could push a finger inside her. She shuddered, close to the edge. She tightened around him then pushed up and down.

His words ground out, harsh with hunger. "You're so wet and tight. God, I missed you. Missed us."

She went all in. "You ruined me for anyone else. I want to feel you deep inside me. Now."

"You're killing me." His hands clutched her hips, lifted her up, and slid her down on his cock. She gripped his shoulders, clinging to him, her body taut and hurting. She needed just another touch. He pushed up hard and pulled back slowly, shaking. She tightened. His hand came down between them and he teased her then stroked up hard again.

Her release sent stars showering in her vision. He wouldn't let her stop coming. His fingers were relentless, and he was pumping harder until he tensed and shuddered with a deep groan.

They went down to the floor with him clutching her to his chest, breathing deep gulps of air. She was a noodle.

A very satisfied noodle.

No wonder she'd avoided men. The two times that she'd had sex in the past six years had paled compared to being with Logan.

He held her against him, and she fell asleep with a thought hovering in the distance, waiting to be addressed.

Had they come to any agreement?

CHAPTER 34

Logan filled a plate with eggs, smoked ham, grits and drop biscuits. He'd never acquired a taste for grits, but Nitro had told him that Margaux liked them. Nitro knowing something Logan didn't about Margaux rankled, but Logan wasn't about to let on.

Moose was exceptionally quiet this morning before he struck out to walk the perimeter.

Party Man finishing off his breakfast. He'd fixed the truck, but with a little help. When he dug around in the cab, he found a note from Margaux explaining how to repair the wiring.

Angel was honing one of his knives, lifting it to eye the edge.

Logan turned to walk away from the campfire.

Nitro said, "Just remember that we do deliver to the love shack. You know, if you get *tied up.*"

Logan turned and sent him a scathing look that shut down all jokes then kept walking toward said love shack.

What kind of idiot had sex with no condom?

One that loses his mind around Margaux.

He opened the door and stepped in to find her buttoning up her shirt. She stood up and smiled. "I was heading out to eat with the guys."

Logan placed the plate on the bed. "We need to talk."

Her face lost all signs of happiness and he wanted to kick himself. Why was he constantly making her unhappy?

She moved over to sit down and put the plate on her knees. "Is this the 'we made a mistake' talk?"

"We did. Or, I did."

"Well, I didn't. I enjoyed it." Her chin shot up to put an exclamation point on that last part.

"I'm not saying I didn't enjoy it."

"Then what was wrong with it."

"*It* was fine."

"What are you so pissed off about then?" She kept eating, but stared at him the way someone would when they were hearing a new language for the first time.

"I didn't use a condom."

She waved her fork. "Oh, that. Not a problem. I'm on birth control. Have been for six years even though it was a wasted prescription for the past three. I wouldn't risk being in situations like the jungle without it."

The idea that she took birth control because of the chance of being raped sucker punched him. But his brain locked on her not having sex for the past three.

She paused, blinking then looked up at him slowly. "Or are you concerned about disease?"

"I'm clean, but I've never done that. Without a condom."

"But you're not sure about me?"

Margaux would rant and curse you up one side and down the other, but when it came to anything that touched her true emotions, she kept those locked up tight.

Vulnerability peeked from her gaze, as she waited to be judged lacking.

He stood on the edge of a dangerous cliff.

The wrong answer would shake the foundation of whatever was going on between them. "No, I'm not worried about that with you."

Her face eased into a picture of contentment.

One that he was going to destroy.

He was destined to keep hurting her and hated every second of it, but when he woke up this morning, he had to face that he had no choice but to do what was best for her *and* his men.

She cleaned the plate, set it aside and started pulling on her socks. "We didn't really finish our conversation last night."

He tried to break in. "About that."

She kept on without taking a breath. "I know you're not use to having a woman around but I'm not your average woman."

No, she was extraordinary. "Margaux."

"I'm a hell of a shot and good with hand-to-hand combat. You know I don't have much jungle training, but I learn quick and—"

"Margaux!" He was dying with every word of enthusiasm that spilled out of her.

"What?"

Before everything between them went down in flames, he had to try to get something out of her. "Would you please tell me why you want to meet the Banker?"

"Oh, that?" She pulled on her other sock and picked up a boot that she propped on her lap. "He owes me."

"Too vague."

She stopped futzing with her shoes and stared at him. "Then you tell me what your interest is in him."

Logan considered how much to share to get her to open up. "I need him to help me save someone."

She studied him, and from the look on her face she was working through the same debate he'd just gone through. She said, "There was an op in Atlanta. He had someone killed and it cost me."

Logan didn't know what to make of that, but it sounded as if she really was not looking to work for the Banker. He'd decided that last night but wanted clarification. If she was looking for revenge, he could kill that bird for her with his stone. He was already going to have to explain his actions once he captured the Banker and failed to hand him over to INTERPOL.

And speaking of INTERPOL, if they ever found out that Logan had someone in his custody whose fingerprints were part of the Paris bombing investigation and he failed to hand her over, he'd end up in prison himself.

But he couldn't bring himself to give value to those suspicions or to put her through any more agony.

Even if he could explain all that, Margaux would still not forgive him for what he was going to do. "You can't go with me and the team."

She still held the boot and hadn't moved, but her shoulders were rigid in defense. "What are you saying? Just get to the bottom line."

"I'm sending you to a safe location until I complete this mission, then I'll come get you."

"I'm not stupid, Logan. If you're sending me somewhere, it's because you don't trust me. And if that's the case, you won't be coming back. Or if you do, I won't like where you take me next."

That pretty much summed it up. "You'll be safe."

"Right. Like last time when you sent me off to the States. I made myself safe at that point. But you told me to forget you. I guess this is what it takes for me to finally listen to you."

He waited for her to pitch her boot or curse him, but it was far worse than that when her face shifted with cold disdain.

"You may not believe me, but I'm doing this because I can't risk anything happening to you."

She put her boots on and stood up. "Save it. You were right last night. I was a fool to come back, but I'm done being a fool."

Someone knocked on the door. "Truck's ready, Cuz."

Margaux sighed. "Fine. Tell them I'm ready."

This next part was going to kill him. "Put your hands out front."

Confusion raced over her face then her eyebrows drew tight. "You're going to cuff me?"

He shouldn't have to explain any more at this point and didn't think he could talk past the lump in his throat.

She picked up her hands, wrist-to-wrist. "You really think I'd hurt one of your men?"

No, but she would get injured if she tried to escape. He'd made a mistake once and wouldn't do it again. He unrolled the flannel sleeves she'd turned up twice and put the flex cuff around her covered wrists. Then he bent down and cuffed her ankles.

When he picked her up in his arms, she looked away from his face. This was tearing him up. He started to put her down and cut the cuffs, but Nitro knocked at the door and called out, "Nine minutes."

He meant for the sat call from the Banker.

Logan said, "Open the door."

He carried Margaux out and across the camp to the truck to deposit her on the seat. Party Man had driven the truck through the road they'd uncovered this morning.

Party Man sat in the driver's seat and Angel slid in to ride shotgun.

This wasn't the way he wanted to see Margaux for what could very well be the last time if this mission went badly, but she wouldn't look at him and he had a terrorist to make nice with.

Logan told Angel, "Call in when you head back."

"You got it, Cuz."

The truck drove away, dragging Logan's heart behind it through the ruts and dirt.

He was already regretting sending her away a second time. Logan walked back to Nitro who handed him the sat phone.

Logan checked his watch. "If he calls on time, it should be in twenty seconds. *If* we had synchronized time."

They stood there, waiting. The call came through dead on the second. That was disconcerting in itself. Logan answered, "Dragan."

A refined male voice that sounded fortyish said, "I am the Banker."

"But anyone could call themselves the Banker," Logan pointed out, letting his caller know that he expected some form of confirmation.

"I was quite impressed with your escape in South America."

That wasn't the first thing Logan had expected the Banker to say, but it had him curious. "What do you know about that?"

"Everything. It was your test. I arranged the entire event. I had to decide between you and the unfortunate losers."

Shit. The bastard had set him up to be killed just to decide who to hire. But what about Margaux? "Was that test for only me?"

"Actually, it was, and I was surprised by the woman. She is something special."

Logan gripped the phone hard enough to crack the case.

"Clock's ticking. Where are we meeting?"

The Banker gave him the address of a signature hotel in downtown Denver. "A car will pick you up downstairs at 0900 tomorrow morning."

And that car would be filled with three armed men and a bag to put over Logan's head. "What's my assurance that you won't kill me?"

"If I had wanted you dead, I would have had you killed in the jungle. There were several perfect opportunities for my sniper. One was when you two first escaped and sat on that boulder waiting for the tablet to disinfect your Ziplock bag of river water. You looked so peaceful."

The scope of what the Banker had set up just to test him surprised even Logan. But the Banker had a point. He could have killed him—and Margaux—at that point. Logan agreed to the meeting and was ready to end the call when the Banker added one more stipulation.

"Bring the woman."

"No. You deal with me."

"Are you saying you *aren't* a team? That would be ... opportune. I have uses for a woman with her talents and I'm sure she has many."

The sexual innuendo in that prick's voice hit a raw spot. Logan said in a dark voice laced with threat. "She's mine."

Nitro lifted an eyebrow at that declaration.

The Banker's smooth demeanor never changed. "I see. Very well then. Bring the woman and we'll discuss my project." He hung up.

Logan fought the urge to smash the phone against the nearest tree.

Nitro scratched his chin. "I'm going to make a wild guess that you have to take Margaux with you. Is that right?"

"Yes." *And now the Banker thinks Margaux and I are together.*

"How do you plan to convince her to go?"

"Beats the hell out of me."

"She probably will."

Logan sent Nitro a withering look and lifted the phone. He punched the number for the phone in the truck and got Angel. Logan told him, "Bring Margaux back."

Angel called over to Party Man, "Turn around. Logan wants her back."

Margaux released a string of curses that could be heard two continents away.

Nitro cringed. "Good luck fixing that, Cuz."

CHAPTER 35

Logan signed his name as Kevin Sims on the guest documents at a boutique hotel in downtown Denver. Upscale elegance, but quiet and with exceptional service. More importantly, it was a block down from the five-star place the Banker had designated for the pickup point.

He and Marguax wouldn't be spending the night there.

Nitro and Angel were enjoying a room in the signature hotel instead. That way, his men would be in place tomorrow morning when Logan showed up for the car ride.

With Margaux.

He finished the registration at a different hotel then turned to take her elbow. "Ready, sweetheart?"

She smiled and gave him a moment of hope until she leaned in to whisper, "Take your hand off or I'll break every finger that touches me."

Swallowing a sigh, he released her and lifted the handle on an overnight bag while she walked to the elevator. The ride up was as much fun as the ten hours it had taken to convince her to join him, ride down from the mountain camp, and buy decent clothes for her.

Getting gut shot at point blank range couldn't be much worse.

She swept out of the elevator when the doors opened on the fourth floor then waited for him to lead her to the room. The shoulder she turned to him was so cold icicles should be hanging from the ceiling.

Once they were both inside the suite, Logan started in on her. "If we don't work this out, the Banker will get spooked and back out."

"I can do my part. Worry about yours." She pulled off the North Face jacket and tossed it on the sofa. Next went the fluffy gray scarf, leaving black jeans that hugged her sexy ass, a burgundy sweater and weathered-looking Frye boots that gave her three more inches of height.

If only that outfit had come with a sweet personality adjustment.

But truth told, he didn't want that. He just wanted the real Margaux back—the one he'd had when she'd busted them out of that hut in the jungle—back before she'd recognized him. The real her, barbs and all, wanting him as much as he wanted her.

She walked over to gaze out the window that overlooked snow-capped mountains.

"What do you want me to say, Margaux? I was sending you somewhere safe. I still don't want you here, but—"

"You need me for a prop. Again." She turned around and leaned on the window frame with her arms crossed. "I came back to you with an offer to work together. That wasn't enough to change your mind, but now you need me, *and* you want me to be happy about it. I said I'd go with you. That should be enough." Damn it, she was right. He'd have to tell her everything about his background for her to understand, and he'd like to be able to come clean, but he couldn't. Not when he had no idea who had trained her and for what reason.

He tried a logical approach. "I thought you'd be happy about being included in this meeting."

"My happiness has never been part of the equation where you're concerned."

Ouch. He'd earned that. "We can't go into this at odds with each other and survive."

"You might not, but I will."

Logan had hoped things would thaw between them by now, but she was holding onto her fury with an iron grip. Not that he could blame her. From where she stood, he was the same asshole who had destroyed her safe haven six years ago.

Then sent her away thinking she hadn't mattered to him.

He'd do the same thing to keep her safe again, but he regretted how it had ended in Paris.

That was something to be dealt with later on. He was running out of time and had to know what she would do when she stood in front of the Banker. Would she cause a conflict, or would she work with Logan when she had no motivation to do so? *Your fault asshole.*

That brought him back to finding out what was driving her to meet the Banker. First, he had to get her to negotiate. "What's it going to take for you to meet me halfway?"

She pondered his question, tapping her finger against her arm. "The truth about what you're up to."

Leave it to Margaux to go straight for the jugular. No subtly there. "Why do you need those details?"

"Because I need to know what you're planning to do for the Banker."

"And you think I would commit a terrorist attack for him?"

She glanced away. "To be honest, no. If I had thought that I wouldn't have..."

He finished that sentence in his mind. She wouldn't have let him touch her last night.

"This is down to the wire, Logan. It's time to decide if what you're shielding from me is worth blowing this meeting. I've come to terms with what the Banker has cost me and, at this point, I'm more concerned about supporting a deadly plot."

Choosing his words carefully, he said, "I'll tell you what I'm after and trust you to do the same for me." He didn't get any response from that, so he pushed on. "I do need the Banker and I am trying to work a deal with him, but to save someone. Not to kill people. You remember me telling you about my family?"

She was interested now. "Yes. Was any of it true?"

"Parts," he admitted. "I do have a brother and he was in college when I met you, but he was in a Russian university, not in France. He's the baby in the family at twenty-six, but ambitious. I tried to convince him to do something else, anything, but he signed on to be part of the Russian security force."

Margaux's staid expression changed, but to one of suspicion.

Logan mentally edited as he continued, sifting in enough of

the truth that might convince her he meant what he said about not harming anyone. "My brother was part of a team investigating a potential terrorist infiltration. He was leading the investigation. The terrorist figured out who was after him and turned the tables by planting an evidence trail that put my brother in league with the terrorist. He's in a prison in Krasnoyarsk, Siberia. He's been beaten and I don't think he'll survive much longer. I have one chance to get him out and I need the Banker to make that happen."

"How does the Banker play into that?"

This part got a little trickier, but he was determined to be as honest as possible. "I need the terrorist who set up my brother, alive, to make a trade."

"So, you've never been a part of terrorist operations?"

Telling her the truth on this point was a gamble, but no more than Logan had already put at risk to save Yuri. "No."

"What about your international reputation?"

"You don't think a reputation can be manufactured? How else would the Banker consider meeting me?" He watched for a sign that he'd broken through her doubt, but nothing firm showed. "You said I don't trust you, Margaux, but that's not true. I just gave you information you can use against me to destroy my mission, because without your help when we meet this guy, I stand to have wasted eleven months of deep undercover. Not just me, but men by my side to help me. I'm risking that you could cost my brother his life."

"You really are one of the good guys?"

"Yes. I hunt people like the Banker."

"Are you CIA, MI6, or some other international acronym?"

He considered how much he could say and still tell the truth. "No. My team and I are part of what you might call a very old brotherhood. We don't talk about it so please don't be hurt that I'm not telling you more." He had something else to get off his chest. "I was trying to save my cousin when we first met. If you believe nothing else about me, know this—I wanted you more than I'd ever wanted anything, but had to let you go to keep you safe."

Margaux's shoulders lost the tension that had held them stiff for hours. She scrubbed her face with her hands. "I need some time to digest this."

His throat was tight. "I didn't use you in Paris."

She lifted a hand. "Stop. You've said enough. Paris is done. I don't want to talk about it."

"It's not done until you know the truth."

"Why does it matter what I think? That was a long time ago."

Because I can still see the way it haunts you. Because I fell in love with you in Paris and don't want to give you up again even though I know this won't end with us together. That was why he wouldn't tell her just how much she meant to him. He wouldn't do that and walk away again. "What you think matters because you matter. You did then and you do now."

She drove her fingers into her hair, shaking her head. "Don't do this to me, Logan. Don't make noises that sound like this thing between us is more than short-term and disposable."

"I can't offer anything beyond short-term because of the way I live, but it's never been disposable. I wanted to keep you. I left that morning with plans of coming back and—"

She dropped her hands. "What? For us to play house somewhere? You were a merc of some kind then and you're still one now. Besides, even if you could be around on occasion, I couldn't."

"Why not?"

"I don't have a life to pilot. I live at the grace and mercy of others because of past mistakes. When this is done, I'll be gone and you'll never see me again, but I swear I won't say a word about your team or you so long as you've told me the truth."

He still couldn't let her just go back to whatever life she had. Even if she did hold his confidence, she'd be at risk now that the Banker knew she was with him. The idea of not seeing Margaux again after this was going to be worse than losing her last time, but he'd ultimately do whatever was best for her.

Even if she ended up hating him for it.

Until that time came, there was no point in bringing it up

and putting her on the defensive again when she was starting to soften. Curse his worthless hide, he wanted her soft and willing. He wanted her, period.

But touching her again was not happening. She was not leaving him this time feeling used.

Forcing his mind back on business, he reminded her, "I've told you what I want from the Banker. What do you want?"

"Blood. I want the person responsible for killing my cousin last year. She was with the FBI, working on an investigation tied to a terrorist."

Just as he'd thought. She had a vendetta.

He could work with that if she didn't get in his way on this mission. "I'll help you if you help me."

She chewed on her lip, in no hurry to agree, then finally stood away from the window. "Deal. I'm going to bed."

This was a one-bedroom suite with a king size bed, because that was all he could get at the last minute with conferences overflowing. He took a look at the too short and stiff sofa that belonged on the set of *Gone With The Wind* and sighed.

"You can share the bed, but not the booty," she said on her way by, reminding him of her threat to break any finger that touched her.

Sleeping that close to Margaux and keeping his hands to himself would be as uncomfortable as the sofa.

Decisions, decisions and none that offered a decent night's rest.

CHAPTER 36

Logan was only trying to save his brother.

Margaux rolled from her back to her uninjured side. Her arm was improving, but not enough to put her weight on it. The burns on that hand and arm were still tender but were now okay with small bandages. She fluffed the pillow. This whole thing could backfire on Logan if the Banker found out he was being deceived.

Did the Banker know about Margaux Duke from Atlanta or not? Nick said there'd been no attacks on Slye's people. Maybe Snake Eyes hadn't set her up in a trap for the Banker but for someone else. He was greedy—always desperate for money. Had he sold her out to someone working for the pissed-off DEA agent?

She'd know soon enough when she met the Banker.

If he did ID Margaux as the one who had been hunting him in Atlanta, Logan would end up added to the body count as well.

She flopped onto her back again.

Why hadn't Logan taken her up on her offer and shared the bed? She shouldn't have to be miserable alone.

If he was in here, she could give him shit over how much pain he'd put her through for the past six years.

You would have done the same thing in his shoes to keep someone safe.

Spare her from a chatty conscience or she'd never get to sleep. Was he sleeping? Margaux slid off the bed and pulled the thin strap up on her stretchy sleep top that stopped short of her panties.

Using the brush of light filtering in from the nearly full moon, she tiptoed across the bedroom and looked around the corner into the living room.

Logan hung half on and half off that dinky sofa. He wore a pair of sweatpants and had a blanket draped across his bare chest. None of that looked comfortable.

Your fault for telling him you'd break his fingers if he touched you, her conscience reminded her.

Shut up!

Margaux gave in to her guilt and walked over to nudge his leg.

Logan came up with his gun. Hair stood up on end, but his eyes were sharp and deadly. "What's wrong?"

"Nothing. Come sleep in the bed."

He scratched his head with his free hand. "I'm good."

She'd offered. That appeased her guilt.

Admit it, you want him to snuggle up with.

Could she get a conscience-ectomy?

He was keeping his distance, just as she'd asked. She believed what he'd told her about trying to save his brother and even about Paris. She'd welcomed him to her bed the first time and hadn't cared what his life was at the time, because she'd never planned to see him after their affair.

But nine days had changed everything and now she had him back again. For a short time.

Why was she wasting even a minute of it?

Margaux stepped up and hugged her arms around him.

Logan stilled. "What are you doing, Sugar?"

"Telling you to come to bed with me."

His arms came around her and he hugged her. "I can't stand hurting you and you're right about us not seeing each other after this is over. That might happen."

She turned her head and kissed him. He kissed her back, a long, sweet kiss that tasted like a precious memory. She whispered, "I don't care about tomorrow. Just love me tonight."

His body tensed. "You sure?"

"Absolutely."

He hoisted her up and her legs went around him then he kissed her every step of the way to the bedroom. He dropped the gun on the nightstand and tossed her across the middle of the bed.

Then he followed her down, his mouth hot on her neck.

Hooking his hands under the edge of her panties, he slid them down slowly and moved as he did, kissing and tasting his way. His teeth nipped her breasts through the thin material, and she felt it in her womb.

He stepped off the bed and tossed her panties aside then pulled her legs until they hung off the bed with him between them. The next thing she felt was his hands gently opening her legs and he kissed her there.

She made an "mm" sound.

He lifted her legs to put over his shoulders and his tongue slipped across her folds.

She arched and dug her heels into his back. He put his hand over her, pressing to keep her down. While he flicked his tongue across a mass of nerves that were screaming for release, his finger slid inside her. She shuddered, reaching for the pinnacle.

His hand slid up her body until he grasped her nipple between his finger and thumb, rolling it.

She lifted up, her body bowing.

He pinched her nipple, and his tongue stroked her over the edge. She cried out, shaking as her world broke apart into a thousand pieces of crystal.

Then he lifted her to him and carried her as he moved to the middle of the bed, dropped her legs on each side and lowered her slowly onto him.

She pushed her knees against the bed and raised herself, then drove down, squeezing as she did.

He growled and pumped hard up into her. She met him stroke for stroke and felt the coil tightening again. He was making that sound that said he was close.

His fingers touched her, and the tension burst again. She called his name. He slammed into her, the strokes getting harder and harder until he made a guttural sound as he came.

They were soaked with sweat and the sweet smell of their sex took her back to the nights they'd first shared.

He rolled to the side, taking her with him and huffing

breaths. "God, I missed you. Not just this, but you. Meeting you made me want to walk away from what I did so many times, but ... I can't."

He was a warrior.

He would be one until the day he decided he was no longer capable of standing with his men.

She was running her hand over his chest. "I get it. I really do. I'm just glad to have you here now."

His lips touched her forehead in a sweet kiss, but he didn't offer her empty promises. She had loved him once and that love came bursting to the surface again. No matter how much she told herself this would probably end badly, she couldn't help the way she felt. Couldn't talk herself into keeping this light and casual any more than she could back in Paris.

She was stroking his hair and thought he'd drifted to sleep when he asked, "Tell me what happened here. Why you had to hide in Paris."

"I'd made my first major mistake at eighteen and let someone I thought I loved convince me that I should walk away from my family and fight for a better world. I met him in school in a little town in nowhere, Arkansas down near the Louisiana border. But he turned out to be the son of a man who had built an anti-government anarchist group. They were going to make a better world by destroying this one."

Logan's fingers were sliding across her back, turning her content body into a lethargic rag. Feeling him close made it easier to tell what she'd kept hidden all these years. "They had a plan to blow up the capitol of Arkansas to make a statement. When I found out what he was going to do, I tried to leave. That was mistake number two."

"What did he do?" Logan asked in a quiet voice, barely above a whisper.

"It wasn't what he did, but what *they* did."

Logan slowed his hand over Margaux's back. Her head was

tucked against his chest. Her hair fell everywhere. He picked up a strand to feel it between his fingers. "What did they do?"

"Lonnie, my so-called boyfriend, told his father I wanted to leave. His father said I not only couldn't leave, but I had to earn my keep."

Maybe it was so many years spent with the worst scum of the world, but Logan made a mental leap he hoped he was wrong about. "How?"

"We were in a nasty house. His father locked me naked in a closet for two days while they planned the bombing. I screamed at spiders and things I couldn't see crawling on me until I was hoarse. When his men showed up to get their orders, he unlocked the door and said they should take what they wanted because there would be no time for fooling around later."

Logan closed his eyes and had to be very still, or he'd crush something. He wanted to kill every one of them. He would find this man and make sure that she never had to hide from him again. Logan forced his emotions back out of the way so he could hear it all. "Tell me you killed them and got out."

"Oh, no. That was long before I had the ability to maim a man who tried to hurt me." Her voice sounded small for his Superwoman.

They had hurt her viciously.

But they hadn't broken her. "What happened to them?"

"The bombing went off, but not the way they thought. SWAT showed up so all of them didn't make it out in time. The blast killed three of the pro-anarchists, including his son, Lonnie. All the other bombers at the attack site got caught but Lonnie's father."

He took it all in and asked, "The authorities found out in time to contain it?"

"Yes. His men had left me bleeding. Thought I was dead. When I regained consciousness, I crawled to a phone and called 911. I told them what was going to happen, but I wouldn't tell them who I was or where I was. I passed out again. The next time I woke up, I heard boots outside the door, and it burst open. This woman came in and got down to talk to me. I told her I had to leave, or my boyfriend's father would kill me."

"Who was she?"

"You know how you can't talk about your brotherhood? Don't ask me about her, because I don't want to lie to you, and I owe it to her to protect her identity."

Out of admiration for Margaux's loyalty, he let it go. "What happened?" He wanted to hear how the bastard who had done that to her was caught.

"I must have passed out again, because I woke up in a safe house. I spent six weeks there. The woman became my friend and kept me hidden. I told her everything I knew about the man who led the anarchist group. He'd gotten away with six of his men, but he'd lost two sons. She talked about the WITSEC program, but the DA would have put me in protective custody because I'd been seen with Lonnie when he was buying supplies. That meant I'd be locked up until his father was caught and prosecuted."

Logan could almost see the rest of it playing out. "You didn't take that deal."

"No. I asked her to help me with a new identity and to get me out of the country. I told her I just wanted to live in peace. That's how I ended up in Paris."

Then he'd screwed that up. The morning of the bombing, she'd lost her sanctuary because of him. "I'm sorry I messed up your plan."

She waved a hand in the air and dropped it back. "I found my friend again and she said she'd train me to work with her people if I promised to stay on the right side of the law."

"How did you end up at the Trophy Room?"

"Because the B—" She snapped shut. "I'm tired. Let's talk later, okay?"

Logan had a feeling Margaux was holding back something significant about the Banker. But she'd given him more than he expected tonight. He'd keep getting it a piece at a time and when he was done with freeing Yuri, he was going to find that bastard who had her gang raped.

He'd told her he didn't kill innocent people.

Monsters like that deserved the worst Logan could do to them.

CHAPTER 37

"Does this flight come with service?" Margaux smarted off, not caring if she got backhanded. She'd asked for water right before the Banker's men had covered her head with the black bag and she was still thirsty.

"What's your problem?" a heavy voice said close to the side of her head. He sat behind her in the helicopter. A six-seater jet model used for corporate transportation that had a reasonably quiet interior.

"Same thing I wanted an hour ago. Water."

A plastic bottle landed on her hands that were clasped in her lap. Not bound, though. Cuffs weren't needed when you'd had three weapons pointed at you from the moment you were picked up outside a hotel. She unscrewed the top and lifted the bottle to her lips, taking a drink.

There was no telling where they were headed.

The limo had rolled up to the hotel where they'd been instructed to be ready at nine. A driver had hurried around to open the rear door. Tinted glass wrapped the limo, leaving the interior almost completely dark.

Party on the outside and lethal on the inside.

She and Logan had climbed in to face armed men who'd been out of view from the exterior.

Even if Logan's men had followed the limo for the forty-minute ride out of Denver, there was no way to keep up with a helicopter once she and Logan were searched in the hangar then walked out to where the helicopter was parked at the small airport.

It didn't lift off until she and Logan wore the black bags.

She noticed the change in rotor noise and felt the helicopter begin a descent.

A hand covered hers.

She might have reacted if not for recognizing Logan's touch. He gently squeezed her hand. Some things had changed last night, like Logan's convincing her that he *had* cared after all.

But other things hadn't changed.

Margaux still had to hand the Banker over to Sabrina, if she didn't kill him first.

She couldn't quiet that part of her that begged for him to resist when the time came to take him down. A fatal flaw in her personality, no doubt.

Of all the variables she couldn't control in this operation, she could depend on one thing for sure. Once Logan got what he wanted to free his brother, he would help her capture the Banker.

The helicopter touched down. She climbed out with the help of men who handled her with sterile professionalism. Brutal cold clutched at her exposed hands and neck. The coat she'd picked yesterday and bulky sweater she wore were doing their jobs keeping her warm. Corduroy pants protected her legs, but the wind still cut through them. Her teeth chattered.

No gloves or hat had been allowed. They'd taken her scarf.

Someone led her up a slight incline then said, "Take a step. Another step. Walk straight ahead."

Her boot heels clicked on a hard surface.

The hand let go of her. "Stop there."

She did. A door shut out the cold air. The bag came off and she raised her hands to brush loose strands off her face, pushing her hair over her shoulders. Her eyes adjusted to the sconces illuminating a foyer that had a stairwell going down instead of up. The room was oval. No windows. Felt like a fortress.

Logan stepped up next to her. "You good?"

"Yes."

One man had called the shots from the minute they'd entered the limo. He was Logan's height, but thicker with no neck and a long Slavik face with sharp cheekbones and a short nose. He said, "You will go downstairs for the meeting."

Logan put his hand at her back, and she moved forward, ready to meet the man who had ordered Nanci's death. In her mind, she attacked one of his men and snatched away his FN

P90, took out the three of them then charged downstairs to blow their boss's head off.

In reality, she put one foot in front of the other and remembered the part she was to play. She was Logan's woman, she was deadly, and she worked as a snitch. At the bottom landing, she stepped into a room that was a twenty-foot-wide half circle with a curtain running across the flat wall.

Two home-theater-style chairs with a console between them faced the curtain.

Her hand itched for a knife or a gun.

"Please have a seat," a male voice announced through a speaker system.

She exchanged a look with Logan. No turning back now.

He'd dressed for the weather in wool pants, a collared shirt and a black leather jacket. A civilized look for any man, but for Logan it was like putting a doggy sweater on a tiger. Be prepared to be ripped apart when you made the mistake of thinking he was pet material. He took the far seat, and she sank into the one next to him.

If they were going to be executed, at least they'd be comfortable.

The curtain separated in the middle and drew apart to each side, revealing a wall of glass as tall as the ten-foot ceiling, and at least two inches thick. Almost certainly bulletproof. Might even take a .50 caliber round.

One chair faced them from the other side of the window ten feet away from the glass wall, but it might as well have been the other side of the world. No getting through that barrier.

Stealing a guard's weapon would have been useless.

A door opened on the other side and a man strolled in. He was bald and slight of build with a pair of half glasses propped on his narrow nose. The nonchalant stride fit his slacks, silk shirt and cable-knit sweater. All he was missing was a pipe and newspaper.

Was this the man who brokered bulk murder?

When he reached the chair, he pulled the glasses off, sat down and two eyes so dark they could be black looked at them through the glass. "Welcome, Dragan. And your lady friend's name is?"

"Not important. This isn't a social call," Logan replied.

Margaux kept the surprise off her face. So maybe the Banker didn't know she was Margaux Duke from Atlanta. Snake Eyes might still be alive if he'd only sold her out to the DEA, as if that wasn't bad enough.

"Very well, we'll get down to business." The Banker folded his hands over his chest and propped his elbows on the chair arms. He had no accent as if he'd been raised in midwestern America and his words were so precise Margaux wondered if he had trained to change his voice to fit in wherever he went.

He addressed Logan as he spoke. "I require you and your team in two places at once that are fifty-seven miles apart."

Logan wouldn't want to split his team, but Margaux kept a mildly disinterested look on her face as agreed. Logan had said he could figure a way around actually killing anyone for the Banker.

She hoped he could back that claim.

The Banker had paused and when Logan didn't comment, he went on. "One team will set up a bomb attack for the convention center in downtown Seattle."

Her gut squeezed, but she kept her face neutral as the Banker continued. "The other team will protect a Wilder Exploration drilling site south of the city."

"Protect the site from what?" Logan asked.

"Technicians on site will need a window of time with no interference. No unexpected inspection. No one coming into work early. These men are on Wilder's payroll. I have assured Wilder that his people will be safe once they finish sabotaging the drill site. Your men are to enter the command center for the site at a precise moment and escort the technicians out, making it look like a kidnapping."

That part didn't sound so bad. What was this guy up to and who was he representing this time?

Logan stuffed his next words with impatience. "That's simple enough. Let's talk about Seattle. What's the area targeted, and the body count expected so I can plan effectively?"

"I know you'll be disappointed, but there will be no deaths in this attack."

Margaux almost asked him to repeat that, but Logan got it out first. "Say again."

"This is to be a terrorist threat, but there will be no actual attack. You will kidnap the speaker at a natural gas technology conference, but it will be easy. He's in on the whole plan, even sabotaging his own drilling site."

"Who?"

"Svenson Wilder of Wilder Explorations."

Margaux realized why she knew that name and glanced over at Logan. He frowned, acting as if he didn't recognize the name, but she'd bet he knew exactly who the guy was. Still, any questions about Wilder would sound like he was too interested in the wrong thing.

She, on the other hand, could pump for information.

Margaux asked the Banker, "Isn't Wilder that guy who has a revolutionary design that's challenging even horizontal drilling?"

"Precisely."

"Why would he do this? At the rate he's going, he stands to be the Steve Jobs of the natural gas industry."

"Someone is always willing to pay more. China is growing economically so fast it's becoming much like the US. They're dependent on oil like never before while things are shifting here with the recent discovery of enough resources in North Dakota to sever this country's need for Middle East oil. China does not care to be dependent upon the US as they move forward. They have their own reserves, but they lack the extraction technology that this country possesses."

Margaux wanted to hurt Wilder. He'd benefitted by living in a country where he could develop a system which was now worth billions. There would be time to deal with him and the good news was no one had to die.

The Banker waved his glasses as he spoke, a professor

explaining economics. "Wilder's technology has taken retrieval a step further than the horizontal drilling with the additional diagonal cut and his patented system. He's fine-tuned hydraulic fracturing, which will likely appease the environmentalists who whine about it even though it's been around for over forty years."

"I don't understand," Margaux said, playing along. She'd read about Wilder. Smart guy. Too bad he had no morals.

The Banker explained, "Wilder came up with a superior method of developing unusual hydraulic fracture points that creates less impact on the environment and protects the water table from methane. It will revolutionize natural gas extraction. The process takes more time up front, but the production flow is higher. Take him *and* his technology away, and this country is left with its present, archaic methods."

Logan asked, "Why sabotage his drilling site? What does that benefit?"

The Banker pointed his glasses at Logan. "Good question. This particular location is his premier drill site with the deepest drilling yet. If it remains intact, his leaving the country will have no impact. But with the right setting, the minor explosions used to break loose the natural gas will instead be magnified to generate enough damage to leak methane into the water table and blow up the drilling site. Once his people are safely out, they will travel with him to China."

"And the US will think he was kidnapped so they'll have no reason to suspect sabotage at the drilling site."

"Precisely."

Logan smiled in appreciation. "Plus, there's the added benefit of China's improving their relations with the Middle East by impeding the progress here in the US."

"A win-win all the way around." The Banker smiled, clearly pleased with himself. Dress him any way you want, but there was no humanity in that face.

"Let's talk money." Logan sat back, relaxed.

Margaux listened as the two men hammered out the zeroes and Logan negotiated as if he took deals to commit acts of terrorism and kidnapping every day.

But of course, he did.

Watching him, she wondered how many times he'd walked into a viper's nest with the odds against his survival? He had to be exceptional at what he did to stay alive, but this job would divide his men and that upped the risk factor.

Logan asked in an incredulous tone, "*You're* going to make the payment in person?"

The Banker announced, "Yes. I will hand you the money when you walk Wilder up to the Learjet that will be waiting to take both of us out of this country. I don't care to be involved on that level with an operation, but China has very deep pockets and the only way they would agree to this was if I personally handled the exchange. My reputation is such that they paid a significant amount as an advance, which means that I will not suffer failure in any form."

"My men are the best. They won't fail."

"That's good because you would not like what happens to them if you do fail. I'm a man of my word, Mr. Stoli. I have a simple philosophy that guarantees success. Everyone who works for me knows that I never threaten what I can't produce."

Logan showed total disregard for that threat, asking, "What about the specifics? I need locations and time?"

"When you're returned to your hotel, you'll receive an envelope with everything spelled out in detail but be prepared to go mobile right away. You'll also receive some photos I think you'll find interesting."

She didn't like the sound of that. Why had he demanded her presence? As if he'd read her thoughts, the Banker's empty eyes shifted to her. "I will expect to see you with the Seattle team, my dear."

Logan stiffened, but he didn't snap a reply. "I command my team."

"I understand, but having a woman in the operation allows for covering the unexpected. Is there a problem with *her* being in Seattle?"

Nicely played. If Logan refused to bring her on this mission, he raised the Banker's suspicion over Margaux.

"She'll be with me."

"Very good. Enjoy your return trip."

The room on the other side went dark. Margaux stared at her and Logan's reflections as the curtain drew closed. She stood when he did and turned toward the stairs where their guard waited for them.

She had a choice to make. She trusted Logan to do the right thing, but she also had a duty to Sabrina and this country. Sabrina expected Margaux to avoid letting her emotions dictate her decisions about national security, which meant Margaux had to get word to Sabrina about what was going down in Seattle.

Logan would gag her and leave her tied up if he knew she was going to contact someone. She *had* told him she'd help.

But she'd never promised to keep information that threatened national security to herself.

CHAPTER 38

Nick leaned against the door of his Ferrari 458 Spider and checked his watch again. It hadn't been the husky female voice that had gotten his attention and convinced him to meet a stranger, but the short and specific message.

Him: "Hello."

Her: "Meet me on the top parking deck of the Varsity if you want to find Margaux."

Him: "And you are?"

Her: "Hanging up."

He was on time and in another twelve seconds, she'd be officially late.

A silver spacecraft masquerading as land transportation rolled past a lineup of vintage college cars, which sounded kinder than calling them beaters. The Lamborghini Veneno parked next to Nick's fire-red convertible.

The doors slid up and away on the Veneno. A woman wearing a Burberry trench coat over wool slacks and thick knit sweater unfolded from the driver's seat. The boots made her appear tall. She was an attractive mid-forties.

Why did he not want to believe what he saw? "You know I'm Nick. Do I get a name?"

"Talia."

"That's as good as anything I could make up."

Her lips twitched. "All you need to know is that I'll help you if we can come to terms."

"First, I have to believe that you can be of value to me. What do you know about Margaux?"

"I know about the DEA bust that went bad."

He shrugged. "Anyone could get that info."

"I know that she entered the Trophy Room to find the Russian meeting the Banker."

Nick asked, "What's the Russian's name?"

"Dragan Stoli. Do you want to continue twenty questions,

or do you want to discuss how to help your friend?"

"We aren't sure Margaux's still alive," he bluffed.

"She's alive."

Nick scratched his nose and shoved his hands in his pockets. "How do you know?"

"Because she met with the Banker today."

That headache Nick had been trying to kill just came back to life. "Are you trying to say she's working for the Banker?"

"No. She and Dragan met with the Banker about an operation they've taken on."

This just got better by the minute. "What's your interest in all this?"

"I want to capture the Banker."

He'd gone out on a limb for riskier propositions. Sabrina might balk, which was why Nick would have to file this under *doing whatever it took to get Margaux back*. "If I agree, what do you want?"

"A day alone with the Banker when he's captured."

"Margaux has to come out of this alive, too."

"That's possible." She tapped her finger on her cheek. "But for that, I'll need something else in trade."

"Like what?"

"A favor at some point."

As deals went, this one was full of holes, but no one had come up with a better offer. He extended his gloved hand to shake.

She gave him an apologetic smile. "No exchange of fingerprints or DNA. We have a deal. I'll be in touch." She turned toward her car.

"What about Dragan?"

Glancing back, she lifted a shoulder. "I don't need him alive. Do you?"

"Nope."

CHAPTER 39

Margaux ordered food while Logan opened the Banker's envelope. She'd seen Nitro on her way into Sam's Diner on Curtis Street in downtown Denver, but that was only because Nitro had wanted to be seen. She and Logan had to get out of here without being followed by anyone, including the Banker's people in particular.

Logan said it would be simple and quick, but they'd have to split up. She had a moment of anxiety that he was sending her out of the picture, but then she remembered that the Banker required her presence in Seattle.

Reaching into the large envelope, Logan pulled out a black sports watch, looked at it and shoved it back inside. He pulled out papers.

"What's that watch for?" She kept her voice down, but the diner had a comfortable noise level with people chatting and so many hard surfaces.

Logan paused in reading the first of three sheets. "The watch is to coordinate with our *sponsor* during the event." The Banker was their sponsor, and the event was the job. "IDs are included. We just have to add the photos. Security clothes will be on site in a locked room. Must be what one of the keys is for."

Drinks, two hamburgers and fries were delivered as Logan scanned the details. She jumped on her food, starving. Sometimes there was nothing better than fried potatoes and a hamburger.

He muttered, "Shit."

"That good, huh?"

"We're going to be pushed to hit this time frame." He chomped on his hamburger and was picking up fries when she wiped her hands on her napkin. Done.

She looked around. "How long before we leave here?"

Logan stopped reading and lifted his head. "About ten minutes. As soon as I give Nitro a sign, why?"

"Because unlike you and the boys on the way back, I

couldn't just pee at the edge of the woods."

"Damn. Sorry. We've got a few minutes."

"Be back in a minute." She'd been watching a woman struggle with two small kids near the bathroom. The table was covered in food, baby toys for the toddler and a stuffed animal the older one had tossed on the floor.

Margaux approached the table at an angle that allowed her to watch Logan out of the corner of her eye. His head was still bent over the Banker's notes. She swooped down and picked up the stuffed cow that squeaked. The toddler turned at the noise and started calling out, "Mine. Mine. Mine."

The poor mother grabbed for him as he tried to nosedive out of the high chair.

"This is yours?" Margaux asked, waving the stuffed animal and smiling at the little boy who clapped his hands. She leaned over to hand it to him and play squeaky in his face.

The mother's face was etched with relief that said she'd expected someone to ream her for her children making a mess. She said, "Thanks," and turned back to deal with the other one climbing around under the table.

Margaux went on to the bathroom, having only used twenty seconds to swipe the ignored cell phone. She waited for one of the waitresses to leave before she dialed Nick's new burner number.

"What?"

"It's me," she whispered.

"You still in Colorado?"

"Denver, but not for long. I only have a minute." She explained about meeting the Banker, impressing Nick, and wrapped it up quickly with, "I didn't have a chance to get the details. Dragan is reading them now and we're leaving in a few minutes, but the good news is no fatalities planned."

"We'll be there."

"Don't interfere and mess up what Dragan has in motion."

"Why?"

She stopped herself before she said, *Because Dragan needs something from the Banker and must have a plan to get that when he has Wilder to hand over.* Instead, she said, "Because we'll lose our shot at the Banker. Just tell Sabrina that I'm trusting her and the team not to bring the Feds or Homeland in on this."

"Jesus, Duke, why not just put her at the top of the FBI's Ten Most Wanted list when this is done?"

"Bagging the Banker is worth keeping chaos out of this, isn't it?"

"Haven't you forfeited enough to get him, Duke?"

"This isn't about Nanci, Nick. I know the team doesn't believe me, but it hasn't been about her for a long time. There's too much at stake and I don't have time to tell you all of it. Would I like to see him bleed out? Sure. But that's not what matters right now. He didn't know I was the one in Atlanta hunting him, but after this that will change. With his resources, he'll find out about all of us, and we'll all have prices on our heads, just like Nanci did."

"Are you saying you don't think we can handle him?"

"I'm saying I don't want any more blood on my hands. This guy is too powerful and too insane to let walk away when we have a chance to stop him. He's brokering deals to play one country against another. That's someone who can start the next world war."

"Okay. I'm sold that your head is screwed back in the right direction."

She would take that as a glowing recommendation from anyone else, but Nick wasn't the best judge of stability. "Gotta go. Remember, don't close in until the trade is done. I'll call if I can, but I'm going to see this through to the end."

On her way back, she cleared the call off the phone, wiped it down and let the phone drop into the ginormous purse next to the young mother's chair.

Logan stood when she reached the table. "Put your coat on."

"Yes, Dad." When she had it zipped, he reached for the hood and pulled it up on her head.

Then he kissed her, a quick touch that tasted like tasty fries and her man. Before he pulled back, he said, "Start slowly toward the door with me until I say now."

Halfway to the door, a taxi sitting outside burst into flames. The diner sat on a corner. Cars running through the traffic light slowed to look. Traffic dropped to a crawl, clogging the intersection."

Logan's grip on Margaux tightened. "Now." He pulled her into a run. She was with him every step.

Outside, they pushed through the crowd huddling close enough to see the car burn.

Logan whispered at her ear, "It's pyrotechnics. Won't explode." He paused at the curb then gave a tug and they were out in the middle of cars parked everywhere. Sirens whined in the distance, coming fast.

Two black crotch rocket motorcycles wove between cars with a high-pitched whine. They cut across the intersection and whipped up to Logan, both doing stoppies with the rear wheels picking up off the ground.

Logan shouted to Margaux, "Get on that one. We'll meet up later."

She climbed on behind her driver and wrapped her arms around him a second before he blasted into traffic again, juking right and left like a pro running back. Icy air blasted her face. He reached down and covered her freezing hands with his jacket. She kept her head tucked against his back.

The whomp, whomp, whomp of a helicopter closed in on them.

A searchlight beamed down, spotlighting them.

She had a feeling this was Nitro driving and he wouldn't panic. He spun through turn after turn, finally forcing the helicopter to peel off when he turned the bike down a narrow street bordered by tall buildings. He pulled under an overhang where deliveries were made at the back of a building and spun around to face out.

She heard him saying, "Boxed in on the west side." He was quiet, then, "Ten four."

Had the Banker sent someone to follow Logan back to his men? If so, why? He needed Logan to do this job.

Margaux played everything back through her mind from the point of being dropped off, eating and making the call to Nick.

Nick had asked if she was still in Colorado.

She hadn't told him where she was specifically. Not even the address of the house in the mountains she'd called from.

That didn't mean Sabrina had a team here. Between Margaux and Logan, there were a lot of people after them.

"Get ready," Nitro told her.

"For what?"

"To make a run. Logan's doubling back to grab the helicopter's attention to give us a chance to escape."

"What about him and Angel?"

"He dropped Angel off to get the truck. Logan'll lose those clowns in the chopper."

He might not.

She didn't get a chance to argue. Nitro gunned the motor, and she wrapped up against him again. They flew out of the opening. She caught sight of the chopper buzzing down a street going in the opposite direction.

Following Logan who was alone. No backup.

An hour out of the city, Nitro pulled off the side of the road and let her get off before he stashed the bike behind a pile of boulders.

Less than a minute later, Angel pulled up in a dual cab truck.

Nitro took the front passenger seat and Margaux climbed into the back this time. "Where's Logan?"

Angel answered. "Lost contact. He'll show up later."

She grabbed the back of Angel's seat and pulled herself forward. "You *lost* contact? What if he's caught?"

Nitro was peeling out of his jacket with the heat running high. "He's not caught. He'll be fine."

"We should go back."

Angel shook his head. "Cuz gave orders to get you back to camp."

She understood why these men thought Logan was invincible, but Logan was a man who could bleed and die.

CHAPTER 40

Logan was a human popsicle by the time he walked into the camp. He'd left the street bike with Moose at the base of the last hill rather than fight his way up the ruts on a motorcycle designed for highways. Dual sport motorcycles were better suited for the terrain up this mountain, but in downtown Denver he'd take a crotch rocket any day.

Margaux stood near the fire with a mug of coffee. She was staring off into the woods.

But she was safe. He'd had no doubt that Nitro would get her back here, but that hadn't stopped him from worrying about all the things that could go wrong.

Like a coyote crossing the dark road out of nowhere.

Nitro could ride anything on two wheels, but sometimes bad luck happened to the best of them.

Not this time. Logan eased up behind Margaux, wanting to hold her and feel her safe in his arms, but not in front of his men. He wasn't fooling anyone when it came to her, but they had a mission, and she was going to be in the middle of it.

Party Man looked up and grinned at Logan, causing Margaux to turn.

When she did, her eyes told the tale. She was wracked with worry. She dropped the mug and dove at him.

He wrapped her up and the hell with what anyone thought. He hugged her to him.

They stayed that way for several minutes with her drawing hard breaths and him feeling at peace.

Then she hit him in the abs.

He grunted. The woman had a punch. "What was that for?"

She pushed away and unleashed her anger. "Taking off without backup. Don't put your life at risk like that. I'm not fragile dammit. Pull a stunt like that again and I'll make you pay."

She stalked off to her shack.

"You're welcome," he called out.

He got a middle finger salute for his trouble.

"You two should get a room." Party Man chuckled.

"They did," Nitro said. "Doesn't look like it did them any good."

Logan cut his eyes at Nitro. "Shut up."

"Hey, I'm on your side, Cuz."

Logan rubbed his eyes with the heel of his hand. "I know."

"But I don't think you've got a snowball's chance in hell with her right now."

Party Man laughed. Angel snickered.

Logan gave up. "Start packing. We leave in an hour."

All joking ceased. He got a round of, "You got it, Cuz," in response and everyone was moving. He'd thought about giving them a couple of hours sleep before they took off, but the helicopter that followed him wouldn't have been the Banker.

Who was the new player in this game?

He didn't know, but anyone entering the fray at this point would end up collateral damage if they got in the way.

CHAPTER 41

"Why are we meeting the Banker before we go into the convention center?" Margaux wondered aloud from the corner seating she and Logan had chosen. They had a secluded spot in the Wild Rye Café, which was doing a booming business. Location was everything in real estate and this café had the Washington State Convention Center next door.

Outside, people walked past the front windows with not a concern that their world could change in an instant if the Banker threw a kink in Logan's plan.

"I don't know why but meeting him here ten minutes before we go hot was a stipulation spelled out in the envelope," Logan answered then downed his coffee. Eyes rimmed with exhaustion, but sharp as a predator's, constantly watched everything and focused on no one person or object. Not yet.

Margaux sat next to him in the booth and kept her eyes on the door and the foot traffic.

Spring was coming in slowly to the Pacific Northwest, but these people were used to the cold. Some walked around in shorts with a sweatshirt, enjoying their sunny fifty-three degrees.

She snuggled up against his throat, drawing the glimmer of a smile until she asked, "How does all this work to get your brother free?"

"You'll see when we meet to make the trade for Wilder."

She bit down on the urge to push him for more. He appeared calm to anyone watching, but she could feel the tension vibrating off him. He was ready to get moving.

"What's plan B?" she whispered. She didn't have one for herself, but Logan should since he wasn't looking at disappearing as soon as the Banker was brought down.

That was her plan A.

No second chances. Going for broke with this one.

"Plan B would end my brother's life. Even so, I'd like to think my men will use the exit strategy we created if I order them to, but they're a hardheaded lot determined to be heroes."

She smiled over the warmth in Logan's voice when he spoke of his men. All of them a Cuz to each other. She missed Sabrina and her team. All Margaux's efforts to remain alone had failed. She'd grown attached to Slye for more than her own survival.

If that had been her only failure at maintaining total independence, she could have lived with it. But she'd given in to that same weakness when Nanci was still hunting for her after Margaux returned from Paris.

Sabrina had sent Margaux to North Carolina to snoop around for intel the DEA wanted on a suspected meth operation. Nanci's FBI team was in town at the same time to investigate an abortion clinic bombing.

Nanci was worse than a dog with a fresh bone when she was after something. Worried for her cover identity, Margaux had broken into Nanci's hotel room while the FBI was in North Carolina.

Margaux had only gone to warn Nanci to stop looking for her, that Margaux was dead to everyone back home and needed to stay dead. But Nanci screwed it up when she'd walked over and hugged Margaux. No one had hugged her in so long she hadn't known what to do. Nanci got in her face after that and said she'd protect her secret, but family was family.

They'd stayed in touch only by Margaux showing up unannounced. Nanci was fine with it. She cared too much, loved too deeply, and it had cost her.

No, you got her killed. Margaux wiped at her burning eyes. *I'm sorry, Nanci.* And Nanci would say, "Don't make the same mistake twice. Never make decisions based on emotions. Always keep the goal in sight."

Margaux had botched that when she went after the Banker in a haze of bloodlust. She'd ended up putting even more people at risk. That idiocy had been done for a while now, but the fallout was still a danger to everyone she cared about.

Now the goal was simple. Stop the Banker and save lives.

No emotion. No vengeance. No mistakes.

"There he is," Logan murmured, sitting up, alert.

Margaux's Sig Sauer 1911 hid beneath the light jacket she'd chosen for better mobility in a fight. Her hand itched to hold it right now, to gently squeeze the trigger. Two shots between the eyes and he'd be dead.

But so would Logan's brother and any intel on other operations would be lost. More innocent blood.

She brought her hands up, folding her fingers together on the table.

The Banker sat down. What a ballsy fucker. That meant he had backup somewhere in here, ready to kill her and Logan if they so much as twitched.

"My people are in place," Logan said, letting his anger push the words out hard. "What do you need so I can get moving?"

"Do you have enough manpower to ensure success?" the Banker questioned.

"This isn't the time to second guess the choice you've made. If I couldn't do this, I wouldn't have accepted the job."

"Yes, but you have not had a woman on your team until now. I've had some time to reconsider this."

Margaux clamped her jaws shut to keep from asking him if he'd like a demonstration.

She'd promised Logan she'd follow the plan and that plan did not call for her grabbing the Banker by his neck and slamming his head down on the table hard enough to crack his skull.

"What are you getting at?" Logan asked.

"I want to know if you're capable of completing this mission without her."

What was the bastard up to?

Logan answered with a sharp, "No." He must have read between the lines quicker than she had and realized where the Banker was going with this. "You're the one who insisted she be here. Her role now is integral."

"That's a shame." The Banker leaned back with his arms spread over the backs of the chairs next to him. "Because she's coming with me."

"Deal's off."

Margaux froze, wanting to shake the daylights out of Logan. He couldn't call this off now.

The Banker showed his first sign of anger when his eyes narrowed to two slits.

"Wait a minute." Margaux caught the threatening slash of Logan's glare and shoved one right back at him. "I didn't come all the way here to walk away from a big score."

A smile of satisfaction shone on the Banker's face. "See? A reasonable woman."

"What do you need her for?" Logan asked, throat muscles tight and pumped up. One wrong move and he looked ready to pounce on the blood broker.

"Insurance that you will hand over Wilder when you have him. I did not make this long in my business by leaving myself vulnerable at any point. She comes with me and when you have successfully completed both operations, we'll meet to exchange payment and Wilder for your woman."

"That wasn't part of the deal," Logan argued.

Margaux might have a better position for taking down the Banker if she was with him. The idea of spending any time in his presence while he still drew a breath turned her stomach, but she'd waded through sewers to catch a fugitive before.

Breathing the same air as the Banker couldn't be much different.

Logan could set up a fake terrorist attack and snatch Wilder without her help. He had Party Man, Ty and Moose already in place inside the convention center.

Margaux broke the tension with two words. "How much?"

The Banker quirked an eyebrow. Amused. "For what?"

"I only *accompany* a man to bed or to bodyguard, which in your case would be a bodyguard detail. I get paid well for that. If you're pulling me off this job and I can't earn my part, I want my guard fee."

"I have bodyguards."

"Not like me. I could have killed you three times since you walked in that door and neither your boy over there, or the woman in the black power suit behind us could have stopped me."

The Banker glanced at a young man dressed in grunge with iPod earphones who was rocking back and forth, but his eyes had given him away as soon as the Banker entered the cafe.

Determined to sell him all the way, Margaux made another educated guess. "The woman took too long to make a decision once she entered. Her job was to appear as if she came here every day. She doesn't have an iPhone or Blackberry going in one hand while she's sipping her coffee. What businessperson sits alone and isn't online this time of day?"

Margaux swung around to look and blinked when she noticed a hunched over guy further back.

Nick had dressed that way once.

The guy laughed at something and talked to his buddy. Not Nick. He wouldn't get this close and risk the op.

Correction. He would, but only if he had reason to.

She caught herself and finished telling the Banker about his female guard. "Plus, for someone with a body built for the runway, she's wearing an unflattering jacket. It's cut to shield her shoulder holster."

"Well done."

Like I care about impressing you? "To be honest, I'm good with this change. I'm better at killing than kidnapping."

Muscles in Logan's jaw flexed and moved. He didn't like it, but he had to play along to back her since anything else would end with the Banker walking away.

And the Banker didn't leave anybody in his wake who could squeal.

She turned to Logan and put heavy emphasis on her words to load a guilt trip. "You made a promise on this job. You can't change your mind now. This has the potential to be worth a lot more in the long run."

"She's right." The Banker thought she was talking about contracting more jobs from him, but Logan would know exactly what she meant.

Logan looked over at her, pain riding his gaze that no one could see but her.

Oh yes, he'd gotten her message.

She was going with the Banker so that Logan could make whatever deal he had in mind to trade Wilder for his brother's life. He hadn't shared his end game with her, but then she hadn't shared hers with him.

Sabrina and the team would swoop in for the capture as soon as the Banker and Wilder tried to walk away. Margaux had told Nick that was the moment to move.

Not before. *Please, not too soon.*

She had to believe that Sabrina wouldn't risk moving too soon, but if Sabrina shared this with the Feds it could all blow up at any moment.

Logan looked over at Margaux and shrugged. "You can go with him."

It was an arrogant you-belong-to-me comment that Margaux would make another man choke on, but that sold the Banker who sat forward, clasping his hands. "Excellent. You and I will negotiate your fee once I see what you can do, although I don't expect any attacks on my person today."

"I'm liking this job more all the time." Margaux grinned. *Please, keep letting your ego do your thinking.*

Logan stopped the Banker from moving when he said, "If you ever change a deal on me in midstream again, you'll regret it."

"I'll keep that in mind. If you're successful today, I won't require insurance from you again in the future."

Margaux rose and as she rounded the table, she caught the movement of Logan starting to stand. She shook her head and mouthed *trust me.*

Logan still stood and stepped over, pulling her to him. He kissed her the way a man makes a statement. The message wasn't a warning about touching her. Logan was making it clear he would exact retribution if anything happened to her.

Her heart squirmed in her chest.

The timing sucked, but she couldn't say for sure that she'd get a second chance. She whispered against his lips, "I love you."

His grip tightened, but someone—the not Nick guy—bumped them on his way out, in a rush to leave.

She pulled back and gave Logan a quick kiss and a smile, saying loud enough for the Banker, "Make me proud, baby."

Logan chuckled. "Anything for you, Sugar." The effort to hold back from calling all this off showed in Logan's knuckles that were turning white on the fist he balled.

When the Banker stepped away, Margaux fell into step beside him.

The young man with the iPod headphones appeared next to them and by the time they reached the door the female suit strode past to step in front of the Banker. Outside, two men peeled away from the wall to flank Margaux and their boss. A dark SUV that probably had armored panels and bullet resistant windows pulled up and the rear door opened.

Ninety minutes and everything would be over.

She could do this and so could Logan, if the Banker didn't throw any more surprises at them.

If he did, he'd get a first-hand view of Margaux's deadly skills. She'd keep him alive, if she could, but alive came in many forms.

CHAPTER 42

Logan hadn't thought ninety minutes would be enough time, but now it felt like every second dragged by. Changed into the dark blue suits that matched the security detail on the convention center, he moved past the real security for the convention that was focused on the crowd of three thousand waiting to hear Wilder speak.

The head of Wilder Explorations had gained millions of new friends with forward thinking that would revolutionize natural gas extraction, but he'd gained a handful of powerful enemies, too.

Once this went down, Logan would send word through his INTERPOL channels that would be relayed to the FBI. The US needed to know the truth about Wilder's drilling plans and China's part in this.

None of that would happen if he and his men didn't make it out of here with Wilder.

The Feds would be all over this building once the Banker made the call to report a bomb threat.

Logan's cell phone buzzed. He answered, "All set, Cuz?"

Nitro confirmed, "All quiet here. This is some boring shit."

"Consider it comp time."

"Funny. No one has come out of the operations building since three of them showed up this morning with donuts. Nobody brings me donuts on a job."

Logan passed a security guard who gave him a long look and Logan nodded back as if saying, "Carry on." Must have worked. The guy turned back to where the emcee was wrapping up his introductions and everyone was clapping.

When the noise died down, Nitro said, "Got a wide-open area. Good view for a quarter mile in any direction. Based on the information our sponsor supplied, this should be fine for the party."

Nitro was saying he and Angel had secured the area. No one could stroll up into the strike zone without Angel or Nitro seeing them well in advance with enough time to intercept and send them away from the drill site.

Logan still had a bad feeling in his gut about this. He didn't like splitting up his team and was close to a meltdown over allowing Margaux to walk out with the Banker. But there would be no Wilder to hand over if she was so much as scratched when he saw her again.

"Cuz?"

Dammit. No mental wandering. "All good. Just make sure no one changes the plan."

"You got it."

Logan hung up as he reached the access door to the bowels of the convention center. He locked it behind him and worked his way to the level where service people pushed flatbed carts filled with miscellaneous equipment and furniture. Someone passed him carrying an elaborate floral display that trailed a sweet scent to mix with the concrete and cardboard warehouse smells.

He spotted all six "bombs" hidden right where he'd directed Party Man to place them. None of them would explode, but only a pro would be able to determine if they were genuine at first glance. Party Man had used cold pyrotechnics for the one that had been placed to 'ignite' next to the power center.

When that one went off, it would make noise and put on a show.

That was the spot the Banker would send law enforcement first—to find a bomb.

Logan reached the door that would lead to the side of the stage where Wilder was talking.

Party Man, Ty and Moose were standing with the rigid posture of security and had curly wires running to their ears, but only to listen to the security's chatter. Not to talk.

Wilder had images flashing on a large screen behind him. His enthusiasm over a new way of accessing resources was contagious. The audience clapped, leaned forward listening, then clapped again.

Logan intended to see Wilder get what he deserved after the

way he'd planned to screw this country. Wilder had a shock of blond hair that he brushed back with his hand at times. He smiled and had a rugged look to him, like he went out and drilled the sites himself. At thirty-eight, he had a future here that most men would envy, but he was greedy.

In eleven minutes, he'd get everything he wanted.

Until the Feds locked him up.

CHAPTER 43

Margaux followed the Banker into the elevator that filled up quickly with his four guards. Overkill considering they'd taken away her Sig the minute she stepped into the Banker's car.

The eighteen-story building they were now in had appeared to be under renovations in the lobby. She played it as relaxed as she could, considering the circumstances, and asked, "Is there a restaurant here?"

"No. Not for another few months."

"Where are we going?"

"You've heard the term bird's eye view, right?"

She rolled her eyes. "Yes."

"I want a front row seat to the show."

He had a spot where they could watch Logan? That might not be so bad. She stepped out of the elevator car at the top floor and the six of them walked through a hall to a door. On the other side were metal steps that went up ten feet to a landing. The guard leading them opened the door and held it as they all stepped out into a brisk wind.

No matter how calm it was on the ground, it was always windy up top.

The building was an old mix of glass and steel. Nothing special and a squatty shape that took up most of a block, but it did have a wide-open roof.

The Banker strolled over to the edge and stopped at the parapet that came up to his waist. He looked down.

One push and she could watch his head crack open like an egg.

The guards fanned out in a half-circle behind him, all within ten feet, weapons handy. What good would standing there do if someone had a sniper rifle?

Of course, someone would have to know the Banker was coming up here.

She walked over to him. "How'd you know we could come up here?"

"I had someone acquire this building just for the view."

She caught the smirk in his tone. He was so proud of his ability to snap his fingers and make people jump. She wondered if he'd been behind something else. "Just like you had someone chase us in a helicopter through downtown Denver after our initial meeting with you?"

"Of course, but that was unsuccessful. Unfortunate for those I'd paid."

"I hope China's making it worth your time for this." Because they would have diplomatic issues out the wazoo once this got out.

The Banker turned to lean his hip against the wall. "China isn't paying for anything."

Warning bells clanged so loudly Margaux thought her head would burst. She kept her composure, barely. "Trust me, Dragan doesn't give a shit whose money ends up his pocket. He only wants to know that it's going to be paid on time."

For the first time since meeting the Banker, he broke out a genuine smile. The kind a person had when he realized everything he'd ever wanted in life was coming true.

Not the expression Margaux wanted to see on his face right now. "Something funny?"

"Yes. You and Dragan are quite the pair. I would have been happy finding one of you, but both was unexpected." He'd put on sunshades, but now he pulled them off, squinting a moment in the glaring overcast skies. "Did you really think Snake Eyes could locate someone like me, Duke?"

No. This couldn't be happening.

Margaux's skin felt clammy. She started searching back in her mind to before she walked into the Trophy Room. Logan told her the Banker had set up the kidnapping as a test.

It hadn't been just for Logan.

"Ah, I see you're figuring it out." The Banker stood there, confident of his immortality. "It took some arranging, but I only sent you in to see what Dragan would do if he thought you were the contact. I had no idea you two would team up and make this job even more delightful."

Her insides were shaking.

After all this, Sabrina and the team were still going to be hunted down.

And Logan was in a trap.

She had to keep her wits about her and find out how much trouble Logan and his guys were in then she had to get away from the Banker to help everyone. Before that happened, she needed intel. "You're not so clever, you know. You don't have Wilder yet."

"Wilder is unimportant to me. He and his drilling patents just need to go away. All I have to do is to make sure that when this is done Wilder is considered a terrorist and that this country fears his drilling technology enough to shut it down for years."

He didn't need Wilder? "So what? You're just going to call the Feds in on Dragan and Wilder? Dragan's too smart to be caught. He'll sacrifice Wilder and get his men out."

"Oh, he'll try. But he won't be able to leave a city that is panicked."

"Over a bomb scare? It'll cause some traffic issues down here, but that's not enough to stop Dragan." She taunted him with a smile. *Come on, Banker, get pissed.*

He lost his happy face. "That's the problem with peons like you and Dragan. You think so small. At the same moment that I have someone calling in the bomb threat at the convention center, I also have someone calling in the explosion at Wilder's drilling site."

"So? The drill site is fifty-seven miles south of here."

"And close enough to a fault line for a potential earthquake."

She gave him a frown of disbelief and waved her hand in dismissal. "Isn't that a stretch? Fracturing isn't the big threat it's touted to be if they're careful about how they flood the water and chemicals through the system."

He twirled his glasses, too comfortable again. "Yes. In a normal operation, the charges set to break up shale are minor and controlled. But Wilder's technology drills a diagonal off the horizontal cut. He also creates wider holes in the charge points by setting off multiple charges in one area that are not deep. The idea is to then shoot a lot of mini explosions from there, creating longer but thinner cracks in the shale. All very clever and green conscious."

Time was wasting. She needed a damn sketch, and he was painting the big picture. "Is there a point to this geological lesson? I'm still not seeing the punch line."

"The technicians sabotaging Wilder's signature site will shove a specially developed explosive down the hole that will detonate in a continual charge. The earthquake at that point is only a fifty-fifty possibility, but once the drill site blows it will take a very long time to determine exactly what happened. Those technicians believe they will activate the charges and walk out before they're in any danger, because they have no idea what they've sent down in that hole."

"You're going to kill the techs."

"And let's not forget Dragan's two men. Never, ever, leave witnesses."

Oh, shit. Nitro and Angel were going in expecting to kidnap techs and they'd rush into a detonation. She saw red. Blood red. She could kill the Banker. Right now. His guards would mow her down, but this abomination would be dead.

"You're thinking about killing me. But you won't."

"Oh, why not?"

"Because you and Dragan are more than business partners. You're a woman in love and he has that crazy-eyed, touch-her-and-you'll-die look. I'm willing to bet you won't commit suicide by attacking me if there's a chance to save Dragan. And there's always a chance. Just like when you two were in the jungle."

He was right. She wouldn't let Logan down by letting emotions control her decisions.

The Banker explained, "Dragan has until the first news report leaks about a possible earthquake along the Cascadia Subduction Zone that runs parallel to the Pacific coast. That is not just possible, but probable. The tsunami that hit Japan struck less than an hour after the earthquake."

He couldn't be serious. "You can't know that exploding that drill site will set off any earthquake, much less one large enough to cause a tidal wave."

"Oh, please. Give me more credit than that. I would never leave anything up to chance. I have one more trick up my sleeve you haven't seen yet, but you will."

He was serious. He had a plan to launch a tsunami on the Pacific Northwest.

His watch started beeping. "Show time."

Margaux struggled not to throw up. She had no way to warn Logan or Nitro.

Another thought slammed her in the solar plexus.

Sabrina and the team would be here.

A helicopter approached fast from the south. This location made more complete sense now. The Banker was exiting by air.

Margaux had to figure out how he intended to create a tsunami and stop him. She had her doubts, but not enough to waste time thinking about possibilities when this man dealt in absolutes.

She wouldn't underestimate a death merchant who had built his reputation on never making a threat he couldn't back.

CHAPTER 44

Nick stared down Josh and Tanner who glared at him while they waited on the call from Talia. He repeated, "She'll come through. She's invested."

"Sabrina sent two full teams to Seattle on the word of a woman you met one time."

Nick shouldn't have told Sabrina about Talia, but Sabrina wouldn't have mobilized a team without all the information. Talia had called to tell him Margaux would be in downtown Seattle today and forced to play a role in a terrorist plot.

His phone buzzed. "Start talking."

"Dragan and his team are planting fake bombs as a cover to kidnap Svenson Wilder. You have thirteen minutes to intercept him. If it were me, I'd pull Wilder out through the loading docks if they plan to exit once a bomb alert is released."

"Where?"

"Washington State Convention Center. Three thousand in attendance."

"You're sure the bombs are fake?"

"I'm sure the intel is good, but I can't be sure about what's planted without looking at them in person. Don't forget our deal."

"I won't."

Nick snapped the phone shut. "Call Ryder and tell him to bring the other four Sabrina hired to the back loading docks of the convention center. Let's go." He led the charge to the loading docks for the convention center but couldn't take the chance of faulty intel.

He told Josh, "Call in a bomb threat for the convention center. We're going in locked and loaded as soon as we have everyone."

If SWAT showed up, things would get dicey since Nick and his team were wearing the same gear, right down to protective face shields that were tinted to protect their identity.

CHAPTER 45

Keeping an eye on Wilder as he strutted back and forth across the stage, pointing as images scrolled on the mega-screen, Logan explained to Moose, Ty and Party Man why Margaux wasn't with him.

Moose had thick eyebrows on his wide forehead. He pushed one up. "She did that? Took one for the team?"

"Yes."

Party Man leaned over to Moose. "Still thinking about ways to torture her?"

Moose hesitated a second too long and Logan cleared up any confusion. "No one touches her."

That drew a smirk from Moose who had just baited Logan.

He wasn't in a joking mood. "Two minutes."

His men took their positions, moving closer to the stage to wait for an interruption from security that would send people out due to a bomb threat.

Logan and his men would step up to escort Wilder. They'd take a route back through the service area where they had a GMC Yukon waiting that Party Man had already confirmed as on site. From that point—

An explosion rocked the room.

Party Man shook his head. "Not my shit, Cuz. Wrong location, too."

People were standing up at their seats and looking around, not sure what they'd just heard and felt. Security was rushing around, hands at their ears listening.

Logan took in Wilder who had that confused dog look. Why wasn't he anxious and searching the security to see who was going to kidnap him?

Another blast hit further away.

People started running for the exits, shoving and yelling.

"Let's get him," Logan told his men and leaped up on the stage to hook Wilder by the arm before the star of the show took off toward the exit.

Wilder's face had lost color. "What's happening?"

He sounded genuinely terrified.

Logan kept his voice professional. "We're going to escort you out, Mr. Wilder. Just come with us."

Security was ushering the attendees out but two of them were fighting against the tide to get to the stage.

Party Man held his ear and announced, "Exits are getting blocked. We need to go."

Logan put his hand up in a stop motion, hoping those two security guards were too busy to argue. Then he gave Wilder a tug.

Wilder didn't balk this time. "Hurry up. Let's get out of here."

"Just stay calm, Mr. Wilder," Logan told him as they moved to the service exit.

As soon as they reached the service area, Logan pulled his Glock 21 and stopped Wilder. "We're taking you to the Banker."

"What Banker?"

Logan got that sick kicked-in-the-nuts feeling. "The one who cut the deal between you and China."

"Who the fuck are you people?" Wilder tried to back up, but Moose was there shoving him back toward Logan. "I don't have a fucking deal with China."

"Drop your weapons. Hands in the air!" shouted from behind Logan.

A SWAT team in tactical gear and carrying M4 Carbines converged on them from every direction.

Logan lowered his weapon to the concrete floor and raised his hands.

One of them stepped up ahead of the others and removed his face shield. Hard eyes that gave no quarter stared back. "Where are the bombs, Dragan?"

Fuck me.

CHAPTER 46

The Banker's helicopter had lifted off amid a buzz of news helicopters hurrying toward the news story of the day at the convention center.

It all played out so normally, right down to the pilot calling in his flight path and getting approval.

Margaux sat between two of the Banker's guards, but she could hear him talking to someone on his sat phone.

He listened a moment then said, "Everything's right on time. Call me as soon as the drill site blows then you've got forty-five minutes to clear out."

He turned around. Just couldn't get enough gloating in. "I do love when everything goes according to plan."

She'd seen a real bomb blow out second-story windows at the convention center as the chopper had lifted off. "Why send in a team with real bombs if you're so sure Dragan will be caught with Wilder?"

"It's bad to threaten a fake terrorist attack. Word might get out that I was involved and that could reflect badly on my reputation."

Something had bothered her since leaving downtown. "Why Dragan? You don't hit me as a man who does something without gaining plenty of benefit from a deal."

"It's taken a while to lure Dragan Stoli into my web. He crossed me nine years ago when he destroyed my entire operation. I was just rolling good. I was well on my way to becoming a legend when he wiped me out."

A legend in your own mind. But she wanted to know how he and Logan were connected so she let him talk.

"I swore he would pay. It took me all this time. He's not easy to draw out of hiding. I had to use his brother Yuri. I have not decided if I will let him linger in prison or terminate him, but I spent a great deal of money to frame Yuri. I need a return on my investment in pain and suffering."

She was speechless. The Banker knew who Logan was if he

knew who his brother was.

The Banker nodded. "We go way back. He forgot about me, but I never forgot about him. This is going to be the trifecta of all plays. I'm paid to ensure Wilder Explorations is a nonentity, that the relationship between China and the US is put in conflict and, as a bonus, I land Logan Baklanov and Margaux Duke. Logan actually thinks he's going to trade me to the Russian Federation for his brother. I'm insulted they would place such a low value on my capture."

So that was Logan's end game. He'd planned to capture the Banker for the Russians.

Sabrina and the team would be his next target. The Banker was going to murder everyone Margaux cared about. He'd started with Nanci.

He had an audience and wasn't letting it go. "But you want to know what makes this one of my premier events?"

"What?" She asked out of habit to get information more than caring at this point. What more could he possibly do?

"I've had two thousand feet of deep charges set into the part of the Cascadia Subduction Zone that runs closest to the Pacific Northwest. Took seventeen months to do that. Engineers in Germany have guaranteed me when I send the detonation signal to those explosives, there *will* be a massive earthquake and there *will* be a tsunami. Every model they created shows a wave great enough to wipe out everything from the coast all the way through Seattle. It might even set off a second earthquake along the Seattle fault, but that wasn't part of the deal. Just a potential extra."

Please let me have one chance at his throat. "Who can ensure that?"

"People with small children and wives they want to keep alive. They won't be wrong. You'll see as soon as we get airborne. I received word the drill site explosion was a success. I needed cause and effect. First the drill site is compromised. Then the threat of an earthquake. Then a real earthquake. No one will question that it was caused by the failure at the Wilder drilling site. That will send drilling in this country back to the dark ages."

She wanted to shove every smug word from his mouth down his throat. It wasn't enough just to kill innocent people. He intended to wipe out an entire state.

Nitro and Angel were already dead.

With no way to get out of the city, Dragan, Party Man, Ty and Moose would end up captured.

They wouldn't go to prison. They'd all die with Sabrina and the team when the tsunami hit.

The Banker had made a bad calculation. Margaux had nothing left to live for if those people died. The Banker controlled the detonation, but only if she didn't stop him.

She would watch for her chance and take it.

The helicopter began its descent to a mid-size airfield with a set of hangars and three buildings on one side. A Learjet was parked on the far side of the runway as if it owned the place.

Or maybe the Banker had paid to have the only flight in or out today. That wouldn't surprise her.

When they landed, the guard squad stepped out and surrounded them. They walked as a unit, facing away from the Banker as he strolled toward the Lear that glowed white against a forest of evergreen backdrop.

CHAPTER 47

"What the hell's going on?" Logan barked at the man who identified himself as Nick, a friend of Margaux's. But that was only after Dragan showed them a fake bomb and convinced Nick the Banker had double-crossed him and Margaux.

He'd heard from Nitro and Angel, who had followed his instructions and pick up the technicians exactly on time and exited safely. The drilling site blew with three minutes to spare.

Nick was driving Logan, Party Man, Ty and Moose in a paneled van with two of Nick's men in the back covering them with M4s, because Nick wasn't letting his guard down until he was convinced Dragan was telling the truth.

Some techie named Dingo was on the radio, giving Nick directions as Dingo cleared traffic and routed him out of Seattle heading west.

Nick scowled at him and took another curve on two wheels at the same time while he punched numbers into a computer mounted to the dash. "Can you feed the video to me?"

The voice known as Dingo called back, "Workin' on it, mate. They're out of the chopper and headed for the Lear."

Logan watched the monitor that flickered then the image of a sleek white aircraft came into focus. The Banker's four people covered Margaux and the Banker, walking them to the jet. "Where is that?"

"About five miles south of the city."

Party Man called out from the back, "How'd you know they'd be there?"

Nick cursed at a driver that was half on and half off the road then answered Party Man. "I dropped a tracker on Margaux at the café while your boss was trying to swallow her tongue."

Logan recalled the moment and snarled, "If the Banker had found that tracker he'd have killed her."

"The alternative is not knowing where she is right now, so I don't fucking want to hear it." He punched the accelerator when he hit the interstate, and the van took off like an Indy racer. "Our team had eyes on her when the chopper took off from the downtown building and caught the flight plan. We had someone alter the security camera to keep eyes on the Lear."

"Shots fired!" Dingo called out.

Logan leaned down to the monitor and watched a horror show unveil. "*No, don't ...*"

CHAPTER 48

The Learjet sparkled like a jewel in the sun. That was the end game for the Banker that Margaux couldn't let happen.

The Banker's four-person guard squad held their positions as a unit as they approached the jet.

No help in any direction.

Margaux didn't need it.

She stumbled, going down to her knee. One of the guards whipped around and grabbed her arm to yank her up.

The Banker turned, grin in place.

She shoved up hard, head butting the guard and wrenched his weapon.

The power suit woman dove toward her boss. The Banker grabbed her to use as a shield.

Margaux took her out first, then the next closest guard as he shot back.

Something hot burned Margaux's arm. Her good one, dammit.

Shots fired everywhere, hitting the Lear and the other two guards. Who was shooting now?

Margaux turned her weapon on the Banker. If she stopped the tsunami, Logan might survive. If he did, she couldn't destroy the chance for saving his brother. She shot the Banker in the leg. More bullets peppered around her.

The Banker froze, grabbed at his chest and fell backwards.

That wasn't supposed to happen.

He couldn't die. Logan needed that miserable death merchant. She took a step toward the Banker and felt the bite of something hit her hip. She ran forward.

Sirens and cars exploded onto the runway.

She took two more steps that dragged.

Her vision swam. She couldn't be losing blood that fast, could she? Her adrenaline would ... would ...

She crashed face first onto the pavement, staring at the Banker who finally stopped smiling.

He wasn't breathing.

Don't die, you miserable dog. Not yet. Logan needed him.

But she couldn't move to check his pulse or try to keep him alive. She was the one dying. Her body wasn't even trying to move. Her heartbeat had been racing. It was slowing down with each tiny breath she took.

Someone shouted and two fingers touched her neck.

Too late. She closed her eyes.

CHAPTER 49

Logan stared at the video feed on the monitor in horror. It all happened in seconds and Margaux was down. "Get up, Sugar. Get up. *Get the fuck up!*"

Black vehicles slammed into view. Everyone jumped out with FBI on their windbreakers.

Logan wanted to reach inside the monitor and pull Margaux to him. "Get out of the way," he shouted at someone on the screen who was standing in front of Margaux's prone body.

A female agent came up and the asshole moved. The woman put her fingers on Margaux's throat. One second ticked off. Then another and another while he gripped the sides of the monitor.

The female Fed turned to a man who must have asked her something. He pointed at Margaux and the woman shook her head then stood up and walked off.

Logan jerked on the monitor. "No. Go back. She's alive."

Everyone in the van was quiet.

No matter how much Logan tried to will her to move, Margaux just lay there. Not breathing.

The feed died and he beat the dash with his fists until he crushed it and his fists were bloody. Tears stung. The pain was like nothing he'd ever endured.

He'd let his team get fingered for a terrorist attack.

He couldn't save his brother.

And he'd lost *her*.

CHAPTER 50

Chatton watched the sun set on the Pacific Ocean. People in Seattle had suffered damage she couldn't prevent but it could have been a wasteland at this minute. Instead, a catastrophe was prevented today. She waited for the clicking to stop that ensured she and Wayan had a secure line.

When he came on, she said, "You dodged a nasty bullet today."

"I had very disturbing phone calls over the past hour," Wayan said.

"Understandable, since the attack in Seattle is only six hours old, but the calls have ceased, right?"

"Yes."

"That's because it takes time to maneuver the details so that the truth comes out. The Banker intended for the US to believe that Russia had been behind the terrorist attack funded by China to put your relationship with the US and Russia in conflict. I have averted that disaster. True?"

"Yes, but what of the Amber Room panel?"

Amazing. The man's country has just barely managed to avoid a military conflict with the United States, and he's worried about a bloody artifact. She really had to get her hands on that piece. "It's beyond the General's reach. At the moment, he is busy trying to explain an email that was sent to his Pentagon computer from the Banker. A traceable email."

"He will turn that around on someone else."

True, but she'd enjoyed sending it. "You now know who is devoted to revealing Orion's Legacy."

"And I presume my information on how to get to the Banker's helicopter pilot was useful."

"Very much so." The pilot turned out to be a stand-up guy and that had been the weak link in the Banker's organization. The Banker's guards had hired an out-of-work pilot who had just lost his home, offering him enough money to ignore what he saw since they wouldn't leave him alive. Once Chatton got to the pilot and explained how he would be making his last flight ever unless he followed her instructions, the pilot was all too happy to do her bidding. He relayed the flight plan to a ground team and took a wide arc around news helicopters that had been unnecessary.

As promised in their agreement, Chatton had located the pilot's significant other and moved that partner to a nice place in the Caribbean where he waited for the pilot to arrive.

"I must go," Wayan said just before the line disconnected.

Chatton smiled with satisfaction she hadn't enjoyed since meeting the General and Wayan. She punched in another number.

"What?"

"Hello, Nick. I kept my end of the deal." She scratched at the edge of her latex mask but wouldn't take it off until she was finished with the Banker.

"It didn't go down exactly as expected."

"These things never do."

"What time will I get the Banker back?"

She looked over at the building where the Banker waited for her. "I'll call you tomorrow, as agreed."

"He'll be able to talk."

"Yes, he should be quite the conversationalist by then."

"Good. I've got everyone up my ass for him right now."

Chatton turned and headed back to the building, smiling. This Nick was some character. "Don't forget you owe me."

"You'll have your favor. I always pay my debts."

CHAPTER 51

"Get up. Time to roll."

Margaux had always known she'd end up going to hell, but she hadn't expected Nick to go with her. She opened her eyes and blinked.

Paneled walls. A comfortable bed. Modest furniture. Hell had decent rooms. She looked to her left to find Nick leaned back against a door, arms crossed. "Water?"

Nick came over and poured a plastic cup half full.

She held it in a trembling hand until he put his fingers on hers to steady the cup. "That's enough."

"What time is it?"

"Two in the afternoon, give or take a few minutes."

"I've been out for twelve hours?"

"You've been out for thirty-two hours while Singleton monitored you. He managed to keep both of your feet out of the grave."

Leave it to Nick to give it to her straight, but she appreciated that and what Singleton had done. She had a feeling she owed many more thanks. "I'm clearly missing a few details. Want to tell me what happened?"

He put the cup down. "What do you remember?"

"Fighting with the Banker's guard. Lot of shooting. I got hit in the arm." She rubbed her hip. "Feel like a pincushion. I must have been hit there, too."

"Yeah, that's where Sabrina shot you."

"I didn't hear that right." Margaux pushed up on her elbows, moving the most-recently injured arm slowly. Just had to be the other one this time.

"Sabrina had some test ammo from her friend."

"More stuff from what's his name ... Tigger?"

"Right. He's filed for a patent on ammo that carries drugs like tranquilizer darts do."

"Thought someone else had a patent on that."

"They do, but Tigger's bullet design is different. Anyhow,

he loaded different drugs and she used one on you that was supposed to slow your heartbeat enough you couldn't function, but would send you to the hospital."

"Thought I'd died."

"Sabrina wasn't sure she hadn't killed you. The first Fed called you dead. Fortunately, White Hawk and Singleton showed up with an ambulance and hauled you off before the Feds called the morgue."

She hurt everywhere. "So now I'm a guinea pig?"

"You're a live guinea pig. Lucky for you she agreed to test the ammo or she wouldn't have had it."

Margaux would have to think on that one, because feeling her heart slow down had been hairy. "Hey, I'm not complaining when the alternative was to end up jailed as a terrorist, but she should tell her friend to work on a smaller diameter round." Margaux sat all the way up and flinched at the headache. She wouldn't be head butting anyone else for a while.

"Need help getting to the john?"

"No. At least, I hope not." She swung her feet around and lowered herself to the floor, pushing up to stand. She listed to the left.

Nick made a move.

She held up her hand then noticed she had on a soft gray tank top and sweatpants. By the time she reached the bathroom, she felt her step get stronger. Shutting the door, she glanced at the mirror.

"So that's why my cheek hurts." She had a greenish-blue bruise on the side where she'd hit the pavement. The scary hair could be fixed with a shower. She turned on the hot water and took her time in the steamy space.

Fifteen minutes later, she'd brushed her teeth and her damp hair, put on the T-shirt and jeans that had been waiting in the bathroom and looked more human than she had coming in.

She didn't do makeup unless the job called for it.

And she no longer had a job. Not with Slye.

Swallowing her pride was tough with the lump in her throat.

No whining. This was no one's fault but hers. She would accept whatever Sabrina handed her and thank her for it.

She stepped back into the room. No clothes to pack. No weapon to holster. To mentally prepare herself, she asked Nick, "What's she going to do with me?"

"I'm in enough hot water for sharing intel with you."

"Good point. Sorry, Nick. I appreciate all you did." The question she'd been avoiding wouldn't wait any longer. "Any word on Dragan and his men?"

"You mean Logan?"

Guess his cover was totally blown. Thinking of him as Dragan hurt. But hearing Logan's name made her eyes swim for a moment.

Stop thinking about him.

That would be her goal for the next hundred years.

To find a minute that she didn't think about Logan.

"What was the deal between you two?" Nick asked.

Guess he wasn't going to share any intel on Logan either. She pushed a handful of hair off her face. "We go way back. I met him in France when I was still capable of caring about someone the way I felt for him. He was—" *Sweet, loving ... special.* She cleared her throat. "He was different."

"You don't think you'll feel that again?"

"Not for anyone else." She had to change the subject, or she'd do something insane like cry. She hadn't hurt this bad since losing Nanci. "How'd Sabrina manage to get my body away?"

"That was easy. We pulled you out of the ambulance down the road and blew it up." Nick grinned at that.

"What about the Banker? Did he make it?"

"Barely, but yes. Sabrina shot him with a tranq, too. We smeared a bloody trail to make it look like he'd been dragged off. That explained what happened to everyone else."

Maybe Logan came out of this with the Banker. "But what did happen to him?"

"I had to hand him off to a woman who helped us find you. But he's not going to be a problem for anyone ever again."

Her heart sank at that. Logan had probably ended up in prison as a terrorist and his brother would die in Siberia.

She held up a hand. "Nothing is ever free. Did Sabrina have to give up anything else for me?"

"No."

"Nobody owes a debt from this?"

"I do, but I'm looking forward to finding out what it is."

That would sound normal coming from only one person. Nick.

He looked at his watch. "Might want to get moving. Sabrina's waiting."

Margaux grabbed a light jacket thrown across the bed and Nick helped her put it on. She was headed to some form of lockup, but she really didn't care anymore.

Anywhere without Logan would be a prison.

Nick kept the pace slow as they wound their way through a long hallway that looked familiar. When he stopped at a door, Margaux realized where she was. "This is the basement of Slye."

"Yep." He opened the door to the war room.

The room was full of agents who called out greetings and came up to hug her. Margaux fought back the surge of emotion clogging her throat. Her eyes stung, but she would not allow a tear to fall. Not even when the idea of walking away from her Slye team was killing her. She'd done this to herself and would face the consequences with what dignity she had left.

She owed it to everyone here to make this as easy as possible.

Sabrina stood at the back of the room leaning against the wall, arms crossed. When everyone settled back into their seats, she said, "Four people were badly injured in the bombings, but no deaths. Seattle did suffer a mild earthquake."

Margaux argued, "But he didn't detonate the sunken charges."

"I know." Sabrina walked around the long conference table as she spoke. "The Navy has a SEAL team that found the charges. It would have very likely caused a major earthquake as a minimum and a tsunami at worst. Seattle was spared a terrible disaster."

Something to feel good about finally. Margaux had made more than her share of mistakes, but her father was wrong about her being nothing. She'd saved lives and *that* was something.

She turned to the agents. "Thank you all for what you did. There were times I didn't deserve your support, but I got it. I won't say I'll never make stupid mistakes again, because we're talking about me after all."

They chuckled, but there were nods of appreciation around the room.

Sabrina had made it all the way to Margaux's end of the table. She hugged her and Margaux had to blink to keep her eyes dry. She told Sabrina, "Thank you for being my friend no matter what."

"Always."

Then Sabrina stood back. That was the closest to touchy feely she had ever been that Margaux knew of. Sabrina said, "Time to hand you off."

Margaux cut her eyes at Nick who had a noncommittal expression. Guess this was it. "Goodbye."

"Goodbyes" and "Stay out of trouble," echoed around the room.

They all wished her well and seemed happy for her to be leaving. Really?

This sort of sucked. *No sad faces.* Margaux took a deep breath and nodded at Sabrina. "I'm ready."

She followed Sabrina out the door and down to a private room Margaux had been in for planning sessions. Sabrina opened the door and Margaux followed, her eyes on the floor until Sabrina said, "You can do what you say, right?"

A male voice replied, "Already done."

Margaux's head snapped up.

Logan was standing there, shaking hands with Sabrina who turned around and told Margaux, "We'll talk before you leave."

She left and closed the door behind her.

Logan didn't say a word.

Margaux's heart was trying to beat its way out of her chest. She swallowed and found her voice. "What's going on?"

His lips moved, but he seemed to struggle to find the right words until he finally said, "I love you, Sugar."

She leaped into his arms, and he caught her, kissing her face and hair. Tears streamed down her face. She didn't know what was going on, but as long as she was in Logan's arms she didn't care.

He held her that way for a while, kissing her and whispering how glad he was to hold her again. When he lowered her back to stand, he kissed her once more with a sweetness that rocked her and cupped her face in his hands. "I watched you die. I thought I'd never get to touch you again."

A tear ran down his cheek.

"No one will tell me what's going on. Are you on the run or what, Logan?"

His eyes twinkled. "I owe Sabrina for helping me extract my team and for her people catching the true bombers that the Banker sent in."

"I'm still amazed at what she and the team did."

"She brought an army to save you."

Margaux had never been a watering pot, but she'd also never realized how much she was loved. Everyone had come to her aid, but she'd let Logan down. The Banker was gone. "I tried to keep the Banker alive and stop him, too."

His arms tightened around her. "You almost died trying to do that."

"What about your brother?"

"Nick had to give the Banker to someone who'd fed him intel, but he got the bastard back twenty-four hours later. Sabrina and I came to an agreement when I assured her the Banker would never be able to harm anyone again and in exchange for giving me the Banker, I would give any aid to protect the US in the future. I negotiated a trade for my brother and sent the Banker to Russia with my men. They're bringing my brother back here."

"Yuri will be here?"

"Yes, with my mother and sisters."

"Are *they* here? In Atlanta?" Margaux was starting to sound like an idiot.

"Not in Atlanta. There's a lot I have yet to tell you."

Her heart fell. "That's why Sabrina gave us this time. So we could talk before I went away."

"Oh, Sugar, I'm never going to lose you again." He hugged her and kissed her again, longer this time.

She put her hand on his lips. "I don't want to lose you either, but there are things you don't know. I can't stay with Sabrina."

"No, you can't. In fact, Margaux Duke doesn't exist anymore."

"What do you mean?"

"She officially died in an ambulance back in Seattle. Fingerprints found at the Trophy Room and in Paris have vanished." He brushed his hand over her hair. "You don't exist anywhere."

"What are you saying, Logan?"

"I do occasional work for INTERPOL, special projects. I've built a profile for you there like mine and my men's that will protect you in the future. But just like with the WITSEC program, you can never go home."

"There's nothing for me there. The Banker killed my only family. I don't want to go back to where I grew up." It felt like a stampede going on in her chest. "Are you saying I can stay with you?"

"If you want. If you don't—" He caught her when she leaped again and squealed, kissing him everywhere she could reach.

He was laughing. "And here I thought you'd miss Atlanta."

What about her Slye family? She was torn between wanting to be with Logan and losing touch with people she cared about. He'd said she couldn't go home, but what about Atlanta? She asked, "Uhm, now that you know Sabrina, is there any chance—"

"Yes."

"You don't know what I was going to say."

His eyes twinkled. "Yes, I do. You want to know if you'll ever be able to come back here. Sabrina and I have talked. I'll tell you more later, but we've agreed to share resources when necessary for a common goal. For a bunch of covert agents, they've sure got a mushy side, because I had to threaten your team with bodily harm if they said a word to you before I got a chance to tell you all of this myself. They know you aren't leaving them forever."

If Margaux wasn't so happy, she'd give them grief over letting her think they were happy she was leaving.

Logan brushed his hand over her hair and smiled with such raw happiness her heart did a flip. He teased, "Sabrina might pay me for taking you off her hands. We decided that you can be our liaison as well as my better half."

Margaux stopped and looked him in the eyes. That sounded like some safe, stashed away position. "I'll never be wife material. I'm not cut out for weddings and staying home or doing normal wife things."

"Do I look like I'm ready to settle down yet?"

"No, but I don't want to be left behind or stuck somewhere safe. I'll be miserable."

"You don't think I know that by now?" He turned serious. "It would kill me if anything ever happened to you, but only a fool would try to make you be someone you're not. I love who you are and how you make me feel. I would marry you in a minute, but if you're not ready for that I want you with me any way I can have you, Sugar."

"What about the team?" If she had to be there just because she was the boss's woman, that was okay because she wanted Logan no matter what. But it would suck to be on the fringes of the work she'd come to love.

"They know about this, and they respect you more than you can imagine. I told them I would go solo if they didn't want this and they all voted to keep the both of us."

She arched an eyebrow at him. "They want me on your team? Even Moose?"

"Especially Moose. Nobody's ever had the skill to get the drop on him before. After you put your life on the line for the team, his was the first yes vote." He grinned. "Just don't taze him again."

Could a heart burst from happy overload? She was willing to test hers. "I love you, Logan."

"I love you, Sugar."

"You have to take me just the way I am." She needed him to understand. This man was all she wanted and needed, but she was no prize. Nothing, according to her father.

"I wouldn't change a thing. You're exceptional."

Looking into his eyes, she felt as special as he made her sound. But she wasn't through negotiating. "And no sticking me with pansy-ass assignments."

"Whatever we have to face, we do it together," he told her, using the words she'd given him in the jungle when they escaped.

She shuddered at that memory. "But no more jungles."

He kissed her cheek and whispered, "Not this week."

What?

THE END

Keep reading for an excerpt of DECEPTIVE TREASURES.

Thank you for reading my book.
I hope you enjoyed it and would appreciate a review
wherever you buy books.

You can order signed and personalized copies at
www.**DiannaLoveSignedBooks**.com

To be notified first about any news, new releases,
and special deals, sign up for Dianna's occasional
newsletter at
www.AuthorDiannaLove.com

The complete Slye Team Black Ops romantic thriller series:
Prequel: Last Chance To Run
Book 1: Nowhere Safe
Book 2: Honeymoon To Die For
Book 3: Kiss The Enemy
Book 4: Deceptive Treasures
Book 5: Stolen Vengeance
Book 6: Fatal Promise

DECEPTIVE TREASURES

While leading an extraction team deep inside North Korea, Tanner watches his escape route disintegrate minutes after encountering a suspicious female who claims she knows another way out of the dangerous country ... if she can exit with his team.

CHAPTER ONE

Tanner Bodine stared at the three heat signatures on the thermal-imaging camera and cursed.

The idea was to *not* kill anyone tonight.

I should have known this mission was rolling along too easily. Not that there had been a damned thing easy about a HAHO, or high altitude, high opening, night jump into North Korea four hours ago. Now his team crouched behind an unfinished concrete wall in the one country no one should enter without an invitation.

Definitely no American.

If he and the other three Slye team operatives got caught while they were gate-crashing Pyongyang's annual citywide April celebration, the fallout would be bad. Much worse than just having the US government deny knowledge of this mission.

Tanner's team would be painted as nothing more than mercenaries trying to kidnap two North Korean physicists for financial gain. And the world would believe that lie, since Iraq was known to pay top dollar because *their* physicists got sniped all the time.

Tanner nodded at Dingo Paddock, who angled the thermal-imaging camera so that Nick Carrera and Damian "Blade" Singleton could also watch the monkey wrench shoved into their operation.

Who was that third figure following the two physicists at a covert distance?

All three continued across the empty plaza toward the first

floor of a 330-meter-tall, pyramid-shaped structure that soared through the black skies above the Pyongyang skyline. The Ryugyong Hotel.

Or better known as the Hotel of Doom because it remained a giant, unfinished money pit, under construction for twenty-four years.

Twenty. Four. Years.

Who does that?

A leader willing to spend billions on a joke of a hotel while his people starved.

Tanner lifted the Velcro flap covering the illuminated face of his watch.

Twenty-two-hundred hours, five minutes. The physicists—the packages—were right on time. So where had they picked up a tail?

It wasn't either of the two guards on duty at the hotel's front gate.

Over the last two hours and ten minutes, each guard had taken turns making a casual pass around the area once an hour. The last patrol had included a smoke break in the plaza sixteen minutes ago.

Eluding the security to reach this point had been laughably easy for his team, but who would send their best personnel to watch an empty hotel?

Hadn't some UK journalist just blogged about making it right past the standing guards a few months ago to get inside the hotel before daylight?

Yep, everything about this op had rocked along smoothly … until now.

But one uninvited guest to this party was *not* going to screw Tanner's mission.

With temps hovering around thirty, he had to cover his mouth with a gloved hand to hide the frosted air when he gave orders. His throat mic easily picked up his whispered words. "You three enter by the second access point, secure the packages and head to the rendezvous location."

If anything went FUBAR, Tanner had a backup plan, but the

last thing he wanted was to divide his people. He'd volunteered to run this op because of his knowledge of North Korea.

Knowledge he'd earned as a member of Delta Force.

But the real reason he'd volunteered for tonight was to save a young girl his sister had grown up with, whose dying mother had been deported. Saving that girl hinged on a successful mission here.

Tanner added, "Give me a sixty-second head start to intercept the unidentified. We rendezvous and exit at twenty-two-thirty hours."

"Roger," echoed in Tanner's ear. He lowered his night-vision monocular into place, leaving his other eye as the only body part exposed. He wore gray wool that blended in with the locals, just like the rest of his team, all custom-made clothes to cover the gear he needed for the op.

He pushed up slowly.

The roar of a cheering crowd in the distance drew his attention for a second. Lights glowed above where a hundred and fifty thousand citizens of the Democratic People's Republic of Korea, or DPRK, filled the May Day Stadium three kilometers away to celebrate the birth of their leader's grandfather.

A packed house in the largest active stadium in the world.

That's why this op had to happen right now while so many of the DPRK military were on show for their dictator.

That and the fact that the North Korea nuclear threat finally had teeth and their pit-bull leader was ready to bite someone this week.

Not happening.

Tanner lifted his Chinese Norinco rifle and moved carefully, melding from shadow to shadow. The team carried nothing that smacked of the US or South Korea. The suppressor on his rifle was Russian. Even their clothing was made without tags and with materials sourced outside the US.

Two young men waited inside that building, ready to defect to the US and trade what they knew of Project Jigu-X.

Translated, it meant Project Earth.

Did the head Nork behind Jigu-X really believe that name would camouflage his true plans? *Live on in your dream world, buddy.*

Tanner placed one careful step after another. No one could know that his team was extracting the two physicists and delivering them to the US. Plausible deniability wasn't an option. There could be no connection whatsoever to the US government.

The State Department had cashed in on a debt Sabrina Slye—the head of Slye operations—owed another government agency to get this job done off the books, so to speak.

Sabrina could have backed out by claiming she owed the DEA, not the State Department, but she'd never leave the US exposed if she could prevent it. The op had a thirty-percent chance of success and Sabrina wouldn't ask anyone to go. In fact, she'd planned to run the op herself, but Tanner had convinced her to let him take point.

Nick, Dingo and Blade had volunteered next.

Sabrina accepted the job, but only after the State Department agreed to do a favor for Tanner once he handed over the two physicists.

Tanner had told his mother he had a plan to save Martina. He would belly crawl over hot coals to fulfill his end of this deal and then he'd use the State Department's pull to cut through red tape for what he really wanted.

The silence sharpened his senses. Tanner skirted the weak lighting and hugged pooled shadows.

Get the package, get out, echoed in his mind.

Entering North Korea had been fairly simple.

Exiting would be a challenge even with transportation waiting on them a half mile away.

He hoped it was actually there when he arrived.

The two egghead physicists in this doomed hotel better be able to provide proof that North Korea had finally developed a nuclear warhead small enough to fit on a long-range missile. If so, they would live in anonymity in the US by entering the equivalent of a super-secret WITSEC program. They'd never see their home country again, but where they were going would be Utopia compared to life here for anyone other than the elite.

The leader of this country had the ultimate zero-tolerance policy when it came to defectors and anyone accused of espionage, so Tanner hoped the two eggheads would follow orders and keep up.

He'd protect the physicists at all costs, but he couldn't allow his team to be captured. Capture meant execution for all of them.

He paused near the main entrance, then continued to one of four access points his team had located and stepped through the opening of an unfinished window. Inside, he wove through a forest of scaffolding set up for the workers and stopped short of the vast, circular lobby.

The ceiling was hundreds of feet up.

Light from a half moon dodging clouds struggled to filter through empty space covered with glass walls.

Not enough light to bother his night vision.

Just enough to sneak around inside without it.

On the far side of the unfinished room, two figures huddled together. They were dressed in the dull colors of poor citizens who lived in portable cabins outside the hotel and worked as supplementary labor alongside the military who were building this fiasco. Intelligence reports had stated that locals would help the physicists reach this point, which appeared to have happened.

If the local people who'd played a role in this defection were discovered, they'd be executed or sent to a prison camp that made hell look like a tropical vacation.

Why would people here risk their lives to help?

He could understand the physicists' motivation. Who wouldn't want to defect to a country where they ate regularly as a minimum?

These two claimed they didn't want blood on their hands.

Scientists with a conscience.

What was the world coming to?

Tanner tamped down bitter memories of one female

scientist who sure as hell hadn't possessed a conscience.

He held his position as he swept the interior visually, searching for that third bastard. His team would enter from behind the physicists, which prevented anyone from surprising them. Dingo and Nick would pull the packages out of sight without making a sound while Blade covered their six.

That initial tingle of warning riding Tanner's neck since the minute he'd seen the third heat signature clawed at him harder. *Where are you?*

There.

Moving from right-to-left as silent as a ghost, a figure circled the outer perimeter of the lobby.

He was heading toward the physicists.

Tanner mirrored that movement on this side of the lobby, keeping track of the physicists as well as the unidentified.

In less than a second, two of his team coalesced from the shadows and grasped the defectors, vanishing from sight.

So far, so good.

Tanner eased near the empty space where his men had been only seconds ago, until he was between that spot and the exit point.

He stood in shadows to the side of the path, out of sight unless that third figure also wore night vision. Tanner hadn't seen any headgear.

Keep coming this way for your special welcome, you bastard.

The unidentified was heading forward at a quicker pace. Five-foot-five, maybe five-six, light build and quiet as a ninja mouse sneaking past a cat. At six-three and just over two hundred pounds, Tanner should have no problem containing that scrawny rat.

Tension ran along the tight muscles in his neck.

He froze every muscle, waiting for the intruder to pull even with his position. At that point, he could cold cock the sucker and leave him laid on the floor, none the wiser about what was going on when he did wake up.

If the little guy fought him, Tanner's only other option

would be to snap his neck.

Boot heels scuffed over grit and concrete near the main entrance, dividing Tanner's attention with a new threat entering. Dammit.

The ninja practically flew toward the team's exit point.

Tanner released his weapon to hang from the dummy cord hooked to his vest. He lunged and caught the ninja, hooking his arm around a body that weighed little more than a big kid's. His captive made a soft squeak a second before Tanner covered his mouth. The speed the guy had been moving forced Tanner to spin to handle the momentum. The minute Tanner lifted his captive off the ground, the ninja stilled.

This guy's cheek skin felt too smooth to grow whiskers.

Was it a boy? Hell, he didn't want to kill some kid.

If Tanner left him unconscious, what would the guards do to him?

He moved his arm up for a better grip and bumped into … breasts.

Are you shittin' me?

His ninja was *female*?

Who had he pissed off in a former life for this bullshit? He couldn't leave her here unconscious and vulnerable to male guards who might abuse her, but neither could he leave her to spill her guts about the physicists.

Boot heels slapped the floor where the guard walked from the entrance to the center of the vacant lobby area.

Leaning to his left, Tanner took in the guard who carried a Type 56 assault rifle, a Chinese version of Kalashnikov's AK-47.

Seconds were ticking off the clock for meeting up with his team.

He slowed his breathing to where his chest barely moved. The woman in his arms did the same. She breathed in sync with him.

Another guard entered. Dammit.

The first guard turned around, saying something in clipped Korean to the second one. Tanner could grasp enough Korean to get the gist of what they were saying, but the guards spoke too low for him to hear.

Whatever they'd discussed ended with one heading to the far side of the building and the second one turning in Tanner's direction.

Of course.

No point in going halfway when things turned FUBAR.

Taking down the guard or getting out of the building silently wasn't going to happen with this woman in his arms.

Tanner turned sideways and eased backwards into a pocket of black created by a support beam. He angled his body to shield his captive.

Why? Because of his damned ingrained instinct to protect a woman. As long as she didn't try to kill him.

If she stayed quiet, the guard should pass by without noticing them. But that warm little body of hers was pressed against the front of him, and *his* body was noticing her soft curves.

Not the time for Big John to wake up.

What the hell was this woman doing here? Following a boyfriend?

Had Shin Pang or Jae Har, the physicists, told a girlfriend goodbye?

That would have been stupid. But geniuses were not known for their common sense.

Tanner sorted through ideas for what to do with her and kept coming up with nothing his conscience would accept. First, they had to escape discovery.

That *might* have been a possibility until the guard heading his way flipped on a small penlight.

You son of a bitch.

The beam swung left and right in front of the guard's feet as he moved closer.

Tanner's ninja tensed.

That damned light swept to the left and paused on a pile of construction debris. When it did swing back to the right, the light would land on Tanner and his ninja.

Well, shit.

Toss aside his ninja and go for the guard?

Sure, that'd work. And for his follow up act, he'd pull a helicopter out of his back pocket.

AUTHOR'S BIO

New York Times bestseller Dianna Love once dangled over a hundred feet in the air to create unusual marketing projects for Fortune 500 companies. She now writes high-octane romantic thrillers, young adult and urban fantasy. Fans of the bestselling Belador™ urban fantasy series will be thrilled to know more books are coming from that world with the release of TREOIR DRAGON CHRONICLES. She also has a new paranormal romance series – League of Gallize Shifters. Her sexy Slye Temp romantic thriller series wrapped up with Gage and Sabrina's book–Fatal Promise–but fans wanted more of the HAMR BROTHERHOOD, so Dianna has released Wrecked, the first book in that spinoff series. Look for her books in print, e-book and audio (almost all the series). On the rare occasions Dianna is out of her writing cave, she tours the country on her BMW motorcycle searching for new story locations. Dianna lives in the Atlanta, GA area with her husband, who is a motorcycle instructor, and with a tank full of unruly saltwater critters.

Be sure to visit her website at AuthorDiannaLove.com and order your next print book, signed and personalized, from DiannaLoveSignedBooks.com.

A WORD FROM DIANNA…

No author creates without a great support team and I have the best, starting with my husband, Karl, who has always believed in me and makes it possible for me to do what I love – tell my stories to the world.

Cassondra Murray is on the front line with me for every story, vetting out early versions and reviewing the last pass through for those significant edits that every story needs, but an author is too close to see at times. She sees things that never fail to amaze me. Thankfully, she enjoys traveling with me and makes every trip a pleasure, always doing anything possible to give the readers a great event.

Steve Doyle is so generous with anything I ask for help on. We are so blessed to have men and women like him who have put themselves between us and danger to keep us safe and free. He shares his vast knowledge gained as a Special Forces soldier to improve my action and black ops scenes plus he is amazing when it comes to any discussion on weapons. On top of that, he reads the stories, giving important feedback. Any errors are my own.

I so appreciate USA Today bestselling author Mary Buckham who brainstorms with me during the year when she isn't writing on her own *Invisible* Recruit series.

Every story needs beta readers. I am so thrilled to have Joyce Ann McLaughlin read my stories in the "not quite finished" stage and share her feedback that gives me ah-ha moments while also making me smile over her encouraging comments. Manuella Robinson has read my books since the first one I wrote, back before anyone knew I was writing. She's always willing to read something quick and give me her honest opinion, for which I am so thankful.

Once the story has made it through beta reads, Judy Carney handles the first copy edit read to catch those things word gremlins that sneak in. It's always a joy to work with her.

Thanks to Kim Killion who recently redesigned the covers for my entire Slye Team series that I LOVE! Thanks also to Jennifer Jakes who takes all the text I send her a bunch of files and formats a book from it that can be released.

Any mistakes made or adjustments for fiction are my own, because every one who helped me went above and beyond the call to give me the best information.

Thanks also to Leiha Mann, Su Walker, and the RBLs for supporting all authors!

Love and appreciation goes to my amazing readers who support me all through the year.

A special thanks to Tina Rucci who recently went through the story and caught things that were missed earlier.

Printed in Great Britain
by Amazon

47752503R20175